Logan Belle's first visit to a burlesque club on her birthday inspired her to write the erotic trilogy *Blue Angel*. Her latest novel is the erotic romance *Bettie Page Presents: The Librarian*. Her short fiction has been published in the anthology *Obsessed: Erotic Romance for Women* and the upcoming *Twice the Pleasure: Bisexual Erotic*. Logan Belle lives in New York City, where she is working on her next erotic novel. To read more about Logan Belle and her books, visit www.loganbelle.com.

D1147483

Also by Logan Belle:

Fallen Angel
Naked Angel

LOGAN BELLE

Constable & Robinson Ltd
55–56 Russell Square
London WC1B 4HP
www.constablerobinson.com

First published in the US by Kensington Publishing Corp., 2011

First published in the UK by Canvas,
an imprint of Constable & Robinson Ltd, 2012

A copy of the British Library Cataloguing in
Publication data is available from the British Library

ISBN: 978-1-47210-614-8
ISBN: 978-1-47210-617-9 (ebook edition)

Printed and bound in the UK

1 3 5 7 9 10 8 6 4 2

MIX
Paper from
responsible sources
FSC® C018072

Acknowledgments

Thank you, Alicia Condon, my wonderful editor, who immediately "got" the world of Blue Angel and gave this book the best possible home.

This story would not have been written without the community of burlesque performers in New York City who inspired me. In particular, I would like to thank Gigi La Femme, who generously shared her time and experiences with me. Thank you to Jo Weldon, founder of the New York School of Burlesque, whose book *The Burlesque Handbook* helped me "teach" Mallory how to perform.

In LA, thank you to the amazing producer and performer Courtney Cruz.

Most importantly, thank you to Adam Chromy, my mentor, muse, and parter-in-crime: You taught me how to write a great second act.

Dancing begets warmth, which is the parent of wantonness.
It is, Sir, the great grandfather of cuckoldom.
—Henry Fielding

I'm a free bitch, baby.
—Lady Gaga

1

During the entire cab ride he kept telling her, it's a surprise.

"I don't like surprises," Mallory said, following him into the dark, barely marked building off of Bowery.

"It's your birthday! What's a birthday without a surprise?" He winked at her, and she couldn't resist smiling back. That was the thing about Alec: no matter how much he aggravated her, she loved him too much to stay angry.

And why should she be in a bad mood? They'd finally moved in together after three years of dating long distance while she finished law school. She had a good job at a midsize firm. And yes, it was her birthday—the big twenty-five—and Alec was taking her out for a night on the town, in her new city, just the two of them.

Except...the dark location did not seem to be a romantic restaurant.

A woman with a clipboard greeted them inside the door. She had a butterfly tattoo on her neck and a perfect face. Behind her, a blue velvet curtain prevented Mallory from seeing into the room.

"Alec Martin and Mallory Dale. We're on the list," Alec said, taking Mallory's hand.

Once inside, Mallory saw that the venue was a bar of some sort, with a seating area and a stage and...dwarves. Two that she counted. And a topless woman wearing a garter belt, black-seamed stockings, and red patent leather stilettos. And a man dressed for a rodeo carrying a bullwhip.

"What the hell is this?" Mallory asked.

"It's the Blue Angel. A burlesque club," Alec said, smiling like he'd just presented her with a diamond.

Burlesque—the topic of the article Alec was writing for *Gruff*, the pop culture magazine he worked for. And his latest excuse for constantly ogling other women.

"We're spending my birthday doing research for your article?"

He steered her to the table closest to the stage. The room was packed, but the table had a reserved card on it. Now she *knew* the evening was a *Gruff* magazine gig. The owner of *Gruff* was a rich kid named Billy Barton. Alec had met Billy thanks to the long tentacles of the Penn alumni network. And unlike Alec and most of their friends, who had only been in New York a few years, Billy could open any door, pull any string, and reserve any table.

"No," Alec said. "We're doing something fun and interesting on your birthday that I happen to be writing about but that I know you will enjoy. Wait here—I'm going to get our drinks."

And he was off to the bar before she could protest.

She wished she had worn something different. Her long, houndstooth Ann Taylor skirt suddenly seemed overly prim. There was a lot of leg showing in the room—bare legs, garter-belted legs, legs in fishnets and heels. At least she was wearing a simple black turtleneck, so the overall effect wasn't too dressed.

In the corner at the far end of the room, two women were laughing and talking to the guy in the Western getup. The one in the faux leopard coat was the first person Mallory had noticed in the room. How could she not? Aside from being model gorgeous, she had an ultra-stylized look, with dramatically pale skin, full red lips, and straight black hair cut in a fabulous, razor-sharp bob. As if sensing Mallory's stare, the woman turned and looked at her with sharp blue eyes. Startled, Mallory quickly looked away. But when she glanced back, the woman was still watching her, as if expecting that her gaze would return. Their eyes locked, and Mallory's stomach did the oddest little flip.

"Hey," Alec said, sitting next to her and sliding over a bottle of Stella Artois. "You're not mad, are you?"

Mallory accepted the beer, trying to resist the urge to look back at the beautiful dark-haired woman. "What? Oh, I don't know. A little. Come on, Alec. Admit it—you're just killing two birds with one stone: you want to do research, but it's my birthday and we're going out so this is what you chose to do. It has nothing to do with how I'd actually want to celebrate."

She hated the way she sounded, but she was worried. It wasn't just about her birthday—it was about *them*. She didn't want to admit it, but their relationship hadn't felt right since she'd moved to Manhattan six months ago. Alec was consumed with the cutthroat world of New York media. She was working crazy hours at the law firm and studying to retake the bar exam. And lately, he kept bringing up the idea of their hooking up with another girl—of having a three-way. At first when he brought it up, she had thought he was just being provocative. But she finally realized he was completely serious. She didn't quite know what to make of this, so she mentally filed it under Things I Can't Deal With Right Now.

And it wasn't that she was appalled at the thought of being with a woman; she'd had minor girl crushes when she was younger. There was that one girl at overnight camp, Carly Klein. She wore tube socks pulled up to her knees even in ninety-degree heat, and she spiked a volleyball like she was going for the gold medal. She'd even had a sex dream about that girl and felt guilty about it for weeks. But this wasn't overnight camp, and she didn't have girl crushes anymore. She was an adult, and she was allegedly in an adult relationship.

Alec put his hand over hers, but before he could tell her how wrong she was or whatever he was going to say, Lady Gaga's "Beautiful, Dirty, Rich" pulsed through the room, the lights dimmed, and the thick, blue curtain on the stage slowly parted.

Rodeo Guy stepped into the spotlight, and the crowd erupted in hoots and applause.

"Ladies...and those annoying creatures you felt compelled to bring with you tonight," said Rodeo Guy, "Welcome to the Blue Angel!"

He cracked his whip, and Mallory jumped in her seat.

More hollering. Despite herself, Mallory felt a slight rush. The energy in the room reminded her of being at a rock concert. She didn't want to give Alec the satisfaction of smiling— because no matter what he said, this night was just about his story—but for the first time since stepping inside the club, she was just a little excited to see what would happen.

But her history with these types of places made her less than optimistic. She had gone to a strip club in Philadelphia sophomore year of college and again, reluctantly, when she first moved to New York. She'd hated both experiences. The girls seemed miserable, and she felt like a perv for looking at them, even though there was little else to do. And giving them money had made *her* feel exposed. Both times, her friends had just had a laugh and told her to lighten up. But she'd minored in women's studies, for God's sake. She couldn't just walk in the club and check her mind at the door.

She dreaded that feeling of not knowing where to look or what to do with her hands, of feeling both sorry for the girl and embarrassed for just being in the room.

And so when the first girl came on stage, Mallory was nervous. But the crowd was raucous and exuberant, and she was aware of being the only one in the club not making some sort of noise. Alec, especially, was yelling, clapping. He looked over at her only briefly, and winked.

Mallory turned back to the stage. The song "Diamonds Are a Girl's Best Friend" played, and the stage lights bathed the dancer in fuchsia. She was blond, and she wore a surprising amount of clothes: thigh-high, pink patent leather boots with a platform heel, a white corset, long white gloves, and in both hands, gigantic fans made out of pink and white feathers. She waved the fans around so that sometimes they concealed her face and most of her body. Other times, she just covered her body and looked at the audience with a sly smile. When the hooting and hollering reached a peak, she tossed the fans aside, stood with her feet squarely apart, and slowly tugged off one glove. The crowd roared as if she'd just flashed her bare breasts. Did women get completely naked in these shows? Mallory didn't know what to expect.

Little by little, the blonde pealed away her costume—first the gloves, then the boots, and then she turned her back to the audience and eased down the zipper of her corset so slowly, Mallory was shocked to realize she could not wait for the woman to get it off. And when she finally shook herself free and turned to face the audience with her hands over her breasts, Mallory found she was holding her breath.

The blonde moved her hands away, striking a pose like Madonna in her "Vogue" video. Her breasts were small, pert, and perfectly shaped, the nipples covered in red sequined flowers. When she danced around in her pasties and red thong, Mallory was simultaneously relieved and disappointed—the performer was probably not going to get totally nude, after all.

The crowd was in a frenzy, and Mallory joined in, whistling and clapping. The woman responded to the crowd, seeming to feed off of the excitement, gyrating close to the edge of the stage, where she slowly bent over, flashing her ass to the crowd, playfully squeezing both cheeks.

Once again, the cheers escalated, though Mallory did not think a higher decibel level was humanly possible.

The rodeo guy returned to the stage.

"One more round, everyone, for Poppy LaRue," he said, though he didn't have to ask. The room was still wild.

"What do you think?" Alec asked, squeezing her leg.

"It's ... I like it," Mallory said.

"I knew you would." He leaned over and kissed her cheek.

As the rodeo guy launched into a brief monologue, surprisingly clever, full of sly political commentary and pop culture references, Billy Barton slipped into the seat next to Alec. He wore a lavender shirt and purple suspenders. He was handsome and rich, so he could get away with dressing like Scott Disick on *Keeping Up with the Kardashians*.

"Did I miss anything?" he asked, a little too loudly.

"I don't know. What do you think, Mal? Did he miss anything?"

She rolled her eyes.

"Ladies and gentlemen, please give it up for the gorgeous, the glamorous, the *dangerous* ... Bette Noir."

The regulars in the crowd chanted the dancer's first name. The curtain remained down, but Marilyn Manson's "I Put a Spell on You" began to play. As the low, pounding, eerie first beats filled the room, the curtain slid back to reveal two wooden chairs and a small table with a crystal ball. In one chair, a woman was crouched, a towering black witch hat obscuring her face.

She rose slowly, her figure shrouded in a long, black dress. She swayed and looked directly at the audience, moody and defiant; Mallory saw that it was *her*—the stunning, leopard-coat woman.

Mallory knew the song well—had heard it long ago in a David Lynch film and loved it. It had been years since she'd heard it, but it had an unforgettable early crescendo and when it reached that initial peak, the dancer pulled off her black dress to reveal her perfect body in only a bullet bra, black lace panties, black seamed stockings, garter belt, and six-inch patent leather stilettos. In one hand, she held a shiny black wand. This time, when she looked at the audience, she focused on Mallory.

And then—and at first Mallory thought she was imagining this—she pointed her wand at Mallory and gestured for her to come on stage.

Mallory looked away, pretended not to see. But the crowd was cheering her on, and Mr. Rodeo appeared to assist her. Damn Billy Barton and his front row seats! She looked back at Alec, but he was laughing and waving her on.

The exact mechanics of how she got on stage were details she would never quite grasp. But somehow she found herself seated in one of the wooden chairs, in front of the crystal ball, with Bette Noir dancing around her. And then Bette sat in the chair opposite her, back to Mallory, and gestured for her to undo her bra.

Hands shaking, Mallory somehow managed the metal clasp. Her fingertips brushed the woman's pale skin, as remarkably soft as it was fair. And when Bette turned to face her, bare breasted, Mallory felt she was an audience of one. She did not hear the crowd or the music. She did not know if she even heard Bette speaking to her—but it felt like she was. And Bette was telling her to remove her sweater. The only reason she did it was because she couldn't be responsible for ruining this gorgeous spectacle. She hesitated for maybe twenty seconds, and then, with a rush of adrenaline, Mallory slowly pulled off her sweater.

Bette did not smile, did not even bat her fake eyelashes. She calmly took the turtleneck from Mallory, walked to the edge of the stage, and tossed it to the seat Mallory had vacated. The crowd was roaring—yes, she heard it now, like a television set that had become unmuted. Mallory, now wearing only her Anne Taylor skirt and white Victoria's Secret bra, felt her heart pounding. She wondered how much longer she would have to be on stage, but at the same time didn't want to leave. It was like she was hyper-alive—everything felt louder, brighter, and bigger than life off the stage. It was dizzying, and to ground herself she looked out at the audience to find Alec. She could see that his gaze was riveted on her, only her. She took a deep breath and kept still as Bette worked the stage around her, wearing only a bejeweled thong and impossibly high heels and still holding the wand and dancing—all the while dancing, moving in the most deliberate and perfectly choreographed way.

And then the curtain came down.

Poppy LaRue peeked at the crowd from behind the curtain. She could not believe Bette had pulled that brunette onto the stage. Her nerves had barely settled after her own act—it was flat-out sadistic that Agnes had made her open the show on her second performance ever. She thought about telling Agnes just that, but Agnes was too busy reaming Bette for pulling one of the audience on stage.

"What are you thinking? This is not a circus!" Agnes fumed in her thick Polish accent. Agnieszka Wieczorek, former Warsaw ballerina turned proprietress of the Blue Angel, did not take kindly to broken rules.

"Of course it is," Bette said, calmly lighting a cigarette. "Why else do you think these people come here?" Bette walked past her without another word, into the dressing room. She closed the door with a sharp slam.

Who else but Bette Noir could get away with that?

"I need to get my shoes out of there," Poppy said. Agnes

mumbled something in her native tongue, and waved vaguely in the direction of the closed door with disgust.

Poppy waited until she was out of sight, then rapped lightly on the dressing room door.

"Fuck off," Bette said.

"It's Poppy." She took Bette's silence as an invitation to enter. When she'd started at the Blue Angel six months ago, she would never have followed Bette Noir into a room if she was in a snit. But she'd finally gotten close enough to feel comfortable; she only hoped she could get a lot closer. She'd never been with a woman before, but she knew Bette only liked girls, and, if that's what it took to get Bette to take her under her wing and show her the ropes, she had no problem with it.

"I don't think Agnes's really mad at you," Poppy said. She paused in front of the mirror and couldn't help admiring herself. She'd recently cut her white-blond hair into a chin-length bob, much like Bette's black one. They were both fair-skinned and blue-eyed, although Poppy was a few inches taller. She'd always liked being five nine, but ever since meeting Bette she wished she were a bit shorter. Everything about Bette seemed more perfect, more right for burlesque, more special. Regardless of the height difference, with the black / blond bob thing going on, Poppy liked to think they were like photo negatives of each other. More and more, she imagined what it would be like to be in bed with Bette, her lovelier twin.

"I don't really care," Bette said, looking up from her iPhone, fixing Poppy with her unnerving cat-eyed glare. "I'm not working here to make a hundred and fifty dollars a night for the rest of my life. Do you know who that was at that table?"

"The girl you pulled on stage? No—is she an actress?"

"Not her! The guy in the stupid suspenders."

Poppy was the one who felt stupid. Was he an actor? She'd barely even noticed him. She decided it was best to say nothing. She knew Bette was going to tell her, regardless.

"It was Billy Barton," Bette said. When Poppy still showed no sign of recognition, Bette sighed in exasperation. "The owner of *Gruff* magazine. You know *Gruff*, right? They have that annual 'Hot' issue. I think it was Megan Fox on the cover last year."

"Oh, yeah—sure. I read it all the time," Poppy lied.

"Well, the publisher was here—tonight! That's a big deal, Poppy. If the magazine writes about the club, we could get some industry people in here. Not just these horny NYU kids."

"Cool. So...do you want to get a drink?"

Bette turned abruptly in her seat, looking at Poppy closely. She eyed her up and down, her gaze lingering at her chest. Poppy, wearing a pink satin robe over her pasties and G-string, felt more naked than she had on stage in front of fifty strangers. She forced herself to stand still.

Bette stood so they were almost face-to-face. She reached out and slipped her hand under the robe, cupping Poppy's breast. Poppy couldn't even breathe. After months of being ignored, then barely getting conversation out of Bette...this! Poppy had never been so invisible to another human being.

But not anymore.

"Take these off," Bette said, her thumb brushing over the red sequined flowers hiding Poppy's nipples. Bette sat back in her seat, content to be the audience, while Poppy slowly removed her pasties. In the background, Poppy could hear the chords of "Fever" by Peggy Lee; it was Cookies 'n' Cream's number—the final act. Usually, Bette closed the show. But she and Cookie had made some crazy bet, and Cookie won. They wouldn't even tell Poppy what the bet had been about. She felt like such an outsider, and wondered when that would change. How long would she have to be at the Blue Angel before she understood the place? Before Agnes spoke to her? Before the customers shouted her name? A year? Two?

But none of that mattered right now. All that mattered was

that her robe was on the floor, her pasties were in her hand, and Bette was staring at her bare breasts.

Poppy decided to be proactive. That was her new mantra, proactive. She'd heard it on *Oprah,* or read it in *Cosmo.* Or someplace important like that. Don't wait for things to come to you.

She stepped forward, her eyes locked with Bette's. It was disturbing to admit it, but she was, for once in her life, faced with someone hotter than herself.

"I'm not really in the mood to drink tonight," said Bette.

She turned back to her iPhone.

2

"Never a dull moment with you guys," Billy Barton said, hailing a cab on the Bowery. It was midnight, and it seemed the entire city was out and about. The taxis were scarce, but Mallory wouldn't have minded walking a few blocks. She was still high on adrenaline.

"Getting less dull by the minute," Alec said. She couldn't tell from his tone if he was happy about the evening's turn of events, or annoyed with her. He'd barely said a word since that woman had pulled her on stage, but with Billy Barton monopolizing the conversation, it was hard to read too much into his silence.

"True that," Billy said. Ugh, he annoyed the hell out of her. She hated his foppish clothes and the way he talked down to waiters. She hated that he signed Alec's paycheck, and that he knew so much more about New York City than she ever would. Billy Barton was one of those native New Yorkers who believed he was a breed apart from the rest of the universe. And she hated that he was tagging along on her birthday. "Do you two want to join me? I'm meeting some folks at the Standard. Might be some interesting guys for you to meet, Alec."

Mallory looked at Alec, and to her relief, he didn't hesitate before saying, "Another time."

"Well then, happy birthday, love. I can't believe I almost got to see you in your *birthday suit*." He kissed her on the cheek.

Alone, finally, Mallory and Alec walked silently to the corner. He pulled her to him.

"So, birthday girl. That was quite a show."

"Yeah, it was really . . . interesting."

"I meant your show."

"Oh . . . that. Are you mad?"

"Why would I be mad?"

"I don't know. It showed a certain lack of decorum."

"Mal, you went with it. That took nerve. To be honest, it was hot."

"Really?"

"Yes! What else would it be to me? My God, any guy would kill to see his girlfriend up there like that. The only thing that would be better would be if we got that dancer back to our apartment for a private show."

"Alec!"

"What? I told you I've been thinking about that."

"Do you have to bring it up on my birthday? And I don't need to hear about the specific women you have in mind."

He stopped and pulled her close to him, kissing her on the forehead.

"You're the only woman I have in mind. And speaking of, I was going to take you out for dessert somewhere and toast your birthday over champagne but honestly, all I want is to take you home. Is that okay?"

Mallory looked at him. There was nothing in the world she preferred to do over sex with him. Nothing could compare to that feeling of walking into the bedroom, knowing he was going to touch her. Knowing how he would touch her.

"Of course it's okay."

He hailed a cab.

In the backseat, he took off his seat belt and moved close to Mallory. She resisted the urge to tell him he really should wear his seatbelt. Her friend Julie's ex-boyfriend was an ER doctor at Mt. Sinai, and had told her that not wearing a seatbelt in a car accident increases your chance of dying by some huge percentage that she couldn't remember—probably because she'd blocked it out because it upset her.

Alec started kissing her, and she felt her stomach jump. He still had that effect on her—even after four years. When she told that to Julie, her friend hadn't believed her.

She glanced at the cab driver. He was talking into a hands-free headset. Clearly not paying attention to them.

But when Alec's hand slipped under her skirt, she pushed it away.

"Alec!" she said.

"Shh...he's not looking. Believe me, people do a lot worse in the back seat of cabs."

His fingers brushed over the front of her underwear.

"Seriously, stop," she said. He pulled his hand back and moved to the far end of the seat.

"What? You're mad at me?"

"I wish you could just go with it. You were fine to push the envelope when a strange woman pulled you on stage."

"I just don't want to do it in the back of a cab."

The rest of the ride home was silent.

As was the elevator ride up to the tenth floor of their apartment building on East 83rd Street.

Alec opened the door and went straight to the couch, where he sat and looked at Mallory expectantly. She wondered how to diffuse the situation. *He* should be the one trying to mollify *her*, but she decided that wasn't a fight worth having.

Mallory stalled by rearranging a vase filled with long-stemmed yellow roses. That morning, Alec had sent her three dozen of her favorite flowers. She fanned out the stems, and asked, "What do you want from me?"

"I want you to dance for me," he said with a smile.

"Shut up," she said.

"I'm serious," he said. "When you were up there on stage, I kept thinking I just wanted you to do that for me."

It was classic Alec. He was always pushing her just past her comfort zone when it came to sex. It was one of the things she'd come to love the most about him. She'd slept with a few other guys before Alec, but all of her important "firsts" were with him: First simultaneous orgasm. First sex in a public space (library stacks one weekend when he was visiting her at law school). First time she let someone take a nude picture of her. (She made him erase it, but it was surprisingly hot.) He'd even talked her into getting a Brazilian bikini wax not too long ago. She was angry when he suggested it. She found it offensive that he would tell her what to do with her own body. But after consultation with Julie, she decided she should try it. And she loved it—not the actual process, but the result felt so smooth and clean. When Alec suggested she try something, he was usually right. And everything he opened her up to made her feel closer to him, and closer to her own sexuality. But this whole threesome with another woman thing...she was afraid it would have the opposite effect—on her and on their relationship.

"I thought you were thinking about getting that woman home with us," Mallory said, her stomach tightening.

"No. I was thinking about you." His gray-blue eyes had that cloudy, intense look they got sometimes. It was incredibly sexy. She remembered the first time she got on top when they were having sex, and he had looked up at her with that heavy-lidded, cobalt gaze, and it made her come.

He took her hand and kissed it. "I'm serious, Mal. I'm not going to fuck you tonight unless you dance for me."

She knew he was serious.

"Oh, my God. Fine. Put something on."

"You should pick the song," he said, tossing her his iPod. "I'll get us some drinks."

She scrolled through his playlist while he uncorked a bottle of red wine. It only took her a few seconds to know what she was looking for.

Alec settled back on the couch, handing her a glass. She dimmed the lights and cued up the Mos Def song "The Beggar" on the iDock. She took a gulp, and pressed Play.

It was ridiculous after all the times he had seen her naked, after all the different ways he had fucked her—but standing there like that, she felt nervous taking off her shirt, despite the fact that she had just done it in front of dozens of strangers. But somehow, being on the stage made it impersonal. She had felt, for a few moments up there, like someone else. But now she was just Mallory.

She tried to imagine that she was someone else. She pictured Bette Noir, and somehow that put her in the right frame of mind to sway to the music and slowly unbutton her blouse. Thankfully, twelve years of ballet muscle memory gave her some idea of what to do with her body. Shrugging out of her top, she moved her arms into *bras au repos*. It was amazing to her that, seven years since she'd last set foot in a dance studio, her limbs still ached for the positions that had been imprinted on them.

Alec watched her with a look she'd never seen before, and it made her incredibly hot. She dropped the ballet arms and eased out of her skirt. Wearing only her bra, underwear, and the silver

Elsa Peretti heart pendant he had given her earlier in the night, she swayed in front of Alec to the lyrics about love and devotion.

She tried to think of a burlesque move she'd seen at the club, but she couldn't find the right motion. Instead, she did a *piqué* turn, and even though she felt silly doing it in her underwear, it was exhilarating to use her body in that way. With Alec's eyes following her every move, she felt more beautiful than she had in a long time. Moving to the music, she connected to something she'd thought was long gone, a feeling of power and inspiration that she had pushed away as an indulgence of adolescence. She'd quit ballet when she went off to college. After all, as her parents had constantly reminded her, there was no "real world" application, and it was a major time commitment. Her love of dance was something she packed away with her high school journals.

"Come here," he said softly, pulling her onto his lap. She straddled him, instantly feeling his hardness. She rubbed herself against his erection.

He ran his index finger along the edge of her panties, then slipped it easily inside of her. "You're so wet," he said.

"I know," she said.

"Take these off," he told her. She eased out of her underwear and tossed them to the floor. He pressed her gently back, parting her legs so he could look at her pussy. It used to embarrass her when he did that, but he always told her how beautiful she was and how much it turned him on to see her, so she had stopped being shy about it. Besides, the way he touched her made any moments of bashfulness short-lived. He could send her over the edge in less than a minute, and once he had her in that state she couldn't care less what he was looking at.

She closed her eyes. He rubbed the outside of her pussy with his first two fingers, then eased his middle finger in and out of her slowly, brushing her clit with his thumb. She had the urge to pull his hand in deeper, but he didn't like when she tried to control the pace of things.

"Mal, watch this." He handed her his iPhone.

"What?"

"Just check it out."

She took it from him and looked at the screen, which was filled with the image of Alec's beautiful hands playing her pussy like an instrument.

"What did you do?"

"I taped myself touching you."

"Oh, my God, erase this right now!"

"I swear I'll erase it after you watch." He pressed a button to start it from the beginning. "Lie back down." She complied, and felt his hands on her again. This time, instead of closing her eyes, she held his phone in front of her, watching him stroke her clit on screen as his hands repeated the same motions on her body. Then he inserted his finger slowly, in and out, in and out, onscreen and off... and she dropped the phone down. Within seconds she felt the spasms building in her cunt, contracting against his hand, his fingers feeding her orgasm in their expert, practiced way. *Yes... oh, yes!*

When the tremors died away, she sat up, fumbled with his belt, and he helped her, pulling off his pants and boxers. His cock strained against his stomach. She ran her hand along the length of it. She could tell how incredibly turned on he was, knew that if she took him in her mouth, she would already taste it.

"Put your panties back on," he said, his voice husky. Confused, she looked around the floor and scooped them up, wiggling into them while half on her back. Didn't he want to have sex?

He pulled her onto his lap so she was straddling him, her breasts in his face. He undid her bra, his mouth moving to suck her nipples so hard it almost hurt. She tried to remove her underwear but he stopped her. "No—like this." He pulled her underwear to the side, and she lowered herself onto him.

"Oh, my God," she moaned. There were some nights, like tonight, when he felt so big it made her gasp. She felt like if she moved just an inch she would come again. It was like that with him—so intense, so right every time. She told him that she was embarrassed by how crazy he made her in bed. He told her it was the most beautiful thing he'd experienced in his life.

As she swayed her hips, the friction of her underwear rubbing against her pussy intensified the feeling of him inside her. She opened her eyes to look at him, and as if sensing her gaze, he looked up at her. The expression on his face was filled with such lust and passion and love, it sent her over the edge; shudders moved from her pelvis through the rest of her body, explosive, incredible, better than ever before.

Her release triggered Alec, and she felt him come, crying out the way he always did—loudly, with complete abandon.

Mallory rested her head against his chest and closed her eyes, relishing the feeling of absolute contentment that always washed over her after they made love. It was usually the rare time when her mind was absolutely blank.

"I hope you had a good night," he said, kissing her head.

"Are you kidding? It was incredible."

"I'm thinking of interviewing that dancer for the article," Alec said.

"What?" Mallory asked, although she knew exactly what he'd said—and who he was talking about.

"That dancer who pulled you on stage—Bette Noir. I'm going to interview her for my article." Mallory pulled away and looked him.

"Were you thinking about her just now? When we were making love?"

"What? No—of course not. I just started thinking about

work." Mallory didn't know if he was telling the truth, but what was she going to do? Turn it into a cyclical argument in which she accused him and he denied it? She didn't want to ruin the moment.

Instead, she said, "Thanks for a great birthday," and kissed him.

"I think it's the beginning of your best year yet, Mallory." He smiled at her and stroked her hair.

"I just need one more little, tiny thing from you tonight," she said.

"Anything, my love."

"Erase that video from your phone."

"Aw, Mal, you're killing me. It's an instant classic."

"Erase!" She leaned off the couch to find the phone, and he scrambled to find it first. He retrieved it, and held it up and away from her while she reached for it. She finally tackled him and wrested the phone away, pressing the buttons randomly.

"Hand that to me before you destroy the phone—I'll erase it, scout's honor."

"You swear?" she said, holding it just shy of his reach.

"Yes. Fine. Have it your way. But I think you're underestimating the potential of a law/porn career...." She handed him the phone and watched him erase the video.

"I'll admit, you are a very skilled cinematographer," she said.

"Well, I did have a great subject. Very inspiring. Now I know how Hitchcock felt behind the camera with Grace Kelly. Or Woody Allen with Diane Keaton...or Scarlett Johansson. Yeah, that one I get a little more."

She rolled her eyes at him.

"You know what I'm saying, though—" He smiled—"we're a great team."

3

Mallory used to feel a thrill walking into the tall, glass Park Avenue building that housed the law firm of Reed, Warner, Hardy, Lutz, and Capel—known within the industry simply as Reed, Warner. There had been a time when she'd felt an absolute sense of belonging there—of destiny, even. Since the first day she'd started at Penn as an undergraduate, she'd known she would be an attorney. Like her father and mother. Like her father's father. What else would she be? And then acceptance at Villanova Law. And then the summer associate jobs at Reed, Warner. And then the job waiting for her there when she graduated.

It all fell into place so easily, so thoughtlessly. Until last month.

The wide bronze doors of the elevator opened on the thirtieth floor.

"Good morning, Ms. Dale," the receptionist, Blanca, greeted Mallory.

"Hi, Blanca."

Does she know that I failed the bar exam? Mallory wondered. Did everyone at the firm know—down to the woman who came around every afternoon at three o'clock with the coffee cart?

"At least you're not famous," her friend Julie had said. "When John Kennedy, Jr. failed the bar, the *Post* ran it on the cover with the headline 'The Hunk Flunks.' "

Needless to say, that did not console her. And even though Alec assured her that it happened to lots of people and that she would no doubt pass the exam when she retook it in February, she was flooded with a feeling about her future that she had never experienced before: doubt.

Even her office felt foreign to her now. What used to be a haven of order and purpose to her now felt like what it was: a cold, boxy room without enough natural light and with an avalanche of paper everywhere.

Mallory logged onto her computer. For the next ten hours she would sit at her computer, digging around Westlaw and writing the legal memo she had been working on for the past month. Her boss was part of the defense team for Koomson, the country's largest paint company. She was researching their potential liability in a lead paint class action suit.

"Half day today?" Patricia Loomis, a third year attorney, stood in the door way of her office. Patricia was short, her suits were masculine and didn't fit right, and she bit her nails so badly they looked on the verge of bleeding. But she was the smartest person Mallory had ever met. And she was Mallory's boss.

Mallory looked at the time on her computer. 8:30 a.m.

"I had a late night. My birthday."

"Harrison wants the brief at the end of next week."

"Okay," Mallory said. But Patricia was already gone. Ugh! Mallory didn't know why Patricia disliked her so much, but it had been obvious from day one that she couldn't stand her. And then when Mallory failed the bar, any spec of esteem she might have begun earning with her hard work evaporated. She knew Patricia was just waiting for her to flame out.

Mallory opened her handbag, digging around for the Life Saver she knew was in there somewhere. She was so tired she needed a sugar kick. Her hand closed around something small and boxy. When she pulled it out she saw it was a robin's egg blue matchbook that read *The Blue Angel.* Who'd slipped that in there? Probably Billy, that ass.

She set it on her desk, and thought about that dancer. Bette Noir. What did she do during the day? Did she go to an office like everyone else? If so, did her boss know what she did at night? Or did she just sleep all day like a creature of the night, emerging only to appear at the Blue Angel. Maybe her whole life was just about beauty, and art, and inspiration. She probably never heard of the bar exam. She'd probably didn't know people like Patricia Loomis even existed, never mind having her whole career resting on those slumped and badly clothed shoulders.

Mallory logged onto Westlaw.

The buzz of her cell phone jolted her out of her lead paint fog sometime later that afternoon. She bent down to get her handbag and immediately felt dizzy. As usual, she'd forgotten to eat lunch.

"Hello?"

"Hey—it's me," Alec said. "What time are you getting out of there tonight?'

"I don't know—Patricia is on the warpath. She has me transcribing a deposition for her—can you believe that? She's not supposed to have me doing things like that. *And* she told me Harrison wants this brief by the end of next week...."

"I need you to come out tonight."

"I can't. Whatever it is, go without me—I was late today, I'm exhausted, and this is taking me twice as long..."

"Seriously, Mal, I need you to come out tonight."

"Why? What's the urgency?"

"I e-mailed that dancer, Bette Noir, about doing an interview."

A tug of jealousy pulled at her gut.

"What did she say?"

"She agreed, but said you have to be there."

"That makes no sense. Why would she care if I'm there or not?"

"I don't know. She also said I had to find a cool place that she couldn't get into on her own."

"I really don't have time for these games, Alec."

"I'm not joking. This is my job. Come on, you know I would help you if you needed it."

Mallory looked at her computer screen. The words swam together, the blinking cursor making her eyes blur.

"Where are you going to do the interview?"

"I'm not sure. I'm going to call Billy and see if he will get us into Soho House or if he has a better idea."

"I can't leave here before 8:30."

"Deal. Thanks, babe. I owe you one."

Mallory tossed the phone back in her bag.

She picked up the Blue Angel matchbox, turning it in her hand.

It was called the Boom Boom Room.

Set in the heart of the Meatpacking District, on the eighteenth floor of André Balazs's Standard Hotel, it was the most decadent, intense space Mallory had seen in her life. It was somehow retro and futuristic at the same time, with curved, pale couches, chandeliers like starbursts and snowflakes, and 360-degree views of Manhattan and the Hudson River. It was as if the entire city had been created as a mere backdrop to the room.

Mallory teetered near the floor-to-ceiling windows. Her heels were too high—she rarely wore heels. But Alec had warned her to look good, and so she was thankful she had a pair of black Walter Steigers under her desk from last week. Everyone in that room was straight out of a magazine—sleek dresses, and high skirts, and shoes and bags that cost more than her monthly paycheck. Men in suits, models in every corner, Penelope Cruz deep in conversation with Pedro Almodóvar, Lindsay Lohan and entourage...and still heads turned for Bette Noir.

"Come sit with us," Bette called to her from the cream-colored banquette where Alec had planted her for the interview. Across the room, she saw Billy Barton watching them, then he turned away, pretending he had not been.

He had given them a wave and a wink when they walked in, but didn't cross the room to say hi. It was just as well; Mallory was already a nervous wreck by the time they got up to the room. They had met Bette outside the hotel, and she was oddly quiet as they made their way past the line at the velvet rope that looked like a casting call for *America's Next Top Model.* She wore a black velvet trench coat, and her bobbed hair was so shiny and dark it looked almost purple in the night.

"We're guests of Billy Barton," Alec told the brawny guy at the door with the headset. And with that, the seas parted, and they walked in. Mallory felt the hostile glares of the wannabes behind her, people wondering, *who are they*?

Patricia Loomis and Reed, Warner seemed very far away.

So there they were, in one of the hardest rooms to get into in all of Manhattan—a city run on exclusivity and closed doors. It was not a scene Mallory would have ever thought to seek out, but according to Alec, it was Bette's stipulation for doing the interview. A place she couldn't get into on her own. Like a dare. Or a scavenger hunt task.

"Yeah, come sit down, Mal." Alec patted the space next to

him, on the opposite side from where Bette was seated next to him.

"Over here—I like to have a close witness to make sure I'm not misquoted," Bette said, taking her hand and seating Mallory between her and Alec.

Mallory was startled when Bette touched her. Had it really only been twenty-four hours ago that Bette was pulling her up on stage?

"It's really Agnes's vision," Bette was saying about the club. "It's different from any other burlesque show in New York."

It was too loud for Alec to use his mini tape recorder, so he scribbled notes on a small notepad.

He nodded, and said, "I know—the first time I went I was completely blown away. That's why I wanted Mallory to see it."

"And what did you think?" Bette asked Mallory.

"Um, it was...interesting."

"Interesting? Wow. Damned with faint praise," Bette said.

"No, it was more than that. I mean, I've been thinking about it all day."

"Do tell! What have you been thinking?" Bette focused her cat-like blue eyes on Mallory.

"I think Alec wants to interview you...not have you interview me," Mallory said with a shaky smile.

"Oh, I've got nothing interesting to say. I'm meant to be seen in the flesh, not read in print."

Mallory looked helplessly at Alec. He flicked his eyes toward the other side of the room.

"I'm going to excuse myself...to use the restroom. If I can find it."

Mallory stood up, though walking through that crowd was the last thing she wanted to do. In her white blouse and black pencil skirt she was a pigeon in a crowd of peacocks.

"Where's the restroom?" she asked a cocktail waitress, who

was dressed like the sexiest flight attendant on the face of the planet. She followed the woman's directions to a corridor near where they had entered the room. She'd only had half a glass of champagne, but something about the layout of the bathroom made her completely disoriented. The entire room was glass— floor to ceiling windows! She couldn't pee in front of a gigantic window overlooking Manhattan.

She decided to just touch up her makeup. She wished she'd paid more attention to those magazine articles about taking your makeup from day to evening in two easy steps, or whatever the advice was. A lipstick rolled around in the bottom of her bag, and she uncapped it for the first time in months.

And then there was a knock on the door.

"Um, someone's in here," she said.

"I know. It's me, Bette—open up."

"I'll be out in a second," Mallory said, shoving her lipstick back in her bag.

"Just open the door."

Mallory complied, about to leave the room for Bette to use it when Bette pulled her back inside and closed the door behind them.

"Cool space," she said, walking over to the window and pressing herself against the glass.

"It's a little much for a bathroom," Mallory said.

"Hmm. You must not have very strong exhibitionist tendencies. I thought you might have, after last night."

She locked eyes with her, and Mallory found herself leaning against the sink for support.

"Come over here and check out this view. Might as well appreciate it, even if you don't approve."

Mallory crossed the small space and stood beside Bette. She felt like she was standing at the edge of a cliff.

"Put your hand on the glass. Don't you feel like you're on top of the world?"

"Yes."

Bette turned to her and brushed the hair away from Mallory's face. She ran her hand down the length of Mallory's hair, to a spot between her shoulder blades.

"I'm not usually a fan of long hair. But on you, it's hot."

Mallory tried to keep her eyes focused on the city stretched beneath them, but Bette walked to the toilet and started pulling up her skirt.

"Oh! I'm going to give you some privacy. I'll…"

But before she could leave Bette was peeing, her fishnet stockings around her ankles.

"What's the big deal? We're both girls." She nonchalantly finished, pulled her skirt into place, and washed her hands. She turned to Mallory.

"You can go too if you want. I won't peek."

"No—that's okay. I'm fine."

"I dare you."

"What?"

Bette laughed, a full, throaty laugh that would have been contagious if Mallory weren't so unnerved.

"Just kidding."

Mallory realized she'd been holding her breath a little. Looking for something to do with her hands, she went back to the mirror and pulled out her lipstick.

"Wait!" Bette said.

"What?"

"Don't put that on."

"Why not?"

"Because I'm just going to mess it up."

And with that, Bette put her hands on Mallory's face and brushed her lips against hers. The touch was so whisper light, Mallory could almost tell herself she imagined it.

"See you back out there," Bette whispered. And with that, she was gone.

* * *

Mallory took her third glass of champagne from the waitress. Alec threw her a glance, making sure she was holding steady.

"The best part of the shows happens away from the audience," Bette was saying. "If you want the real inside scoop, you should have Mallory hang out with me backstage."

"I'm writing the article, not Mallory."

"Yes, but you're a guy. I could never bring you into the dressing room. But it's different when it's just us girls, right, Mallory?"

The image of Bette with her fishnets around her ankles flashed through Mallory's mind.

"Interesting idea. Okay, I might take you up on that. My deadline is in a week. Any shows coming up soon where you could make that happen?"

"We're doing our Christmas show next Saturday night. It's pretty crazy." She turned to Mallory. "Are you in?"

"She's in," Alec said.

4

Poppy sat on the edge of her bed, finishing up a second coat of Essie A-List red nail polish on her toes. Her BlackBerry buzzed with a text. From Bette.

Call me ASAP.

Poppy dialed quickly.

"Hi—what's going on?"

"How soon can you meet me at the Angel?"

Poppy looked at her wet toenails. "A half hour?"

"Meet me in the dressing room. Oh, and wear a black skirt and a white blouse. And a long, brown wig if you have one."

Poppy couldn't imagine what this was about, but she wasn't going to waste time asking questions. Bette's rejection of her in the dressing room last night had stung...badly. But now... maybe Bette had just been waiting for a better time. More privacy. On the nights when there wasn't a show at the Blue Angel, it was just a regular bar/lounge, and the dressing room wasn't used.

Of course!

Now she just had to find a white blouse.

*   *   *

Bette was already in the dressing room, seated at one of the vanities. She wore an amazing black velvet trench coat that Poppy had never seen before. Poppy felt like a librarian in her stupid blouse and skirt. Why did she have to dress like a troll? Was it some kind of power play—only Bette could be hot?

"Why didn't you wear a long wig?" Bette asked.

"I don't have one like that."

"Hmm. I thought that might be the case. So I brought this for you." She handed Poppy a brunette wig. Poppy reluctantly secured it on her head with bobby pins.

"Perfect." Bette stood and unbuttoned her trench, revealing her nude and perfect body.

It was odd—Poppy had never hooked up with a woman before, had never particularly thought about it before Bette. But seeing her incredible breasts, creamy and pert and perfectly round, she felt as attracted to her as she had ever felt to a man. And when she touched them, cupping them gently and then brushing Bette's hard nipples with her thumb, she felt her pussy quiver more intensely than it had with the last few guys she'd slept with. Bette pulled her face toward her and kissed her, deep and hard and with a surprising urgency. Poppy felt she couldn't get enough of Bette's mouth—her lips were full and soft, and she could smell her perfume—vanilla and orange and something woodsy.

Bette unbuttoned Poppy's blouse and squeezed her breasts, then slid her hands under her skirt. She stroked her pussy over her underwear, and Poppy was shocked that it was enough to make her wet.

"Take off your skirt, and I'll make you come," Bette said. Poppy fumbled over the zipper, her hands shaking as she eased off her panties. No guy had ever spoken to her like this.

Bette turned her around so that her ass was pressed against her own pussy, and Poppy looked at their reflection in the mirror of the vanity table. But when Bette slid one finger inside her, she closed her eyes.

Her knees felt weak as Bette worked her finger slowly in and out, her thumb stroking her clit. She knew Bette was probably watching her in the mirror, and this would have made her self-conscious if the throbbing pleasure between her legs had not been making her mind a total blank. She moaned as she came, a sound that shocked her because she was usually so quiet. Bette moved to stand before her, then knelt down and licked her pussy with a single stroke of her tongue, like hard candy.

"Oh, my God," Poppy breathed.

Bette stood so they were face-to-face.

"Now you're going to make me come."

Bette pulled her over to the musty green couch and proceeded to stretch out like a cat in the sun.

"Use your tongue," she commanded. Poppy wasn't sure where or how she meant, so she knelt in front of the couch. Her own pussy was still throbbing, and she knew if Bette touched her again even for a few seconds she would have another orgasm.

She took Bette's breast into her mouth and touched the other one with her fingers. Bette slapped her hand away. "Just your tongue."

Poppy moved her mouth to Bette's other breast, flicking her nipple with her tongue, then gently biting it. Bette made a small noise and pressed the top of her head.

"I want you to eat my pussy," she said.

If Poppy hadn't been in such a heightened state of arousal, she doubted she'd have been able to do it. But the way she felt at that moment, she wanted to eat Bette. She wanted to be with her in every way. She wished one of them was a guy, so they could fuck properly—fuck in a way that hurt a little.

She kissed Bette's breasts, then made her way down her

body to her stomach. When she got to her pussy, she licked the outside of it the way Bette had done to her minutes before. The scent of Bette was surprisingly exciting—foreign but familiar at the same time. She pressed her tongue against Bette's clit, and Bette put her hands on the back of Poppy's head, pulling her closer. Bette made a noise, and Poppy moved her tongue to the center of her, thrusting it as deep inside as she could, trying to fuck her with it. Bette's hips moved rhythmically, and Poppy slipped her hands under her to grab her ass. She felt her start to come, could taste it. She moved one hand to her own pussy, fingering herself hard so she came just as Bette shuddered, her orgasm going on and on.

She sat back on her knees and looked at Bette, who had one arm over her eyes. Her chest rose and fell heavily. Poppy's own heart was beating hard. She felt around on the floor for her underwear and pulled it on. She was still wearing her blouse. Now the wig was bothering her, so she pulled it off. Bette looked at her lazily.

"I like your pussy," she said.

Poppy had no idea what to say to that.

"I was at a party earlier," Bette said. "It made me so horny."

"Where was the party?"

"The Standard Hotel. This insane room—the hottest people in the city were there. I told you that guy Billy Barton was worth making an impression on."

Poppy thought of the brunette Bette had pulled on stage last night. She suddenly felt uneasy.

"Billy took you to a party?"

"Not exactly. He was there, but it was that girl I brought on stage and her boyfriend who brought me. Alec—that's his name—wanted to interview me for some article he's writing for the magazine."

Poppy thought of the woman from last night—her plain clothes, her lank, brown hair. Suddenly, she felt sick.

"So the party made you horny."

"It was the party, it was the conversation. I don't know—maybe it was Mallory. I didn't think she was that pretty at first but I found myself wondering tonight if I could get her into bed."

Poppy started looking around for her skirt. She didn't know whom she hated more in that instant—Bette, or that stupid bitch from the audience.

Bette sat up and smiled at her.

"Thanks for meeting me here. That felt good."

"Yeah, sure," Poppy said. "I'll see you later."

She left the dressing room quickly, closing the door behind her. Outside, in the dark and empty backstage area, she leaned against the wall and put her head in her hands. When she looked up, she found Agnes watching her. The older woman shook her head at her slowly, as if saying, *you poor fool.*

Mallory was propped up on pillows, working on her laptop, when Alec came to bed. She closed the computer.

"Thanks again for coming along tonight, Mal," he said, turning off his bedside light.

"You're going to sleep? I'm totally wound up," she said. That was an understatement. The party, the conversation...the kiss in the bathroom. She felt as if she'd drunk three espressos. Or done coke. Not that she'd ever done coke, or would really know what it felt like. But she imagined it would feel something like the way she felt at that moment—like she was jumping out of her skin. Like she would never fall asleep. Ever again.

She also felt turned on. And there was a time when, after a night like this, Alec would have been all over her. He would have told her on the ride home that she was the hottest girl in the room that night—and he would have meant it. But he was deep in his own head, something that happened a lot since she'd moved to New York.

Maybe she was being oversensitive—not to mention hypocritical. After all, she was the one who'd let some strange woman kiss her. Although it barely could be considered a kiss. And besides, Alec always said kissing didn't count—that a kiss to a guy is no more significant than a handshake.

"You really want me to go to that show next Saturday night?" she asked.

Alec rolled over to face her. "Yeah, of course I do. More detail will help the article. Any schmuck can go to a show. But how many people actually get backstage?"

"Okay. Just checking."

"You don't mind, do you?"

"No. I just don't want our whole lives to start revolving around this."

"It's one night out, Mal. I hardly think that qualifies as our 'whole lives.'"

"We spent my birthday at a show, then tonight I had to leave work early to sit there like a prop during your interview. Now we're going again this weekend."

Alec turned the light back on.

"What's this really about?"

"Nothing. I mean, I just told you."

"I think it's hard for you not to be the center of attention."

She sat up. "What are you talking about?"

"When we had the long distance thing while you were in law school, every time we got together it was like a honeymoon— we dropped everything to spend time together. Now that I have work and you have work, you're upset that you're not the focus of my undivided attention."

"That is so unfair. I do think there is a change in our relationship, but it's not about my needing to be the object of your undivided attention."

"Then what? You said you had fun at the show last night."

"I did."

"But now you're complaining about it?"

"It's the principle."

"You want to argue over principle?"

"I don't want to argue at all."

"That makes two of us." He pulled her to him, kissing her face. She looked into his eyes, that complicated pool of blue and gray, and knew she couldn't be angry.

She was hopelessly in love.

5

Six months into her life in Manhattan, Mallory still couldn't understand why people lined up all along the Upper West Side every Saturday and Sunday morning for overpriced eggs. The line outside of Sarabeth's stretched half a block long. The only reason she was willing to put up with this insane Manhattan ritual was that Allison and Julie wanted to have a belated "happy birthday" brunch. Finding a night when all three of them were free was an exercise in futility.

They had been best friends since freshman year at Penn, when they were alphabetically assigned the same dorm room for the pre-term registration weekend: Dale, Diamond, and Delmar. The 3Ds, they called themselves. Still going strong, seven years later.

Her BlackBerry vibrated in her bag: a text from Allison: *RU here? We're in the front of the line and don't want to miss getting seated—hurry!*

Mallory looked at the time: she was five minutes early, and Allison and Julie still managed to act like she was late. It was impossible to keep up with such compulsive, control freak over-achievers.

I'm in line half a block down. B right there, you early bitches.

Allison turned from the front and waved to her. No wonder Mallory had missed them—they were dressed in nearly identical jeans and long black coats that blended in with the rest of the crowd.

"Happy birthday, Mally boo!" Allison said, pulling her into a hug,

"How long have you been waiting?" Mallory asked, slipping in line.

"Fifteen minutes."

"Why did you get here so early?"

"We knew there'd be a long wait."

The hostess waved them in, and showed them to a prime table near the front window.

"Did you have a great birthday? I hope Smart Alec found something worthy of your twenty-fifth." Allison had coined the nickname senior year, when she decided Alec was arrogant. "Arrogant, but hot," she always said.

"It was interesting."

"Interesting?" Allison and Julie echoed in unison.

"Yeah, he, um, brought me to a burlesque show."

"Wow. Happy birthday to *him*," Julie said.

"Seriously. Where will you go on your anniversary? Scores?"

"You guys are so harsh. It was fun! Seriously, it was something different, and I really had a great time. I mean, it was a show just like if we went to a play or something."

"Yeah, a play with strippers."

"They weren't strippers—or, not the way you think. It's very artistic—the music, the costumes . . . each dance was a narrative."

Julie and Allison looked at her like she was crazy.

"Can I have a mimosa, please?" she asked the server.

"Make that three," Allison added.

"I've actually been thinking about it a lot. And then last night Alec interviewed one of the performers for an article he's doing. We went to this crazy room on the top of the Standard."

Allison nodded knowingly. "The Boom Boom Room. Fabulous space."

"Yeah. Well, we went there. And I don't know—she's very interesting. I'm going to a show Saturday night. You should come."

"No, thanks," Julie said. "So not my thing."

"I'm in," Allison said. "Can I bring someone? Or is this a bad idea for a third date?"

Mallory and Julie looked at her.

"Third date? You're holding out on us! Who is he?"

"He works for Bloomberg. We did this amazing event for the Mayor's office at the Guggenheim." Allison worked for a very glam, top-notch PR firm. Her BlackBerry was a who's who of New York, and every guy she dated was wealthier and more connected than the last. "We just hit it off. What can I say?"

"Name?"

"Andrew. Goldmark."

"Jewish?" Julie asked. Allison nodded. "Your mom will be so relieved."

Allison had a bit of an obsession with Italian guys that had started during junior year in Florence.

"It's only been two dates. We'll see." When Allison said "we'll see," it wasn't due to her worry that the guy would stop calling but that she would lose interest. "So can I bring him?"

"Sure. I'd say seeing how a guy reacts to hot women wearing only tassels and a G-string is a good litmus test," Mallory teased.

"Hmm. I guess that raises the bar for me. Better make a trip to La Petite Coquette."

"I would never spend that kind of money on underwear," Mallory said.

Allison flipped through her menu. "If your boyfriend is bringing you to burlesque clubs on your birthday, maybe you should start."

The Blue Angel was transformed. Glittering, plastic snowflakes hung from the ceiling. Fluffy, fake snow dusted the floor; holly and tinsel lined the bar; and the dwarf Mallory had noticed the week before was now dressed like an elf.

The clipboard woman at the door was dressed like the sexiest Santa's helper imaginable, in a tight, short red dress cinched at the waist by a wide, black belt with a heavy brass buckle; white fur trim and bells hung off the quarter-length sleeves.

"I think we're on the list," Alec said, giving their names.

"How many people are you?" A woman with long white hair appeared from behind the curtain.

"Three," Alec said.

"Who put you on list?" The woman's accent was thick Eastern European. Russian? Polish?

"Bette."

"She never listens. Only two guests per person. So one of you has to pay," the woman said, then disappeared.

Alec handed the door girl a twenty.

"Enjoy the show," she said.

"I think you guys have a reserved table," a woman said to them as they entered the main room. Mallory recognized her as the girl who picked up all the discarded clothing after each performer's set. The MC had introduced her as "Kitty Klitty." Tonight, she wore green sparkly antlers on her head, was topless, and wore a green garter that framed the largest bush of pubic hair Mallory had ever seen. "You're Mallory, right?"

"Um, yeah."

"Bette saved you guys seats. Over there—in front of the

stage." She walked off, and Mallory tried not to stare at her bare ass.

"Interesting," Allison said. "Andrew is going to be kicking himself for not coming. And I think I need a drink."

"Me too. I'll get a round. But Mal, I want to prep you for backstage. Just take note of what everyone's wearing, what they're talking about, if there's any debate about who performs in what order... any fighting over costumes... Are they drinking alcohol? Any details that make the culture come alive."

"I'll do my best."

Alec kissed her on the forehead and left for the bar. Mallory read the one-sheet program on her table. It was green poster board with the drawing of a woman wearing a short elf costume, bending over far enough to reveal her ass, and pressing what looked like a flyswatter against one cheek. It read, *Ho, Ho, Ho... Blue Angel Burlesque presents its third annual Holiday Spanktacular. Featuring: Bette Noir, Cookies 'n' Cream, Scarlett Letter, Missy Pink, Poppy LaRue, Kitty Klitty, Dustin the Dwarf... and hosted by your favorite MC: Rude Ralph.*

"Glad you could make it. Ready to come backstage?"

Bette stood next to the table in the leopard coat she had been wearing the first time Mallory saw her. Her lips were bright red and impossibly glossy, shiny like the pottery Mallory used to make in arts and crafts and coat with shellac. She thought how odd it was that Bette's mouth had touched her own, but shook the memory away.

"Yes. Are you sure it's okay?"

"Absolutely. Hi, I'm Bette," she said, extending a hand to Allison.

"Oh, I'm sorry. Allison Delmar, Bette Noir." Mallory felt a little ridiculous introducing Bette with her stage name, and she wondered what her real name could possibly be. She couldn't imagine any "real" name suiting her.

"Have fun," Bette said. "It will be a great show."

Bette took her by the hand. She felt the other patrons staring at her, and she glanced at the bar to try to catch Alec's eye, but he was talking to the white-haired Polish woman.

"Who is that older woman?" Mallory asked.

"Agnieszka Wieczorek. She's the owner. And ballbuster extraordinaire. She used to be a ballet dancer and is very into the art of performance—which is what I love about the Blue Angel versus some of the other clubs in town. But she doesn't like a lot of the modern music the neo-burlesquers use. She has to loosen up about that because I think the audience enjoys it more than traditional stuff."

Mallory didn't understand what Bette was talking about but nodded anyway. Still knowing the club was owned by a former ballerina gave her a heightened respect for it.

The dressing room was smaller than Mallory had imagined it would be. She had anticipated something like what she saw on E! or NY1 News during Fashion Week, backstage areas at fashion shows with rows of mirrors and organized racks of clothes and maybe a bottle of champagne or two. But the space was smaller than Mallory's living room, and looked like a drag queen's closet had exploded. Shoes, boas, makeup kits, wigs, bottles and aerosol cans, and undergarments the likes of which she had never seen before were strewn *everywhere*.

"Hey, everyone—this is Mallory Dale," Bette said. "She's here to observe us in our natural habitat. Her boyfriend is writing an article for *Gruff*."

Mallory got a few half-interested hellos—and a death glance from a blonde standing in the corner. Mallory recognized her as the dancer who'd opened the show last week.

"Are you sure I'm not intruding?" Mallory said to Bette.

"It's fine. Just sit over there." She pulled a folding chair from against the wall and Mallory sat quickly, wishing she could turn invisible.

"Where's the airbrush?" a well-endowed blonde with a Mohawk asked the room. Someone handed her an aerosol can, and she proceeded to spray her legs.

"What is that?" Mallory asked Bette.

"It's like panty hose—in a can. Makes your legs look flawless."

"Really? That's amazing."

Bette looked at her like she was from another planet. Mallory reminded herself to stop talking and just observe. She watched the women apply false eyelashes, body glitter, and feathers in their hair, watched them fasten wigs on their heads, climb into shoes that seemed more like stilts, fasten stockings with clips and hooks, and pull their bodies into tight corsets. It was as if these women were a different species, one that knew how to use plumage and pots of glitter and paint and delicate garments to make themselves something greater than women— they were the physical embodiment of the very *idea* of womanhood.

And they seemed to have no problem displaying their womanhood; even with Mallory, the interloper, in the room, no one seemed to think twice about walking around in just underwear and bare breasts, or in the case of one curvy brunette, nothing at all but red patent leather heels. She supposed nudity was not a big deal to them since it was their job to take their clothes off on stage every night. But just hanging out with their coworkers like that? And a random stranger?

She was even more surprised when the MC, Rude Ralph, entered the room carrying a bucket of Stella Artois, and no one made any effort to cover up.

"Missy, you're changing your number to 'Jingle Bell Rock'?"

"Yes—and Scarlett is going to go before me." Missy Pink was dressed like a giant snowflake.

"Okay, but that's it—no more changes. I'm getting the music queue set."

"No more changes," the curvy brunette said, making a cross my heart gesture. Ralph handed out the beer.

"And for you?" he said to Mallory, offering her a bottle.

"Oh—thanks," she said.

"Are you being reprimanded? Sent to the corner for a time-out?" he teased.

"Um..."

"Yes—she's been very naughty. I just might need to spank her. Now go," Bette ordered, and ushered him out the door. Mallory waited for Bette to glance her way, but she didn't. As soon as Ralph was out of sight, the dancer turned her attention to applying false eyelashes one by one. Mallory thought of the time she'd tried false eyelashes on Halloween, and she just glued the whole set on at once—like a fan of lashes stuck on the rim of her eyelid. It had looked terrible, and she took them off before she even left the apartment.

Mallory didn't feel that she was gathering any useful information for Alec. She doubted the readers of *Gruff* were eager for false eyelash application tips or the secret to long lasting body glitter. Maybe she should be writing the article for *Allure* or *Glamour*. She could become a writer, too—and forget this whole bar exam debacle.

"I'm going on last—I might go out and watch the show from the side of the stage. Feel free to stay back here. But I want you to try to catch my act," Bette said, and gave Mallory a wink.

"How did it go?" Alec asked, squeezing her hand.

Mallory made her way back to the table just as Dustin the Dwarf's stand-up routine ended. She knew from the set list posted backstage that he was the last performer before Bette Noir.

"Great. I'll tell you all about it." Alec looked so hand-some—she felt a surge of love for him and thought of what Allison had said to her at lunch about buying better lingerie. Maybe she was right. They lived in a city full of beautiful women—she should probably step it up a notch. Maybe it was her fault their sex life had hit a plateau—or what did Jennifer Aniston call it in that Ed Burns movie? A "downcycle." Except in that movie Jennifer Aniston's husband was leaving her for Cameron Diaz. This, years before her real-life husband would leave her for Angelina Jolie.

Note to self: get better underwear.

"What do you think of the show?" she asked Allison.

"Amazing! Absolutely beyond. In an alternate universe, I would *so* do this!"

"Um, don't quit your day job," Alec teased.

Allison punched his arm. "Ugh! You are such an asshole. How do you put up with him?"

"And now, ladies and gentlemen, the moment you have all been waiting for—the tassel queen, pinup dream, and mistress of the night...Put your hands together for Bette Noir."

The room erupted, the stage curtain rose, and the stage was set with four boxes in a row, arranged in increasing size. Each was wrapped with a thick red bow. Bette appeared to the opening strains of the song "You're a Mean One, Mr. Grinch," wearing a candy cane-striped minidress, long white gloves, red high-heeled half-boots curled up at the toe like elf boots, and a red velvet Santa hat.

She gyrated toward the first small box, undid the ribbon, opened it, and turned it upside down to reveal it was empty. She shrugged, pushed the box aside, and slowly pulled off her gloves. The crowed yelled encouragement.

She untied the ribbon on the second box, and revealed that it, too, was empty. With a pout, she threw the box behind her, then angrily tugged off her dress, revealing sequined candy cane-shaped pasties covering her nipples. The crowd whistled and yelled. She turned her attention to the third box, and pulled off the lid to once again find nothing. She tossed the box into the audience, and someone stood to catch it.

She stood facing the audience, hands on her hips, frowning like a petulant child. She stomped her foot and pulled off her pasties, standing there in only red lace panties. The crowd went ballistic. Alec and Mallory looked at each other.

"Omfg," Allison said.

Mallory couldn't believe the perfection of Bette's body. She was skinny with curves; her breasts were large but had small, delicate nipples.

Bette opened the final, largest box. She faced the audience with a huge grin, and pulled out a wide strip of red velvet fabric. The crowd laughed and applauded as she proceeded to wrap herself in the fabric as if it were a giant bow. She crossed it between her legs, over each breast, and tied it behind her shoulder blades. When she turned her back to the audience to exit the stage, the only thing visible was a giant red bow atop a perfect ass.

Rude Ralph returned to the stage.

"How do you top perfection? Clearly, you can't. So that's the end of our show for tonight."

The audience let out a collective, "Aaww!"

"I know, it's hard," Ralph said. "I know *I'm* hard. And something tells me I'm not alone. Right, my friend?" He pointed to a guy at the table next to theirs. The guy clapped. "Easy, fella. It's not that kind of show. Okay, ladies and gentlemen, our stagehand Kitty Klitty will be coming around with the tip jar. Give generously. Support nudity in your neighborhood."

When Kitty Klitty made her appearance at their table holding a Christmas stocking, Alec handed her a few twenties.

"Great show," he said.

"Thanks! Oh, and Bette wants to see you backstage," Kitty told Mallory.

"Me?"

Kitty nodded.

"Be right back," Mallory said.

"Meet us out front when you're done. See if she wants to go have a drink," Alec suggested. Mallory rolled her eyes.

"What? I'm sure they're all going out somewhere."

Mallory ignored him and made her way to the back of the club. The blonde with the sharp bob was sitting on the steps that led to the backstage area.

"Where are you going? It's not a show backstage, you know," she said.

"Oh—I'm sorry. Someone told me Bette asked me to come back."

"Who told you?"

"Um..." Mallory couldn't bring herself to say the name *Kitty Klitty.*

"Yeah, that's what I thought."

The curtain rustled, and Bette strode out. She wore a black silk robe cinched high, under her breasts.

"You're such a flirt, Poppy! Don't mind her," she said to Mallory. "She's always cock-blocking me."

Bette laughed a quicksilver laugh, and Mallory could have sworn the blonde went pale under her stage makeup.

"I should go, anyway. Thanks for having me backstage. I'm sure it will be useful for the article," she lied.

"Really? Then it will be a pretty boring article." Again, the laugh. "What did you think of the show?"

"Amazing."

"Yeah, the holidays get us all sentimental. Last year Scarlett Letter wore an assless reindeer costume. It was very cute. Anyway, I'm going to my friend's show in a half hour. You should really see it—quite a different burlesque experience."

"Let me check with Alec...."

"No, don't bring him. I don't want him writing about another club's show. Keep him focused on the Blue Angel, okay?"

"Thanks, anyway, but I'll have to do it another night."

Bette turned to Poppy. "She drives a hard bargain. Fine, bring Alec. But this is strictly off the record!"

"What show?" Poppy asked.

"The Slit."

"I'll go with you guys."

"I'm only on the list plus one, and I'm already bringing two. Another night."

Mallory knew she was getting another look from hell out of Poppy.

"See you out front in ten minutes," Bette said.

Alec and Allison were huddled in the vestibule of the club entrance.

"It's getting really cold out. You ready?" he said.

"Bette invited us to a show she's going to after this...at some place called the Slit."

"I can't take any more. You guys are crazy," Allison said.

"I don't think I could get you in, anyway," Mallory admitted.

"Oh...well, excuuuse me. I'm not cool enough for the late-night burlesque scene?"

"Believe me—I'm not cool enough for the late-night burlesque scene. You know, I'll just tell her we'll do it another night."

"Don't be ridiculous—it's a Saturday night. Why are we rushing home?" Alec said.

I don't know, Alec. Maybe watching an hour and a half show could be enough for one night, and we could go home and take our clothes off for each other?

"Fine," Mallory said. "We'll go."

"It'll be worth it—believe me," Alec said.

"How do you know?"

"I've been there."

Mallory and Allison looked at him.

"When were you there?'

"A month ago. Maybe longer. Billy brought me. He's friends with the owner—total society brat named Penelope Lowe."

Mallory wondered where Alec had said he was going the night he went to the Slit—because she would certainly have remembered that destination.

She also wondered if that was around the time he woke up one morning and suggested she try a Brazilian wax.

"Since you've already been there, don't feel obligated to go. I'm fine going with Bette."

"Are you mad?"

"I'm not mad that you went—I don't even know what it is. But I feel like you purposely didn't tell me, because we always talk about our nights, and I would have remembered a venue called the Slit."

"I'm sure I mentioned it."

"Okay, you two lovebirds. I'm going to get going." Allison kissed Mallory on the cheek and hailed a cab.

"Don't be upset with me," Alec said. "It was a few months ago—we ended up there in the course of some long night out. It's not a big deal."

"Is it like the Blue Angel?"

"Um, no. Not exactly."

"What's it like?"

"It's a show, but it's a different vibe. And it's hard to get a table there, and it's a five-hundred-dollar-bottle service minimum. It's more like a private club. And the tenor of the shows is more...intense."

"How so?"

"You'll see," he said.

6

The sign outside the club did not say "The Slit." Instead, it read "dance hall." And like the entrance to the Standard Hotel, the door was managed by a bulky man in a suit with an earpiece.

"Bette Noir plus two," Bette said at the door. The man said something into his headset, then opened the door for them. Mallory couldn't help noting that she had spent twenty-five years simply walking into clubs and restaurants, and suddenly it was all about being on a list.

Bette led the way. A woman dressed as a flapper greeted them with a clipboard and asked them to sign in. Mallory was amazed by the baroque interior—she felt as if she was stepping into the film *Moulin Rouge*.

And then Alec whispered to her about love, quoting the film. She smiled at him in amazement—she was so happy when they were perfectly in sync like that. He was the first guy she'd ever had that with—experiencing small moments in the exact same way. She'd had that with her best friend in high school, but never with a boyfriend.

The hostess led them up a winding, carpeted stairwell leading to the mezzanine. On stage, two women wearing crotchless dominatrix gear tossed a flaming baton back and forth.

They were shown to a curved, red leather booth. Alec squeezed her hand, then gestured for her to slide in first. She expected him to follow her, but instead he waited for Bette to sit next, and he took a place on the end.

A waitress, also dressed in a flapper dress with ropes of pearls and a feather headpiece, appeared instantly with an open bottle of champagne. She poured them all glasses, then set the bottle on the table.

"Cheers," Bette said.

Alec said something that made Bette laugh, but Mallory missed it. She was too distracted by what was going on on stage; she could have sworn she saw one of the performers put the flame out on her vagina, but then she thought she must be seeing things. And the audience, unlike at the Blue Angel, was stoic. No applause, no yelling—just cool observation.

And then she felt Bette's hand on her thigh.

Mallory glanced at Alec, and he was looking at her in a way that, given their ability to communicate wordlessly, made her strongly suspect that Bette's other hand was on Alec's thigh.

"I'm going to use the restroom," Mallory said, sliding out.

She made her way back down the staircase. Passing all the elaborately dressed women on the way to the restroom, she once again felt plain and unprepared for where the night had taken her.

The seclusion of the bathroom was a great relief. She didn't have to pee, so spent a few minutes looking at the display of hair care products, powder, combs, mouthwash, candy, gum, and multicolored condoms set out for the patrons' use. Mallory took a peppermint candy, and left.

"Hey," Alec said.

"Jesus! You scared me. The men's room is on the other side."

"I know—I wanted to talk to you."

"What's wrong?"

"Nothing's wrong. You doing okay?"

"Yes. I'm fine." She could tell he wanted to say something, that he was assessing her readiness to hear it. "What is it?"

"Are you open to the possibility of a three-way with Bette tonight?"

Mallory lost her breath. "You think that could really happen?"

He looked at her very seriously and nodded. Mallory wished she hadn't drunk the first glass of champagne so quickly. It was hard to process what he was asking of her. Yes, she knew he fantasized about having sex with her and another woman—but didn't all guys say things like that? She'd never thought the moment would actually arrive. And now maybe it had. And it felt like a moment of truth. Here she was, complaining—at least to herself—that their sex life had grown rote and was on the wane. And there he was—the man she loved more than anything— telling her what he wanted sexually. If she said no, she would have no one to blame but herself if their relationship lost its spark.

"If that's what you want," she heard herself saying.

Alec looked into her eyes, kissed her forehead, the tip of her nose, her lips.

"I love you, sweetheart," he said. "I only love you—you know that, right?"

She nodded.

"It's an adventure I want to have *with* you."

"I know," she said.

"Do you trust me?"

"Yes," she said. And it was true.

He held her hand, and they made their way back to the table.

Two women and a guy were standing by the side of the booth and chatting up Bette. Bette introduced them as Camille, Valerie, and Max.

"Max is an amazing costume designer," she said. "He is a genius with zippers."

Mallory's mind was racing too fast for her to process new people. She let Alec make the polite conversation, poured herself another glass of champagne, and she watched the show. A woman was taking off her Santa costume to the the Mel Tormé song, "Chestnuts Roasting on an Open Fire." She wasn't wearing pasties, and she was soon out of her G-string. She sat on a chair, spread her legs, and proceeded to remove what looked like a chestnut from her vagina. Mallory stifled a laugh and turned to see Alec's reaction, but he was not watching the stage.

He was kissing Bette.

Mallory didn't want to look, but she couldn't pull away—it was like watching a terrible accident at the side of the road. But before she could really get upset, Bette turned and fixed those cat blue eyes on her, and, with a smile, started kissing her. And not just the faint brush of lips like in the bathroom of the hotel, but a deep, real kiss. The first thing she thought was that it felt different—she was aware of how soft Bette's skin and mouth felt. And she was surprised at how much she didn't want Bette to stop. But Bette did stop, pulling back after a minute.

"I have to run," she said. "Camille and Anton are taking me to a party. You guys stay—enjoy the rest of the show."

Mallory nodded, gulped more champagne, and dared not look at Alec. She watched the finale of the chestnut lady—she was now juggling three of them, and Mallory didn't even want to think about where the second and third nuts came from—and felt Alec slide next to her. He pulled her hair away from her face and whispered in her ear.

"Go the bathroom. Close yourself in a stall but don't lock the door. Take all your clothes off. Text me when the coast is clear."

She looked at him like he was crazy.

"Seriously—go," he said.

And she did. And so maybe she was the one who was crazy. Or maybe she was just relieved it wasn't going to be the three of them in the bathroom. Because even though she'd said it would be okay, she knew the way she had felt when she saw him kissing Bette; the thought of having to see him do anything more than that made her stomach knot.

A woman was reapplying lipstick in the bathroom. Mallory pretended to touch up her own makeup, and found that her hands were shaking. She closed herself in a stall, locked the door, and took off her stockings, her skirt, and her blouse. She hung them all on the single hook the best that she could manage, and then put her shoes back on. She hoped standing barefoot for just a minute on the floor wasn't long enough for her to catch anything. Her mother had always warned her of the dangers lurking on unclean floors.

She closed the toilet lid and sat on it, waiting for the woman to leave. She heard crinkling as the woman sorted through something—candy? condoms?—and then finally the click of the door as she exited. Mallory pulled out her BlackBerry and texted Alec.

Coast is clear. I'm in the last stall.

She unlocked the door, wearing only her bra and underwear. The whole situation made her uneasy—what if someone came in before Alec got there? And what did he think they could get away with doing in that small space, with anyone able to walk in and hear them or worse, notice the two sets of legs under the door!

And yet, she felt incredibly turned on. She pressed her hand between her legs, testing the waters. She was wet already.

Someone came into the room, and she tensed, holding the stall door closed.

"It's me," he said, knocking lightly. She stood and opened it. The way he looked at her made all the unease worth it. "God, you're gorgeous," he said.

She put her arms around him, and they kissed. It was confusing to her that twenty minutes ago he was kissing Bette, but she tried to keep her mind blank. She felt how hard he was through his pants, and she rubbed her pelvis against him. He cupped her ass, then slipped one finger inside her from behind. He worked it in and out, and she moaned a little, knowing she could come just standing there like that.

"Take these off," he said.

After she pulled down her panties, her hand fumbled with his belt, and he helped her get his pants off. She took his cock into her hand, stroking it firmly and rubbing her thumb gently over the tip.

"Hold on," he said, and took her blouse off the hook, spreading it out over the closed toilet seat. He eased her back so she sat on it, and he stood erect before her. She took his hard cock into her mouth, using her tongue and her lips the way he liked. He thrust gently, and she held his ass, pulling him to her. He wound his fingers through her hair.

And then the door to the bathroom opened. Someone entered the stall next to theirs.

Mallory pulled away from him and looked up. He shook his head and mouthed, "It's okay." But she couldn't continue.

He pulled her to her feet.

"Turn around," he whispered.

Alec bent her over, and she braced herself with her hands on the toilet seat. He ran his hands down her back, over her ass, and then started rubbing her clit while he moved one finger inside her. Mallory bit her lip so she wouldn't moan.

The person in the next stall began to pee. Mallory wanted to stop, to just wait until she left, but Alec was already easing his hard cock inside her. He slid in and out slowly, the way that he knew always brought her to the brink of coming. Then he gave her one hard thrust and stayed inside her and she came instantly, and—to her horror—loudly. She had lost track of whether or not the person was still in the next stall. Would she tell someone who worked at the club what was going on in the bathroom? She had visions of the management calling the police, who would put them under arrest for lewd conduct, or indecent exposure...or both.

She could tell by the steady, hard rhythm of Alec's thrusting that he was close to coming. Usually, she could climax at the end, too. He was the first lover she'd ever had who made her come again and again, easily two or three times when they had sex. But she was too distracted with thoughts about what the stranger in the bathroom might be hearing or doing.

Alec came, and Mallory felt relieved that they would soon be out of the bathroom.

They quickly pulled on their clothes, and when they stumbled out of the stall, Mallory was appalled to find a young woman standing in front of the mirror. The woman didn't bother pretending to be applying makeup or combing her hair or doing anything but exactly what she was obviously doing: listening to Alec and Mallory.

"Have a good night," Alec said calmly, while Mallory rushed out of sight.

"It's off to a great start," the girl said.

"Damn," Alec said outside the bathroom. "I think she would have joined in."

Mallory shook her head.

"I hope you're joking," she said as they left the club

"Why would I be joking?"

"That wasn't enough for you?"

"Babe, it was amazing—and yes, you are enough for me.

More than enough. But sometimes I'm just open to different, interesting things. I think you are, too. That's what makes us a good match. Didn't you like it when Bette kissed you?"

"Um, yeah. I mean, I think so."

"Did you mind that she kissed me?"

"It was a little weird for me, Alec. I don't like seeing you kissing someone else—to think that someone else is turning you on. That you think about having sex with someone else. That's supposed to be between us."

"Are you upset?"

She *was* feeling a little upset, now that he called her on it.

"Yes," she admitted.

"Mallory, listen." He tried to steer her to a bench outside of a falafel restaurant, but she resisted.

"It's cold. And it's two o'clock in the morning. Let's just get a cab."

She hailed one, the big minivan kind where they wouldn't even be sitting close together in the seat. That was fine by her.

"Can you listen to me now?"

She knew she might as well agree to hear him out because he wouldn't stop talking until she did.

"Fine. I'm listening."

He pulled on her arms, which were crossed in front of her chest.

"Jeez. Your body language is terrible."

"Just say what you have to say, Alec." The champagne buzz was souring to a sugar crash.

"You know I love you. You're my partner—have been since the day we got together four years ago. Anything we do with another person is just adding on to what is between us. It's not about them—it's just something different. Fun."

"The subtext is that we're not enough—I'm not enough."

"Are you less attracted to me because you kissed Bette?"

"No."

"Are you less in love with me?"

"No."

"Then why can't you accept that it's the same for me? I adore you, Mallory. You are my soul mate, and kissing some other woman or bringing some other woman into bed with us for a fun night doesn't diminish that—not even close. Look at it this way—you got up on stage at a burlesque club. It was something you'd never done before, and it was thrilling. But it didn't change who you are. It's not like you're going to drop everything, stop being a lawyer, so you can get on stage every night. It was just a fun thing to do. It didn't change anything, did it?"

"No," she said.

But deep down she had to wonder.

7

Mallory closed the door to her office.

"Okay, I can talk now," she told Allison.

"I just wanted to hear how the rest of your night was."

"Why were you MIA yesterday? I called you three times."

"I was with Andrew. He's a big fan of the Sunday afternoon date. Such a romantic."

"Ahh...*Andrew*. When do we get to meet *Andrew?*"

"Soon. And that's another conversation. So spill it—what happened at the Slit?"

"It was...interesting." She glanced at her office door. Patricia Loomis had just e-mailed her that she would be stopping by to discuss the memo that was due at the end of the week. "I can't get into it now. But Allison—I cannot focus on work. I don't know what it is. The past few weeks...the hours pass so slowly here. I used to get lost in the research, it was like a great puzzle, and when I was done putting together the cases and wrapping up the memos, I felt a rush. Now I'm dragging myself to the finish line."

"We all feel like that sometimes. Work sucks. Just focus on

doing a decent job, make some bank, and you'll live your life outside of the office. You don't have to live for work."

"I know. I just...If I feel like this now, what will I be like in five years?"

"You'll hate it more, but will be well compensated for hating it more."

"Yeah. That's not really consoling me right now."

"You just have the Monday blues. Let's grab a drink later."

Patricia opened the door and marched into the room. Mallory quickly hung up her cell.

"Harrison wants the memo tomorrow," she said—no greeting, no preamble. She wore a putty-colored suit, her hair in a bun. Her T-zone was shiny even though it was only eleven in the morning and thirty-five degrees outside.

"What? Last Friday you said end of this week?"

"And now it's Monday. And I'm telling you tomorrow." She turned on her heel and paused by the door. "And we expect strong work, Mallory. Don't think this firm will keep lowering its expectations to meet your performance level. Have you reregistered for the bar?"

"Yes. It's in early February."

"I know when it is. Harrison wants to make sure you're on track."

"I'm on track."

"Well...good. Let's just hope you can cross the finish line this time."

Mallory slumped in her seat. She texted Alec.

I'll be home really late tonight.

Back at her computer, she logged onto Westlaw. Her cell rang.

"What's going on?" Alec asked.

"The memo I thought I had another week on is due tomorrow. Alec, I'm stressed. Patricia never liked me, but now that I failed the bar she's like contempt walking. She's just waiting for me to fuck up."

"Don't let her get to you."

"I'm trying not to. But I don't know—I'm really doubting myself lately. I never questioned doing this—of course I would be a lawyer like my parents. And law school was difficult but, you know, stimulating. It felt right. But this..."

"You can't let failing the bar throw you off your game like this, Mal. You're going to be a great lawyer. You *are* a great lawyer."

"I don't know. I'm not even sure I want it anymore." It was hard for her to admit it, but there it was—it wasn't just that she questioned her ability. She was questioning her choice of career. And it was terrifying.

"This isn't you talking, Mal. You're tired; you're stressed.... Just get through today, and tomorrow things will look completely different."

"Okay." She hung up the phone, put her head on her desk, and let herself cry.

Her phone vibrated. She hoped it was Alec. Texting her what? Saying it was okay to think she'd made a colossal mistake choosing to become a lawyer? Or maybe it was Allison, reiterating not to worry—everyone hates her job. Better yet, Julie could chime in with her usual game plan: marry rich and then quit.

But the text was from none of the above. It read:

Want 2 have some fun? We're costume shopping. Xo Bette

Mallory paused, her hands holding her BlackBerry as if it were a lottery ticket.

I'm at work, she typed.

Blow it off. Meet us at M&J Trimming, Sixth Avenue.

She looked at her watch. There was nothing wrong with taking an early lunch break, right? She'd be at the office until the middle of the night regardless.

See you there.

*   *   *

Poppy and Bette walked against the wind up Sixth Avenue. Poppy didn't mind the cold—she was wearing an ultra-heavy faux fur coat that she'd bought at Trash and Vaudeville—but Bette kept stopping to text every few feet, and the fact that she couldn't give her undivided attention for more than two minutes at a time was irritating.

"Who are you so busy texting?" Poppy asked.

"Just checking my e-mail," Bette said.

Poppy decided to let it go. After all, one hook-up did not give her the right to know whom Bette was texting or e-mailing. And it was only that—one hook-up. There had been no repeat performance after the night backstage. But Poppy had been thinking about it every day. She was a woman who prided herself on being able to fuck like a guy—no emotions, no attachments...no problem. But suddenly she was like a lovesick schoolgirl...for this crazy bitch! Maybe it was because guys were always chasing her, and Bette was, well, *not*. Or maybe it was the way she'd touched her, that perfect combination of gentle but expertly confident. And the way she smelled...kind of earthy, and sweet like vanilla. The fact that she was so beautiful didn't hurt. Poppy had been with a lot of hot guys, but none who awed her with his perfection.

"This is the place."

Poppy needed a stretchy ribbon of black sequins and some beaded fringe for a Morticia Addams costume she was working on. Agnes said she would help her with the costume, but she needed to buy all the material. It could get really expensive, but Bette said M&J Trimming was a reasonable place if you didn't get too carried away.

"Just go in knowing what you are going to buy and don't get any extras—no matter how cool or how sure you are that you will use it 'someday' for a costume," Bette warned her. "I have drawers filled with impulse buys—fringe in colors that never work, bags of sequins, tassels that are gorgeous but too big. Just stay focused."

Even though she wished Bette had given some hint that she wanted to have sex with her again, at least she'd gotten one thing she'd wished for: Bette was taking an interest in helping her make it as a performer. This shopping trip proved it. Poppy planned to secure her place as one of the lead girls, and then no newcomer would be a threat. Especially with Bette as a mentor—Agnes knew Bette was the best thing she had going, and would do anything to keep her exclusive to the Blue Angel. And Poppy would do anything to keep Bette exclusive to her.

It was a good sign that she'd invited Poppy to go shopping. As far as she was concerned, shopping was always foreplay—at least with men. Was it different between two women? Probably not.

Just as she pondered the equation Bette + Poppy + shopping = hot sex, she spotted her. It couldn't be. Why would Mallory Dale be at M&J Trimming?

"That looks like Mallory Dale."

"That is Mallory," Bette said, waving her over.

"What's she doing here?"

"I invited her."

Poppy felt her face turn colors.

"Wow. This place is amazing. It makes me wish I could sew," Mallory announced.

Poppy hated to admit it, but the other girl was terribly pretty, even in her stuffy wool coat and with lank brown hair that needed a good cut. Or highlights. Or both.

"You can't sew? Like, even a button?" Poppy said. Bette shot her a look.

"No. Nothing. Isn't it terrible? My mother could make some things and of course hemmed all of my skirts. I just take everything to a seamstress on 82nd and York."

"I didn't sew that much until I got into performing. It's too expensive to buy costumes off the rack. And it's more personal this way. Although none of us can make costumes like Agnes."

"She makes things for you?"

"Once in a while. If we have a clear idea and give her the material. I'm having her make an Alice in Wonderland costume for me."

"She mostly does it for Bette," Poppy said.

"You're still fairly new," Bette said. "She'll make something for you one day. You just have to earn it." She smiled at Poppy. Was that a sign? Even though Bette had invited that mousy interloper, there was still something special between them.

The best thing to do was just cut this ill-fated shopping excursion short. Poppy headed to the register with her sequins and fringe, hoping that Bette would follow her. Instead, Bette took it upon herself to give Mallory a tour of the place. Even from the front of the store, she could tell the Mouse—and that was what she would call her from now on, at least to herself— was oohing and aahing at everything, as if Bette had given her the keys to the Emerald-fucking-City.

"Okay, ready to go," Poppy announced, waving her shopping bag.

"We need to take Mallory somewhere to cheer her up," Bette said. "She's having a career crisis."

Great. Now the Mouse was latching on to Bette with some sob story about her job. From the looks of her clothes, it had to be paying pretty well.

"Are you allowed to just wander off in the middle of the day?" Poppy asked, as sweetly and innocently as she could muster.

"No, actually. I'm technically taking lunch, but I should get back. I have a huge thing due, and I'm going to be there half the night as it is...."

Poppy nodded, the picture of understanding.

"It's good to be responsible," Poppy said.

"Don't be ridiculous! If you're going to be there late tonight anyway, what difference does another hour make? Let's shop some more. Is there anything you need to get?"

Now the Mouse was the one turning colors.

"Well," she said slowly. She had this way of speaking that made you focus on her mouth. "My best friend was just telling me I should invest in better underwear."

No! What an operator. But what was her game? Why did she want to get close to Bette? And how did she know Bette was obsessed with underwear? I mean, they all liked underwear, all bought their share of garters and thongs and the whole bit. But Bette had a collection that necessitated outside storage space.

"Done. Have any particular place in mind?"

"Um. Maybe La Petite Coquette?"

Poppy and Bette exchanged a glance.

"You can drop that kind of coin?" Poppy asked.

"Yes," Mallory said. "The only good thing about my job is the paycheck."

And the fact that you have to get back there soon, Poppy thought to herself.

But not soon enough.

Mallory didn't want to be paranoid, but she could swear Poppy was glaring at her from across the backseat of the cab. What had she done to piss the blonde off so badly?

"Give me one good reason to stay in a job you hate," Bette said. At the fabric store, Mallory had confided how rattled she was by her recent doubts about her legal career. Somehow, it was easier to admit this to Bette than to her closest friends—even to Alec.

"Well, money for one thing. I need to support myself."

"Bullshit," Bette said. "The most successful people are people who do what they love."

"Yeah, but a lot of people are broke doing what they love. That's why they have expressions like 'starving actor.' And 'golden handcuffs.' And I went to law school. You don't just throw that away."

"Ah. The psychology of previous investment," Bette said.

Mallory looked at her.

"What?" Bette said. "You think I didn't have choices to make when I decided to perform full-time? I went to Michigan. I was an English major, psych minor. I could have an office job, a steady paycheck. But once I got a taste of this life, I couldn't go back."

The cab pulled up in front of the store on University Place, its hot pink awning unmistakable. Inside, Poppy picked up a pair of black lace French knickers.

"This place is expensive," she sniffed.

"I know. That's why I need my job!"

Bette made a beeline for the back of the store, calling over her shoulder, "If you're going to be negative, Poppy, why don't you do us a favor and just leave?"

Mallory cringed. Poppy looked as if she'd been slapped, and tossed the underwear on a table.

"Fine. I will," she said, and then, sotto voce, "Have fun spending all the money you make at your miserable job."

Poppy stormed out, and Mallory thought maybe she should go after her.

"Mallory—come on back here," Bette called. "I'm by the dressing rooms."

"This way," a young salesgirl said, leading her to Bette.

"Try these on." Bette handed her a pile of black lace. "Oh— and these." She added a package of thigh-high black stockings.

"Poppy left. Maybe you were a little harsh with her?"

"Oh, she's such a diva. She'll be fine. By tonight we'll kiss and make up."

For most people, that expression was a cliché. Coming from Bette, Mallory suspected it was a bit more literal.

"I'll be right out here if you need help," Bette said.

She closed the curtain on the small dressing room, leaving Mallory to contemplate the pile of underwear and . . . what was that thing?

Mallory opened the curtain.

"What is this?"

"You're kidding, right?"

"No." It was black and had hooks like a bra, but had four straps hanging from it. It was like some strange lingerie arachnid.

"It's a garter! Don't tell me you've never worn one before."

"I haven't. And it's really not my style."

"How do you keep your stockings up?"

"I wear . . . you know, panty hose."

"Okay, well, that has to stop immediately. That is *not hot*."

She thought of Allison's parting comment after brunch, *if your boyfriend is bringing you to burlesque clubs on your birthday . . .*

"Okay. Just . . . show me how to wear this thing."

"Absolutely. But you have to take off your clothes first."

"I'm just going to try it on. . . ."

"Over your suit? Mallory, I can tell you have a hot little body. Why are you so bashful? I'm going to help you get some things to show it off for that gorgeous guy of yours. Believe me, he won't be touching my leg under the table next time when he knows what you're rocking under those lawyer clothes."

Mallory's stomach knotted up. So he had been touching

Bette's leg under the table. Well, of course—they had kissed, so it should not surprise her. Still—it stung.

"Okay—give me a minute, and I'll call you in when I'm ready."

Mallory closed the curtain again, and faced herself in the mirror. God, she was glad she'd worn decent underwear today. Nothing spectacular—just cream-colored, lace boy shorts from the Gap and a white demibra. But it was better than the five-year-old, well-worn, floral cotton panties she sometimes fell back to when she was behind on her laundry.

She unzipped her blue pinstriped skirt and let it fall to the floor. It was a little too warm in that small space, and her skin was already slightly moist under her white blouse, but she wasn't taking that off. Observing herself in the mirror, she thought, *not bad*. Not as good as Bette or Poppy—they were nearly perfect. Not all of the dancers were like that. But those two—their bodies were art as surely as the costumes and the dances themselves. But for a twenty-five-year-old lawyer (or almost lawyer), Mallory had to admit she was in good shape. Still, she resolved to go back to Pilates the following week. Maybe even twice.

She removed her panty hose and replaced them with the sheer black thigh-highs Bette had picked out for her.

"What's the holdup in there? I know you need help getting the new stuff on—I didn't know you needed help getting the old stuff off!"

Mallory opened the curtain.

"Ready," she said, holding out the garter.

"Okay—now put it around your waist. It should just rest on your hips. No—those straps have to hang down. You really are lingerie illiterate!"

Mallory hooked the contraption around her waist and then

turned the hooks around to the back—the method she used when she first got used to wearing a bra.

Bette knelt by her side and pulled one of the straps.

"Okay, now these latch onto the stockings," she said, fastening one. "Now you try one."

Mallory bent down and tried to secure the metal latch against the thin fabric, but it wasn't working. She felt like an idiot. Did other women really do this routinely?

"Here—you slide this back, put the stocking here, and then slide this up. There! You got it. I'll do the ones in the back because that takes a more experienced hand."

Mallory felt self-conscious having Bette behind her like that, but less so when she saw herself in the mirror. She liked what she saw—more than she had in a while. Maybe more than she ever had.

Bette adjusted the length of the garter straps, then stood behind her and appraised her in the mirror as well.

"Wow. You were made for this stuff."

And then Bette ran her hand against Mallory's lower back, and over her ass. Mallory shivered, the thin layer of perspiration under her blouse turning cold.

"Wait right here. I want you to try something else," Bette said, leaving her alone with her tumbling thoughts.

Mallory turned and looked at her ass in the mirror. How was it possible that another woman was making her feel more feminine than any of her boyfriends ever had?

She slipped back into her heels, then looked herself over from her toes up to her flat stomach framed in black lace.

"You're definitely going to need help with this!" Bette said breathlessly, and produced, with a flourish, a black satin corset.

"That is gorgeous!"

"Wait til you see how it feels." Bette got to work loosening the elaborate back lacing. She glanced up. "You're going to have to take off your shirt and bra to wear this, you know."

Mallory began unbuttoning her blouse, hands shaking slightly. She hung it on a hook, then removed her bra. Bette, finished with her preparations on the corset, made no attempt to disguise the fact that she was watching her.

"Why are you so bashful?" Bette said.

"I'm not," Mallory said.

"Well, that's obviously not true. Come on—you've seen me take my clothes off twice already."

"Yeah—but that's what you do! I mean, you like having people watch you take your clothes off, right?"

"Of course I do. It's exhilarating to be objectified. Don't you like the fact that I enjoy looking at you—that I obviously think you're beautiful?"

Mallory swallowed hard.

"Here—let's get this on." Bette wrapped the corset around Mallory's torso. "Hold the front while I lace up the back." She pulled the laces tight, and Mallory lost her breath.

"Oh my God!" she laughed giddily.

"I know—amazing, right?"

Mallory looked at them in the mirror. Bette was intent on her lacing task, her shiny dark hair falling across her face. She watched her pale fingers work quickly down the back of the garment, her blood maroon nail polish shiny in the fitting room light. Mallory imagined those fingers against her flesh, but immediately shook the thought away.

"Now, do those hooks in the front."

Mallory started at the bottom. The corset was so stiff it was difficult to get more than a few hooks fastened without one coming undone.

"Slow down," Bette said. Mallory felt herself beginning to perspire again, but she took a deep breath and concentrated on the task. When she finished, she turned to look at herself in the mirror.

And what she saw was someone else entirely.

"I can't believe it," she breathed. There was no difference between the woman she saw in the mirror and the women she saw on the Blue Angel stage.

"I can," Bette said. "This is how I see you. And how you should see yourself."

8

"Anybody home?"

The apartment seemed suspiciously quiet considering Alec had promised to be there when she finally got home from work. But the living room was dark, as was their bedroom. Maybe he'd gotten tired of waiting since she hadn't left the office until ten.

Mallory turned on lights as she moved through the apartment. Maybe it was just as well—she could put away the new additions to her wardrobe and make them a surprise over the weekend.

She heard his key in the lock just as she was arranging her corset in her underwear drawer. It took up a lot of space and probably needed to go on a shelf in her closet but she'd have to leave it for now. She folded up the La Petite Coquette bag and shoved it the drawer, too.

"Hey, I'm in here," she said.

"I meant to be here when you got back, but Billy called me to meet him for a quick drink, and you know Billy.... One turned into four."

"Oh. No problem," she said. But hearing he had been with Billy burned her up a little. Alec knew she'd had a rough day at work and would want to maybe have a glass of wine with him, but once he'd had a drink or two he usually was done for the night. "Do we have any bottles of that cabernet left?"

"I think so. Want me to open one for you?"

"Yes—thanks."

She moved to the couch, relaxing a little. He was home now; he was getting her a glass of wine. . . . They just needed to spend time together. And after testing the waters with Bette by admitting aloud how much she hated her job, she was ready to tell Alec.

"I would have a glass with you but I already had a few beers with Billy," Alec said, predictably, handing her a glass.

"Um," Mallory responded.

"So did you make a dent in the memo?"

"I did. A dent. But this is a major crunch. I should have stayed later tonight, but I just didn't have it in me."

"Did you at least go out to pick up lunch? It's important to get outside for a short break during the day. I know the culture there is very order in / eat at your desk, but if you take a short break it's better for you."

"Actually, I got out for quite a bit this afternoon. Bette texted me that she was shopping for costume material and invited me to meet up with her and that blonde, Poppy."

"You're kidding."

"No."

"Why would she do that?"

"I don't know." Suddenly Mallory felt on the defensive. "Maybe she thought you were still looking for details for your article."

"Well, you can tell her the article is closed, and she can stop bothering you."

"It wasn't a bother. I had a miserable morning and getting out for an hour saved my sanity."

"Don't be melodramatic."

"I'm not, Alec. I hate that fucking job."

He looked at her.

"Since when?"

"I don't know. Lately. Always." She felt tears in her eyes. "I made a huge mistake going into law. It's not right for me. School was challenging and interesting, and I thought I'd be great at putting it into practice. But I hate the firm; I hate the culture. I can't imagine doing this for another year, let alone the rest of my life."

"Okay, you need to calm down. Sweetheart, I think this is just stress talking. You're still upset about failing the bar—which I've told you is not a big deal; you have to let it go and not see it as indicative of your future as a lawyer—and you're anxious because Patricia is busting your balls. But you're going to be a brilliant lawyer. This is just a rough patch."

She shook her head. "I don't think so. And talking to Bette about it today just confirmed that it's not normal to hate what you do every day. To dread waking up Monday morning. I can't live like that. I need to figure out what I want to do and not just continue down the wrong path because it's the one I started on."

"Okaaay," he said, as if talking to a small child. "What else would you want to do?"

"I don't know. Maybe something creative. I mean, Bette went to Michigan, but she found her passion in life...."

"I can't believe you're letting that girl fuck up your head like this. Jesus, Mallory. We spent three years apart so you could go to law school. You spent the last two summers securing your place at this firm. We've planned our future talking about your legal career and my journalism career, and how we would balance the two and make a life together. Now you're going to mess up everything you've built the past few years because you got carried away at a burlesque show?"

"I got carried away? You're the one who had your hands all over her under the table. It's fine for you to want things—but I should just tow the line...not make waves?"

"So that's what this is about. You're trying to make a point—punishing me for admitting that I want to have a three-way."

"Oh, my God! This isn't about you."

"You're right—it's about you being unable to accept that, unlike in college, the real world isn't going to constantly affirm the greatness of Mallory Dale."

"You are such an asshole."

She gulped her wine, slammed down the glass, and stormed off to the bedroom. Alec followed her.

"You've been nervous and nitpicking and basically a mess ever since you moved to New York. You resent Billy for taking so much time away from us; you resent my job for consuming my attention; you want to ditch your legal career because it's not falling into place easily enough for you...."

"And you're escaping into your job because you don't want to deal with our relationship. This whole threesome thing is just a way for you to solve your boredom with us without doing the hard work of breaking up with me." By now the tears that had started on the couch had morphed into racking sobs. She dragged her overnight bag down from the top of the closet and folded her work clothes into it.

"I don't have some magic word that is going to convince you that I love you, that I want this relationship. You're going to have to figure that out for yourself. Along with everything else, apparently."

"Sure. I'll get right on that."

And she left.

* * *

Outside, she called Julie and then Allison, but neither picked up her phone. She hailed a cab and took it to Allison's place in Soho, but when she buzzed her apartment, no one answered.

"Fuck!" She was probably with that new guy. And Julie was all the way back uptown on the Upper West Side. Stupid—she should have tried there first.

She sat on the steps of Allison's building and scrolled through her phone. She paused on Bette's text from earlier—had it really only been that morning?—and hesitated only a minute before typing *Are you around? I need to talk.*

Seconds later she got her reply.

114 East 4th Street. #2A. I'll buzz you up.

Bette Noir's apartment was a small one-bedroom. But it was fantastic, with vivid color everywhere: blue walls, translucent green plastic tables, and a retro white couch. A faux zebra rug covered most of the living room space, and four photos lined the wall behind the couch, a striking series of half-naked women dressed in garters and corsets.

"Your place is amazing," Mallory said.

"Thanks. Now listen, I only have vodka. But since you felt the need to come here at midnight in the middle of the week, I suggest you do a shot. I'll join you."

She disappeared into the alcove kitchen, and returned with two full shot glasses. They sat on the pristine white couch.

"*Svoboda,*" Bette said, raising her glass.

"*Svoboda,*" said Mallory. They downed the vodka. It was perfectly chilled.

"That's 'freedom' in Russian."

"Are you Russian?"

"My mother is Russian. My father is French. Terrible combination, just for the record. But you're not here to talk about my parents, *n'est-ce pas?*"

"No. I'm not. But it might be nice to hear about them just to get my mind off things."

"Sometimes you have to keep your mind on things to solve the problem."

"I know." Mallory looked up at the photograph series. The redhead was stunning. "I always wanted to dye my hair that color," she said.

"Why don't you?"

"Oh...no. I wouldn't do that."

"Why on earth not? It's not surgery. If you don't like it, you dye it back. God, Mallory. What is the point of being a woman if you don't have fun with it?"

"I don't know. That's a good question."

Mallory settled back on the couch. She contemplated asking for another shot.

"I'm guessing that it wasn't a quest for the perfect hair color that brought you here tonight. So why don't you tell me what's up."

"I had a fight with Alec. I know it sounds stupid, but I just couldn't stay there tonight. I called my best friends but neither of them was around. And I thought of you—because you were so nonjudgmental earlier."

"What would I be judgmental *about*?"

"The whole job thing."

"What's the big deal? So you don't like your job."

"I told Alec, and he freaked, basically implied that I don't like it just because it's not falling into place easily for me. I told him I'm having second thoughts about my legal career, and he turned it into a referendum on my character."

"That doesn't make sense."

"Yeah, well, you don't know Alec. He expects a lot of people—himself included. He's not good with failure or weakness."

"You didn't fail."

Mallory nodded. "I did. I failed the bar exam."

"Can't you take it again?"

"Yeah, I'm going to. In February. But that doesn't change the fact that I failed it the first time."

"Do you know how many auditions I went on before I got my first booking?"

"You had to audition?"

"Of course. What, you think I just walked into the Blue Angel and signed up like it was a school talent contest?"

"I guess I didn't think about it at all."

"I had to learn how to perform, practice, feel stupid and bad at it. Then I got better, but I still didn't know how to get a club to take me seriously. I got laughed off the stage when I auditioned at the Slit. Then I got my chance at the Bell Jar, then at a few private parties for a well-known patron of the arts. And then Agnes heard about me and gave me an audition at the Blue Angel. And I've been performing there for two years. But I didn't say 'I failed my audition here or wherever so I'm a bad performer.'" She patted Mallory's knee. "I'm going to get us another shot."

Mallory rested her head on the arm of the couch, gazing up at the redhead in the photograph. She imagined herself with red hair, like the model Karen Elson. It might actually look good. She wondered what Alec would think, then remembered that it might not matter anymore.

"What's the word for freedom, again?" Mallory asked, putting back the shot.

"*Svoboda.*"

"Yeah. Well, you know what they say about freedom."

"Nothing left to lose?"

"Exactly."

"I don't believe that," Bette said. She set her shot glass on the coffee table. "You like those photographs?"

"Yeah. They're amazing."

"I have better ones to show you. Follow me."

Mallory followed her across the living room, almost tripping over the edge of the zebra rug. She would not have another shot—two was enough.

Bette's bedroom was painted robin's egg blue. One entire wall was mirrored. A series of photos in black frames hung above her bed—three in an even row. From across the room Mallory knew instantly they were of Bette. That short black hair and pale ivory skin was iconic.

In the first she wore a black corset, seamed stockings, and long black opera gloves. In the next, she wore just the stockings and high red patent leather heels—her back was to the camera; she was bent over and peaking at the camera from below. The third photo showed her sitting against a white wall, wearing knee-high argyle stockings and black Mary Jane heels, with her arms crossed in front of her breasts but her legs spread to show her vagina.

"Wow. Those are...incredible."

"Thanks. My friend Evangeline took them. She's an amazing fashion and fetish photographer. Next time she's in town I'll introduce you."

"Were you embarrassed to do that photo?"

"No. Why would I be embarrassed?"

"It's so...personal."

"Relationships are personal. That's art." She sat on the edge of the bed, then waved Mallory over to her. "Stand in front of me."

"Why?" Mallory asked nervously.

"Because I want to look at you."

"No," Mallory said with a nervous laugh.

"Why not? You look at me all the time."

"You like being looked at!"

"All women like being looked at. Some of us are just better at admitting it than others. So come on—stand in front of me."

She tugged on Mallory's hand, and Mallory complied reluctantly. "There you go—indulge me," Bette said with a wink. She suddenly looked as animated and excited as a school girl.

"Wait here and don't move!" she said. "Actually, turn this way." She tugged on Mallory so she faced the mirrored wall. "Okay—now close your eyes."

Mallory half closed her eyes.

"No, really close them tight. I want to see wrinkles."

"I don't have wrinkles yet."

"Well, close them so tight you create them! Yes—perfect. Be right back."

Mallory heard drawers opening and closing. "Don't open them," Bette called from across the room.

"I'm not." But she was dying to. For one thing, the two shots of vodka were making it hard to maintain her balance with her eyes shut.

"Keep them closed."

Mallory could tell Bette was getting closer again, and then she felt soft fabric against her face; she was blindfolded.

"Bette! What are you doing?"

"I'm giving you the chance to be like a photograph—observed, not observing. I really think you need to let go and allow yourself to be objectified. It's very liberating."

"This feels a little *too* liberating to me. I like limits....I mean, I'm a lawyer. I need boundaries...structure."

"You're not a lawyer—you failed the bar, remember? Now chill and just go with it."

"So I should just stand here while you stare at me. And this is supposed to be liberating?"

"No, you're supposed to stand there and take your top off. Then we're getting somewhere."

Mallory let out a half laugh, half giggle. "I am not taking my shirt off."

"Of course you are. Don't be ridiculous."

"Only if you leave the room. And I mean it—I want to hear the door close, and you have to talk to me from the other room so I know you're out there."

"How can you experience being observed if I'm not here to observe you, silly? Here, if it makes you feel any better, I'll turn around while you take it off."

"Oh, my God—as if!" Mallory was laughing now. And she was vaguely aware that for the first time for as long as she could remember, she wasn't worried about or thinking about anything beyond the moment.

"Just do it—it will take your mind off of Alec. Seriously, if you wanted to just wallow on a couch all night, you might as well have gone to your friend's place."

"What friend?"

"The Stepford Wife you brought to the show with you the other night."

"Allison? She's not a Stepford Wife."

"She will be—trust me. So I don't see what you're so afraid of—it's not like I don't have tits of my own. Great ones, if I say so myself."

Mallory couldn't argue with her there.

"Besides," she continued. "I already saw you half-naked in the dressing room at La Petite Coquette. So just humor me and take off your shirt. Or do you want me to do it for you?"

Something about Bette's last question made her stomach do a tiny flip. And, as if the other woman could sense that, Mallory felt Bette's hands on the top button of her blouse.

"I like this shirt," Bette said. "Where's it from?"

"Thomas Pink," Mallory said in a whisper.

She felt air on her skin, her shirt fully unbuttoned. Bette moved behind her and eased it off her shoulders. She traced her fingers down Mallory's spine, then up again, pausing to unhook her bra. Mallory considered stopping her, but she couldn't think of one good reason why.

Her bra fell to the floor, and she felt Bette tugging off her blindfold.

"Now look at yourself," Bette said. Mallory opened her eyes, gazing straight ahead into the mirror. But she couldn't look at herself—instead, she was focused on Bette, who had also removed her own T-shirt. Although Mallory had seen her naked breasts twice already, it was as if she was seeing Bette for the first time.

"Don't look at me—look at yourself. See how beautiful you are?"

And then she reached around and cupped Mallory's breasts. Their eyes met in the mirror, and Mallory felt something electric pulse in the center of her.

Bette brushed her fingers across Mallory's nipples, bringing them to points. She pressed her own breasts against Mallory's back, and Mallory felt herself grow wet.

"Turn around," Bette breathed against her neck. Mallory moved to face her, and when Bette pressed her mouth against Mallory's, she eagerly opened her lips. She realized she had been, on some level, imagining this moment since that first butterfly kiss in the Standard Hotel bathroom.

Bette pulled her onto the bed, easing off Mallory's skirt and then her own jeans. Mallory felt a pang of anxiety. Was she supposed to touch Bette? She was lost. All these years of being fucked by men, and she had no idea what to do with a woman. How was that possible?

"Just be still," Bette said, as if reading her mind. Mallory lay back, and Bette bent her mouth to Mallory's breast. Her lips were so soft, and Mallory was aware of how warm Bette's mouth was—it felt different than with a guy. Bette sucked and ran her tongue over Mallory's nipple, then bit her lightly, her hands running down the inside of Mallory's thighs. Mallory lifted her pelvis removing her underwear, shocked at how much she wanted Bette's fingers inside of her.

Bette moved her mouth down Mallory's stomach, kissing and licking her. Mallory arched her back, her hands in Bette's hair. She felt Bette's mouth get closer to her pussy, and it made her tense. But why should she be nervous? Bette was a girl, too—if anything, she should be totally at ease.

And then she felt Bette's tongue brush over her clit, then softly slide lower until she found the spot to push her tongue deep inside. Mallory cried out, arching her back and pulling Bette's head closer. Bette moved her mouth back to Mallory's clit, working one finger in and out.

"Oh, my God," Mallory said, feeling her pussy clench against Bette's finger in waves that made her whole body tremble. Bette moved back up to lie lengthwise with Mallory, the rhythm of her hand not missing a beat. Mallory kissed Bette's mouth, licking her full lips, tasting herself on this strange and beautiful woman.

Bette sensed when Mallory was finished, and she brushed her hand softly along the outside of her pussy, kissing her breasts.

"What do you want me to do?" Mallory said.

Bette smiled at her, her fingers languidly tracing Mallory's thigh.

"Why don't you just watch me?"

"Really?"

"Yes. You know I like putting on a good show."

Bette stretched out next to her, spreading her legs. Mallory felt uncomfortable watching her, but she knew it was what Bette wanted, so she kept her eyes on Bette's hands. Bette cupped her breasts with her left hand and sucked on the middle finger of her right, then rubbed her wet finger all over her open pussy. To her surprise, Mallory felt herself getting excited again.

"I changed my mind," Bette said, her fingers skimming over her clit. "I want you to touch me."

"I don't know what to do," Mallory said.

"Lie next to me." Mallory moved across the bed and pressed her body against Bette's. They kissed, their mouths wide and hungry for each other, and Mallory let herself feel the wetness between Bette's legs. Bette took her hand and pressed it firmly into her pussy, and Mallory gingerly slipped a finger inside of her.

"Yes," Bette breathed, and Mallory's stomach did a tiny flip. Bette guided her hand, pulling it up to massage her clit, then returning it to her center. Mallory moved her finger in and out, and felt Bette clench hard around her hand. Mallory wondered if this was what Alec felt when he was doing the same thing to her.

Bette climaxed with a shudder, and when Mallory withdrew from her, Bette took her wet fingers and pressed them into Mallory's mouth. They locked eyes, and Mallory knew she wanted her to lick her finger, to taste her. She hesitated a second, then sucked Bette's stickiness from her hand. Bette sat up and kissed her deeply, then pulled her down to lie with her against her pillows.

"I'm a little freaked out," Mallory confessed, her head against Bette's shoulder. She could feel the rise and fall of Bette's chest as she breathed, and she was surprised by this intimacy more than by the sexual encounter they'd just shared. She thought of Bette the way she had first seen her, this unimaginably remote creature who seemed almost unreal. And here she was beside her in bed.

"Why? Because I'm a woman?"

"Well, yes. That. And because I haven't been with anyone except Alec in four years."

Bette rolled over to face her.

"I don't think you should tell him about this."

"I have to—I can't just keep something like this from him. That makes it like I cheated on him or something."

"I hate to break it to you, darlin', but he most certainly will see this as cheating on him."

"No, he won't. He wanted me to sleep with you."

"Yeah—with him *there*. I see your logic, but trust me, you will not get a free pass because of that."

"Oh, God. I've just made things worse. Now I have to sort out the fight *and* deal with this."

"Blame it on the vodka. Do you have any Russian in you? I mean, aside from when I'm fucking you..."

"Bette, I'm serious! I love Alec. I don't want to lose him. I think I should just deal with the fight we had tonight, work through that, and then when things are better on that front, tell him that I kind of hooked up with you."

"Sounds like a plan."

They both stared at the ceiling.

"You are really hot, by the way," Bette said, rolling over and kissing her cheek. "I'm going to take a shower and get some sleep. I have to be at the club at noon for Agnes to fit me for a costume, then to practice a new act I'm trying out tomorrow night. Want me to make up the couch for you? Or you can sleep here if you want. I'm not great at sharing a bed, though."

"The couch would be great," Mallory said, knowing full well she wouldn't sleep a wink.

9

Mallory tossed her bag on the sofa, and dropped her coat in a heap on top of it.

"Hello? Alec, are you here?"

It was almost eight o'clock at night, and the day of silence between them had been agonizing. She'd called him twice from the office but got his voice mail. She couldn't wait another minute to finish the conversation that had escalated into a fight, then find a way to move on.

Mallory sank into the sofa, trying to remember the last time she'd been so exhausted. Maybe the night she pulled an all-nighter junior year. Or the first weekend she spent with Alec when she was so excited to be next to him she couldn't sleep. Last night was the same—she would doze off for a short while, then wake with a start, realizing where she was, her body still feeling the thrill of Bette.

She'd slept on Bette's couch, under the picture of the redhead. She had dreamt she colored her hair, but it came out bright purple. The firm sent her home for the day and told her not to come back until she looked like a lawyer, so she left, but when she arrived home in the dream, she looked like Bette, and Alec told her he could never be in love with a lesbian.

She heard the key in the door, and Alec walked in, clearly happy to see her.

"Hey," he said.

"Hey."

He took his time putting his coat in the closet. When he turned to face her, his expression was warm but guarded.

"I'm glad you're here. We need to talk," he said.

"I know."

He crossed the room and pulled her into a hug. It felt so good to be held against him, to breathe his familiar Alec smell, to feel the brush of his lips against her temple. *This is love*, she thought.

"I'm sorry about last night," he said, sitting next to her on the couch. "I was way too harsh. I was thinking about it after you left, and I thought about texting you, but I decided to let us both have the night to cool down. Did you stay at Julie's?"

"Um, Alec, I really feel bad about last night."

"It was my fault. I know you're not a quitter, and if you are this unhappy at the firm, we will talk about it and figure out a way to fix it. I love you—I want you to be as happy in your career as I am in mine. I thought you had that with your law career. It seems impulsive just to change your mind about something after you've invested all these years."

"I know. I've thought that too. But until I got into the firm, I had no idea what it really meant to be a lawyer. I love the law; I like the ideas behind it. . . . I liked learning it. I just don't want to spend my life practicing it. So a part of me is thinking, if I know this now, why spend another five years going down the wrong path? Won't it just be harder and more of a waste to leave then?"

"What else would you want to do?"

"I don't know."

"Then I think you should give it some more time—see if you can figure out something else. But until then, try to give this your best shot. Certainly don't make a decision until after you've taken the bar again. I know you're going to ace it, and I want you to experience that, so you stop feeling so bad about what happened in August."

He hugged her again, kissing her forehead, her nose, her lips. He moved his hand inside her blouse, and when his fingers brushed her nipples she thought of Bette.

"Alec," she said, pulling back.

"It's fine, baby. We'll figure it out," he breathed, his mouth moving down her neck.

"Wait—I need to tell you something."

She pulled back, taking his hand and leading him to the couch.

"I was really upset last night. You and I are supposed to be able to talk about anything, and I was admitting something to you that was hard for me even to admit to myself, and you freaked out. I left here, and I tried calling Julie, and she didn't pick up, and Allison wasn't around. I even went down to Allison's building. I didn't want to come back here, so I thought of calling Bette, and luckily she was home."

"You called Bette Noir?"

"Yeah. I saw her yesterday, and I'd started telling her about my job situation and she was so understanding...."

"Well, I'm glad she was there for you. It's a bit odd that out of all people she's the one who you ended up confiding in, but so be it." He reached out and stroked her hair.

"Yeah. Well, it was a little more than confiding."

He stopped touching her.

"What do you mean?"

"This is hard for me to explain, Alec. I was upset—not just about the fight last night, but about the way things have been between us since I got to New York."

"What do you mean, how things have been since you got to New York?"

"It's hard to explain."

"Try."

"I feel less close to you. I feel like an appendage to your life here instead of really being a part of it. Part of the reason I let myself get pulled on stage the night of my birthday was because I thought, on some level, it would make you finally see me. I don't feel like you want me physically the way you used to...."

"I think our sex life is as good—if not better—than ever."

"Then why do you look at other women all the time? And why are you so fixated on the idea of having a threesome—like I'm not enough?"

"First of all, all guys look at women. It's human nature. And I'm not fixated on the idea of a threesome. I just think it could be interesting, and I would like to experience that with you. If it doesn't happen, it's not a big deal."

"It feels like a big deal."

"I think you're overthinking things."

"Maybe. But that's the way I've been feeling. And so last night I was upset. I went to Bette's, had a few drinks. And then we... hooked up."

Alec smiled a funny smile and shook his head. "What are you talking about?"

"Just what I said. We hooked up."

He pulled back on the couch, looking at her as if she was a stranger.

"Can you be more specific?"

Mallory thought of herself being blindfolded, of Bette unbuttoning her blouse....

"She kissed me and... I let her touch me."

"I can't believe you. You are such a hypocrite! You get offended—angry, actually—because I admit to you that I fantasize about bringing another woman into bed with us—*us* being the operative word here, Mallory—and then you run off and let another woman fuck you the minute we have an argument."

"We didn't...she didn't fuck me. It wasn't sex. She just touched me....It was nothing."

"Did you come?"

"What?"

"Did you have an orgasm?"

"I mean, yeah, but..."

Alec pushed himself off the couch and stalked off to their bedroom. He slammed the door.

Jesus. Mallory put her head in her hands. Bette had been right—this was a disaster. How could she have done this? She'd spent all this time worrying about his losing interest in her, his neglecting her, about their not having the same connection anymore—and then she'd gone off and hooked up with someone else. But did it really count if it was a woman? She wasn't a lesbian. It wasn't as if there was a chance she would have a relationship with Bette, leave Alec for her. That was the basic problem with infidelity—the risk that one person would leave for the new partner. Bette was not a threat to her intimacy with Alec—it wasn't the same as if she'd slept with another man, someone she could fall in love with and have a side relationship with. What had happened with Bette was nothing. And it wasn't the same as his hooking up with another woman, even with her in the room. Alec had relationships with women; she, Mallory, had not—had never, would never. Plus, she wasn't the one asking to do things to spice up their sex life; she was the one focused on him, and on them. So why should he be mad that she'd done something a little crazy? Wasn't that what he wanted from her? Be adventurous—go to the Slit. Be open-minded—let me grope Bette under the table. Be more interesting—let me fuck you in a public bathroom. But the second she'd acted on the adventurousness he'd asked her to tap into, he was freaking.

She followed him into the bedroom.

"You're the hypocrite!" she said. "You ask me to do things that are way out of my comfort zone—you take me to see women take off their clothes on my birthday, an experience you have *no* idea if I'll even like; you tell me to dance for you, as if I need to step it up a notch to be worthy of your interest. You kiss another woman in front of me, ask me to be open to having sex with her, fuck me in a bathroom because God forbid we just come back here and do something pedestrian like make love. And then I have the opportunity to push my own boundaries a little, and you can't handle it!"

He shook his head. "You don't get it. All those things were about us, Mallory. What you did last night was about you. But you're too insecure to see that distinction. Ever since you got to New York, you've been threatened by my life here, the life I established here looking forward to the day when you would finish school and join me so we could share it together. I couldn't wait for you to get here and for us to explore this world together. I'm a journalist, Mallory. A writer. I am always looking for new things, interesting stories, a different way to look at life."

"I know...and I love that about you."

"You love it, but it threatens you, too. So then you run off last night and do something that you know will hurt me. Did you even think about that for a second?"

"No...I mean, I didn't think you would be upset."

He looked at her like she'd slapped him.

"You...didn't think I'd be upset?"

She started crying, realizing what a huge mistake she'd made. "No, I didn't."

"Then we don't know each other the way I thought we did. Maybe you were right. We're not 'clicking' lately. I think we need some time apart."

Now she was the one to look stunned.

"You want to break up? Over this?"

"What do you define as 'this'? The fact that you slept with someone else? Or the fact that you thought I wouldn't care? Or the general lack of connection between us lately?"

"You were just looking for an excuse to break up with me."

"I can't believe you really think that, but if you do, it explains why you handed me the perfect reason to do it."

"Fine. I'll leave." Her sobs were, at that point, inhibiting normal speech. She started throwing random items of clothing into a suitcase.

Alec retreated to the living room. She sat on the bed, hyperventilating, and dialed Julie.

Poppy was pleased. The Morticia Addams costume was a hit. At least, if you were judging by the reaction of the cute guy in the suit in the front row. She would swear she could see his hard-on from the stage.

She was surprised to see Bette chatting him up after the show. Very unlike her.

In the dressing room, she asked, "Do you know that guy at the front table—the suit?"

"The cute one?"

"Yeah—if you go for that Wall Street type."

"That's Justin Baxter. He used to be a regular when this place was totally underground. "

Poppy had heard all about the early days, before Agnes got fined for letting the girls get completely naked and also serving alcohol. Poppy still didn't totally understand the rules, but it had something to do with cabaret licensing. She also knew the Slit got away with their shows because of payola, but Agnes didn't play that game.

Bette continued. "He and his wife are art people—they can make careers—artists, dancers, actors. When the Baxters think you are hot, you are hot. I didn't get my gig at the Blue Angel until after I headlined a Baxter bash."

"What do you mean?"

"Once or twice a year he hires me for private parties. He and his wife have a shitload of money, and they love spending it. They're flying me out to LA in a few weeks for his birthday party. It's going to be insane. They have an...open relationship. To say the least."

Poppy wondered if Bette had ever slept with him. She decided to ask. After all, they were technically lovers now, right? And lovers could ask each other things like that.

"Did you ever sleep with him?"

"Of course not. You know I don't sleep with men. And I especially don't sleep with men who come to shows. And I suggest you don't, either."

That seemed a bit sweeping, but it wasn't a point worth arguing at the moment.

"What does he do?"

"Nothing."

"He doesn't work?"

"Not that I know of. She's got the bank. Martha Pike. Ever hear of her?"

"No—should I have?"

"Kegel Queen? Ring a bell?"

Poppy gave her a blank look. "What's a Kegel? That Jewish noodle dish?" Since moving to New York she'd learned a lot about Jews. She'd certainly never met one in Arkansas, where she grew up.

"Poppy, I need to speak with you," Agnes called from outside the dressing room.

"No. That's *kugel*. Ask Agnes about Kegels. She's the one who taught me all about them."

"Coming, Agnes." Poppy pulled on her pink satin robe. She

hated not being "in the know." And why didn't she ever get invited to private parties by rich dudes? She wondered what Bette got paid.

"Hey, Agnes—what's a Kegel?" she asked.

"Ugh! You American girls. Do your mothers teach you nothing? The Kegel is exercise for your vagina so it don't get too loose. Thank God you have me to help you or in ten years you'd be in trouble."

That couldn't be what Bette meant. How could that guy's wife make tons of money off of vagina exercises? She might have to get more specific with this particular line of questioning.

"Have you ever heard of the Kegel Queen?"

"Of course! Her husband used to be good customer. She invent little ball you put in your vagina, and you squeeze and there, tight."

Good Lord. Yet another thing to tell her friends back home that they wouldn't believe.

"Now we have business to discuss: Kitty is ready to do her first show next week, but I don't have anyone to work as cleanup girl between sets. If we don't find someone, I need you to help out just for a show or two. Kitty has been very patient, and she auditioned for me last night, and she's ready. She's been supportive of all you girls and, since you were the last girl to move up to the stage, I need you to just help her out."

Poppy said nothing. If she spoke at all, she would say something along the lines of, *are you fucking kidding me?* But Agnes couldn't tolerate swearing. Poppy could not think of a response that didn't include at least one expletive.

"Thank you, Poppy. You're a good girl. So remember, next Friday night you're our stagehand. Hopefully just for one show, and we'll find our new girl."

Poppy watched her walk off. She turned to the dressing

room, but decided not to go in. If she saw Kitty in there, she might explode.

She walked out to the main room and sat in a chair. Across the room, Mr. Kegel himself was pacing and talking on his cell. Most of the audience had cleared out, and aside from a few stragglers and Kitty Klitty still trying to get some money in the tip jar, it was just the two of them. He eyed her as he finished his call, then strolled over to her.

"Nice performance," he said.

"Glad you liked it."

"Justin Baxter." He held out his hand.

"Poppy LaRue." She let him take hers. He had beautiful, gunmetal gray eyes.

"I know. You're making quite a name for yourself already."

"Really?"

"Absolutely. I haven't been to this club in a year or so, but I had to check out Agnes's latest and greatest." Things were looking up! Agnes might try to demote her for a show, but it was too late; the word was out. Poppy LaRue had arrived. "We're having a little party back at my place. Care to join? My wife always welcomes the addition of an artist to our little get-togethers."

"Sure. I just have to change."

"My car is outside. I'll be waiting."

Poppy felt his eyes on her as she walked back to the dressing room. She was surprised to feel her heart racing a bit. Was he hitting on her? He did mention his wife, but Bette said they had some sort of open relationship. Of course, she had also said she would never sleep with a guy who came to the shows. But who was she to judge? And she'd made it perfectly clear she wanted to hook up with Mallory—whom she'd met as an audience member. Hypocrite!

Poppy wished she'd brought better clothes, but how was

she supposed to know she'd be going home with some hot rich dude after the show? From now on she had to be prepared for anything. This was how she'd imagined her life in New York would be—and how she had imagined it would feel to be a performer at the Blue Angel. She felt, for the first time since moving to New York, special. It had been easy to feel special in Arkansas—she had always been the prettiest; she had been the most adventurous; and, thanks to her German, film-fanatic grandmother, she had been the most cultured. She knew she had impressed Agnes at that first meeting by knowing about the Marlene Dietrich film, *The Blue Angel*. And no one else in her town had ever heard of burlesque. But her grandmother had grown up in Berlin, and she gave Poppy a cosmopolitan sensibility that drove her to New York. The problem was, once she'd arrived, she had felt invisible. She was no longer the standout blonde, the most interesting, the most ambitious. She was just like everybody else—until two weeks ago when she stepped onto the Blue Angel stage as a performer for the first time. Now she was somebody. Justin Baxter had confirmed it.

"We're going to the Bell Jar," Bette said.

"Thanks, but I have plans," Poppy was pleased to announce. Of course Bette just assumed she was waiting around for her.

"Oh? Anything interesting?"

"I'm going to a party at Justin Baxter's place," she said smugly.

"That's not a good idea."

"You're just jealous that you're not the only one he's interested in anymore."

"You don't know what you're talking about," Bette said. "Fine—go. I'll try not to say 'I told you so.' "

10

The car pulled up to a twenty-two-foot aluminum gate that looked more like a vast modern art sculpture than the entrance to a residence.

"Wow," Poppy said.

"I know. Very Gaudi-esque, right?" said Justin. She had no idea what he was talking about, but she nodded anyway. The structure practically glowed. Behind it, was the glass façade of a building that was straight out of a Woody Allen movie where people lived in impossibly perfect houses.

Although she and Justin had chatted easily in the car, the awesomeness of his home made her uncomfortable, and they fell silent. For the first time since leaving the club, she wondered why Bette had warned her not to go.

"Sounds like the party has definitely started without us," he said. Sure enough, the sound of loud music and laughter greeted them. Poppy tried not to look too impressed with the huge entrance foyer. She was thankful she didn't know anything about art, because she had a feeling that if she did, it would be impossible not to betray how utterly out of her depth she was.

And then she saw it: a giant fish tank hanging high across the room. Except it wasn't a fish tank—it was a glass cube with a girl inside. She wore a tank top and camouflage cargo shorts, and her dark hair was in a high ponytail. She seemed quite content up there, flipping through a thick, hardcover book and painting her toenails.

"What...is that?" she asked him.

"Cool, right? Martha and I kind of stole the idea from André Balazs, but we just couldn't resist."

"Does she...live here?"

"No! She's an NYU student. We pay her by the hour. It works for everyone—gives us some nice, live art, and she gets paid while she does her chemistry homework. I'd offer you a shift, but I'm sure we couldn't afford you." He winked.

Poppy was speechless.

Someone took her coat. (A butler? Did people still have butlers?)

"Please remove your shoes, madam," the man said.

Poppy looked at Justin.

"Yeah, my wife is very protective of her floors. They cost a small fortune, so I can't really argue with her on this one."

Poppy bent down and reluctantly removed her heels. Thank God she was five foot nine and didn't need the height boost. But they did do wonders for her calves. Luckily she was wearing jeans.

Justin steered her to an enormous living room, and she could see what he meant about the floors. They were the darkest, shiniest wood she had ever seen, covered here and there by super shaggy, white area rugs. Pale, low to the ground couches were punctuated with small glass tables. Sure enough, the half dozen or so guests were all shoeless. Poppy was happy to gauge that she was the tallest woman in the room.

She tried to guess from the crowd which woman was Justin's wife. Maybe the well-dressed, slightly older woman with the carefully coiffed blond hair. Or the other blonde—not as put-together as the first, but with a pretty smile and a quicksilver laugh that she could hear across the room.

But then she saw her—with a wink and a wave she greeted her husband. One of the most unattractive women Poppy had ever seen in her life. It wasn't just that she was grossly over-weight, or that her stringy brown hair was in great need of a shampoo, or that her sausage feet were stuffed into ugly shoes (shoes!) that had to be orthopedic or otherwise had no reason to exist. No, it was her facial resemblance to Jabba the Hutt.

The woman hoisted herself from her perch on one of the cream couches, and ambled over to greet them.

"Poppy, this is my wife, Martha. Martha, this is Poppy LaRue—the new girl at the Blue Angel."

"Welcome! Delighted to have you." She took Poppy by the elbow and led her around the room, introducing her to the other guests. After each name Martha would tag the person with a profession or accomplishment—"Poppy, this is Alan Mackler, editor-at-large at *Vanity Fair*...." When people asked her what she did, she replied, "I'm a burlesque dancer." And they nodded and then smiled at each other with looks that said, *stripper*.

Justin showed her to the bar, where a bubbly young woman named McKenzie poured her a glass of champagne. Poppy told Justin it was her favorite drink.

"Hand me a bottle, McKenzie. We're going to take it to the roof if Martha needs me for anything."

Poppy had to admit she was relieved to escape the living room crowd. And if she was being completely honest, she was anxious for some time alone with Justin. She was hot for him. He was better looking than she had even realized at first, with thick, glossy brown hair and a devilishly cute smile.

They took an elevator to the top of the building, and the door opened to a deck with a pool.

"I wish it was summer so you could see how great this place is," he said.

"I can imagine. I can't believe you have a pool! I didn't know this even existed in Manhattan."

So much for playing it cool. What could she do? It was the most insane place she'd ever seen. She thought about her tiny apartment in the Village and cringed.

He held out his hand, and she placed her hand in his. It was big, and when he closed his fingers around hers, she knew she had to have sex with him. It had been a long time since she'd wanted a guy like this. It was different from what she felt for Bette—that was a curiosity, a new type of attraction, and a little careerism. For Justin she had the kind of gut-level attraction that made her feel out of control. It was scary and thrilling— that rollercoaster in the pit of your stomach feeling.

"It's freezing out here—I'd better get you back inside."

She let him lead her back into the elevator. They didn't return to the ground level, but instead stopped on the third floor.

Poppy knew they were headed to his bedroom—and she didn't mind one bit. The only question was—would Martha?

The room was all sleek dark wood and chrome. One entire wall was mirrored, as was the ceiling. Poppy could feel herself getting wet already. And from the looks of Justin's crotch, he was hard for her—again.

He closed the door.

"I wish I could have a tank in here and just watch you all night long," he said. "That is, after I fucked you."

Poppy looked at him, startled. His crudeness made her want him even more.

"Show me what you're wearing under those jeans," he said. She undressed down to her black bra and black lace thong. "God, you're perfect," he said. She loved hearing it. She let him pull the strap of her bra down over her shoulder, freeing one breast. He sucked one nipple while cupping her ass.

He moved up to kiss her mouth, and she felt his erection through his pants. She ran her hand along the length of it. He was huge, and this made her a little nervous. She hoped he didn't want her to give him a blow job. She didn't like doing that when the guy was too big, and Justin Baxter definitely fell into that category. She didn't even know if she'd be comfortable with him fucking her, but he was hot enough that it was worth a try.

"Get on the bed," he said, his voice thick.

She climbed onto the king-size bed. She felt weird being on the expensive-looking comforter in her underwear. And wasn't his wife wondering where the hell they were?

"On your stomach," he said.

She stretched out on her stomach as he asked.

He knelt on the bed beside her and slowly pulled down her panties. He gently pressed her legs apart, and she spread them for him, feeling slightly uncomfortable to be splayed out like that on her stomach. His face pressed between her legs, and his tongue, then a finger delved into her pussy. She was instantly wet.

"I want to tie you up—is that okay?" he said.

"I don't know," she said, uneasy.

"I'll do it very loosely—it's just for fun. You can pull your arms out if you really want to."

"Um, all right."

He pulled a red satin box from a bedside table.

"I'm going to put this on you first." It was a black eye mask, like the kind people wore on airplanes when they wanted to sleep.

"Justin…" Of course she knew people did stuff like this, but she'd never imagined it for herself.

"Let's just try it. If you're uncomfortable, we'll take it off.

No big deal. And it will make me incredibly turned on to know I am looking at you but your eyes are closed, and you are just feeling what I do to you."

Well, when he put it that way!

"Okay," she said.

She sat up, and he secured the cover over her eyes, carefully adjusting the elastic band so it didn't get tangled in her hair.

"Lie back down," he said softly. She got back on her stomach. "Stretch out your arms." She complied, and he gently tied them to the bedpost. Her powerlessness was shockingly exciting. The nervous anticipation she felt was so intense, she knew she would come the next time he fingered her.

Minutes passed, and he did not touch her. She wanted to say something, but felt like she would be breaking the mood. So she waited. And waited.

Finally, she felt his tongue. He lapped at her pussy, his tongue soft and gentle. She moaned, but needed him to penetrate her to give her release.

"Fuck me," she said.

"I want you to come from what you feel right now," he said.

"I don't know if I can."

The tongue pressed deeper inside her, and her pelvis moved of its own accord. She felt her mind detach in that floaty way it got when her body took over completely. A finger pressed into her, maybe two. She groaned.

"I want you to come," he said. "And when you do, I want you to tell me while you're coming."

She felt it building, as his fingers worked in and out, one on her clit. He ran one along the rim of her asshole but didn't press it inside of her. Still, it was enough to push her over the edge.

"I'm coming," she moaned. Suddenly, he pulled off her mask and was in front of her. But it was impossible, because the fingers were still working inside of her, pressing rhythmically with her orgasm.

"What the fuck?" She turned around the best she could manage with her arms restrained.

No.

There, at the foot of the bed, leaning over her, stood Martha. Her gaze was fixed intently on Poppy's ass and pussy; she was oblivious to Poppy's shock.

"Stop!" she yelled. And yet, the spasms continued inside her pussy. Justin moved behind her, taking Martha's place. She felt the tip of his cock against her ass, sliding against her wet lips; she couldn't stop.

"I want to fuck you now," he breathed against her neck, his body pressed against hers, one arm underneath her, bringing her pelvis into position for himself. "And Martha is going to watch," he said.

His cock was poised at her pussy, brushing against her but not going inside. Her head was spinning, but her body was arching back to him.

"Do you want me to fuck you?" he said.

"Yes," she whispered. And with that, he plunged into her, and the size of him made her gasp. He moved slowly enough for her to get used to him.

Martha started untying her wrists.

"Press up on your knees," he said. She listened to him, and with her ass tilted up to him she felt his thrusting grow faster and knew he was going to come—and he did, loudly.

He pulled out, and she immediately turned over onto her back. She looked over at Martha, who was perched on a chair, her gaze glassy and her mouth slack. Poppy pulled the bedspread over herself.

"We'll give you some privacy," Justin said. "The bathroom is right through that corridor. Take as long as you like. We'll be downstairs. We hope you have time for a drink. The night is young." He winked at her, and opened the bedroom door for Martha.

He closed it behind them.

When Poppy was sure they were gone, she reached onto the ground for her handbag. She hoped she had her MAC compact and maybe some eyeliner with her, because God knew she needed a major touch-up after that crazy romp.

And then she saw them fanned out on the edge of the bed: five hundred-dollar bills.

Motherfuckers!

11

Julie's couch folded out into a queen-size bed. Thank you, Pottery Barn, Mallory thought, as she helped Julie tuck the fitted sheets around it.

"Maybe a break isn't the worst idea in the world," Julie said, smoothing out one side and lying down on it. Mallory knew she was keeping her friend up way past her work-night bedtime, but that's what former college roommates were for, right?

"How can you say that? I love him. In what universe is breaking up a good idea when you're in love?" She sniffed and reached for another tissue.

"I don't know. You still haven't told me why you broke up tonight."

Here it goes. There was no way this was going to go over well.

"It started two nights ago. I told him I was having second thoughts about a law career, and he was *so* judgmental and unsupportive and basically attacked my character and said I was giving up just because it wasn't coming easily enough for me."

"He can be such a jerk! Ugh, it makes me mad."

"I know. So I walked out..."

"I'm sorry I didn't answer my phone! I've been going to sleep at eight lately. I'm like a third grader. Anyway—go on."

"I couldn't get in touch with you or Allison so I called Bette, that dancer from the Blue Angel."

"Why?"

"I had seen her earlier in the day...and she was so understanding about my questioning my job. So I texted her, and she was home, and we hung out and we...sort of hooked up."

Silence. And then, "Mal, I think you need to see a therapist."

"Oh, my God, I do not!"

"Yes. It's okay, hon. We're here for you. I'll help you find someone. Obviously, you are having some sort of identity crisis...."

"I'm not having an identity crisis. The only crisis is that my boyfriend and best friend won't listen to me!"

"Well, how did you think Alec was going to react to this news? His girlfriend of four years goes lesbo, and he's supposed to jump up and down with joy?"

"He's the one who is always pushing me to hook up with girls! He's the one who wanted a three-way, who brought me to the burlesque show...who made me leave work early to sit through his interview with Bette like some sort of fluffer..."

"Okay, all I'm saying is this whole dynamic is unhealthy. If you want your relationship with Alec to work, you have to step away from all this craziness."

"When I was sitting home studying for the bar every night, he looked at me like I was a drag...like I couldn't keep up with his lifestyle. Now that I'm in the same arena he's threatened. It's such bullshit."

"Then, like I said, maybe time apart is a good idea. You just got to New York. You're still figuring out your life. How can you know how Alec should fit into it if you don't even know what you want yet? If it's meant to be, you guys will work it out. And a little distance always makes the truth of a relationship clear."

"Maybe."

"Either way, I think you need to get away from this strip club nonsense and figure out what you're going to do with your professional life."

"It's not a strip club. And even if it were a strip club, you're being so small-minded. The Blue Angel is not causing the problem. It's revealing the problem."

"How would you feel if Alec left after a fight and hooked up with someone else?"

"I never said it was okay with me for him to hook up with another girl. *He* is the one who pushed for that open window. And I think it's hypocritical that it's okay when it's in front of him for his amusement, but not okay when it's for my personal experience."

"Did you tell him this?"

"No. I hadn't thought it through. Bette told me he wouldn't be happy, but a part of me really believed we could discuss it calmly and it wouldn't be a big deal. When he instantly jumped to us taking a break, I was shocked."

Julie looked at her with wide, brown eyes full of sympathy. She patted Mallory's hand.

"You have to figure your own stuff out before you can be in a couple. Try to get some sleep. You can stay here as long as you want. Put your clothes in that closet by the bathroom."

"Thanks, Jules. You're the best."

"I'll be in my room if you need me. I set the coffee up for the morning. I'm leaving the spare key on the kitchen counter." She kissed Mallory on the forehead.

Mallory looked at her stuffed overnight bag. She didn't have the heart or the energy to start unpacking. With Julie behind her closed bedroom door, she felt free to start crying again. So she did.

How was she going to sleep? Her life was a mess. And the thought of waking up at 6:30 in the morning to rush to the office made her stomach hurt.

She heard the light bleat of her text alert. Alec! She dug through her handbag to unearth her phone.

We're at Luna Lounge—come out for a drink. Bring your man if you want. Xo B

Bette. Mallory typed back, *We broke up tonight. I'm in hell.*

While she waited for Bette's response, she couldn't resist texting Alec. *This makes no sense to me, Alec. I want to talk. Please call me.*

When her BlackBerry beeped again, it was Bette.

Svoboda! Don't sit there wallowing. Get your ass in a cab. I'll buy u a drink.

Mallory couldn't help smiling through her tears.

She pulled on her shoes.

"Men are all hypocrites. They can dish it out, but they can't take it," Bette said, throwing back a shot of vodka. Mallory couldn't understand how Bette could consume so much alcohol but never appear drunk. Or how Bette could look hotter every time she saw her. Her skin was creamy, pale perfection, and the contrast to her black hair was stunning. Mallory thought again about dying her hair red. She would never be as beautiful as Bette, but hanging out with her certainly made her want to try.

"You were right, though. You told me I shouldn't say anything about it. But I didn't want to lie or have something that major between us."

"So give it a rest for now. He'll come around. Keep busy. You know what you should do? Come to my costume fitting tomorrow. Agnes is a genius. She's doing something with crinoline you wouldn't believe."

"What's the costume?" Mallory asked, stalling. She couldn't blow off work... could she?

"It's an Alice in Wonderland dress. I'm performing to that Zebra song, 'Through the Looking Glass.' "

Mallory loved Zebra—but who didn't? She was the biggest pop star in the country. She was six feet tall, androgynous, racially ambiguous, and dressed in costumes that made Lady Gaga look like the Queen of England. She never did interviews except for one in *Rolling Stone* when her first album was released. Billy Barton had told Mallory that Zebra turned down the cover of *Vanity Fair* and a *New York Times* "Style" feature story.

"I have work tomorrow."

"Can't you call in sick or something?"

It was tempting. She'd never called in sick before. And it *was* flu season.

"Maybe I will."

"I have a brilliant idea—I can get you a part in the show tomorrow night."

"Very funny."

"I'm serious. Kitty Klitty has been promoted to performer, and Agnes can't hold her off anymore. She needs someone else to do the stage kitten bit—wear a cute outfit and pick up the clothes between sets."

"Bette, be serious."

"It's so fun! You need to do something different to get you out of this funk. Come on—meet me at the club at noon, and we'll talk to Agnes."

Mallory discreetly checked her BlackBerry in her bag. Nothing from Alec.

"I'll think about it," she said.

"Bette, what I am going to do with you? You need an audience even for a costume fitting," Agnes said, adjusting the pins in the blue satin bustier that was cinched around Bette's torso.

"Mallory's not my audience, Agnes. I brought her here for you."

Agnes flashed a glance at Mallory, who was perched on a folding chair in the dressing room.

"What do I need with her?"

"She's going to stand in for Kitty tonight."

"I've got Poppy for that," Agnes said without missing a beat. Mallory had expected her to laugh, scoff, scream—react in some way at least to the preposterous notion of Mallory's participating in the show.

"You know Poppy doesn't want to do it. She sees it as a demotion. I wouldn't be surprised if she was a no-show."

"That would be very stupid—unless she never wants to perform here again."

"All I'm saying is she doesn't want to do it. So why not make things simple and let Mallory stand in?"

Agnes eyed Mallory from head to toe.

"How do I know she can do it?"

"She's a lawyer—I think she can figure out how to pick up clothes. And she's hot—I can vouch for that," Bette winked at Mallory.

Agnes rolled her eyes.

"You're a lawyer?" she said to Mallory.

"Yes."

"We could use a lawyer around here. But smarts doesn't make you good on stage. That takes moxie, and you seem like a quiet mouse."

"You saw me pull her out of the audience the other night— she got up on stage and rolled with my performance."

"That was you?"

Mallory nodded.

"Fine. I'll give you a chance. But just *one* chance. No screw-ups. What will you wear?"

"I'll take care of that," Bette said. "You just worry about what *I'm* wearing tonight."

"Don't tell me what to worry about!" Agnes snapped. "This is my show, and everything on that stage is my business down to the panty liners you wear in your thong. So what are you going to wear, Ms. Lawyer?"

"I'm...not sure yet," Mallory said, looking helplessly at Bette.

"We just went shopping at La Petite Coquette," she said to Agnes. Then, to Mallory, "You'll wear that garter and corset."

Just the garter and corset? But she knew better than to open her mouth in front of Agnes.

Mallory heard high heels clicking outside the door, and then Poppy's blond head appeared.

"I thought I heard voices in here. What's going on?" she said.

"We are transforming Bette into Alice in Wonderland," Agnes said.

Poppy glanced at Mallory, but didn't bother saying hello.

"How was the Justin Baxter party?" Bette asked. Poppy's cheeks turned pink.

"Fine."

Bette arched an eyebrow, but said nothing.

"So Poppy, thanks to Mallory you are off the hook," Agnes said.

"What do you mean?"

From the look on Poppy's face, Mallory was sure she wouldn't be getting much thanks.

"She's going to fill in for Kitty tonight."

"That's the stupidest thing I ever heard. Don't you have a job you should be at or something?"

"I took the day off," Mallory said.

"Don't look a gift horse in the mouth," Agnes said.

"Agnes loves American clichés," said Bette.

Poppy turned and walked out.

"Why does she hate me so much?" Mallory said.

Agnes looked at her closely. "She must see something in you. I'm hoping to see it for myself tonight."

Poppy closed the door to Agnes's office and clicked the keyboard on the desktop computer. Quickly, Poppy opened Explorer to Google. She typed in *Mallory Dale, lawyer*.

Bingo. The name of the firm Reed, Warner, Hardy, Lutz, and Capel came up, along with Mallory's name as a junior associate. And the firm's phone number. Poppy programmed it into her BlackBerry and logged off.

She waited until she was outside to dial.

12

Mallory sucked in her breath as Bette pulled the laces on her corset.

"Just breathe normally. If you hold your breath, I'm going to make it too tight." Bette glanced at her in the mirror. "This looks stunning on you. You were made for lingerie."

She tied the last set of laces at the top, then stepped away to let Mallory appraise herself. She looked unbelievable all right—as in, she couldn't believe she was looking at herself in the mirror. Her body was poured into the black satin corset, and a lacy black garter rested on her waist, hooked onto thigh-high fishnets. Agnes had wanted her to wear just pasties, underwear, and the garter with fishnets, but she couldn't do that.

"Size seven?" Agnes appeared beside her, holding out a pair of red patent leather platform stilettos that had to be six inches high.

"Yes! How did you know?"

Agnes rolled her eyes. "Wear these."

Mallory slipped them on. She felt like Dorothy in a bizarro *Wizard of Oz*.

"What's your stage name?" Agnes asked.

"I don't know. I didn't think about that."

"Everyone has a name. You think I can announce you as Mallory? You have five minutes to let me know."

Mallory looked helplessly at Bette, who was busy adjusting her sexy Alice costume. It was genius: Agnes had crafted her a powder blue satin bustier, a short blue skirt with white crinoline underneath to give it structure, and thigh-high white stockings with bows at the top. On her feet she wore chunky, seven-inch black patent leather Mary Janes. Her dark hair was covered with a long blond wig. With the light hair and her fair skin, she looked as ethereal as the young girl who had portrayed Alice in the Tim Burton film.

"Wow. Even the White Rabbit would have a hard-on," Kitty said, smacking Bette on the ass.

"Five minutes I need a name," Agnes repeated.

"You said her name earlier," Bette said.

"I did no such thing."

"Sure you did: Moxie."

Mallory stood behind the curtain, heart pounding. Kitty's number was almost over. Most of the girls had slipped out into the audience to watch her debut and cheer her on, so Mallory was alone with her nervous excitement. The song "Big Spender" was winding down, and Mallory calculated she had about thirty seconds until she had to appear on stage. Rodeo Bob would go out first, lead the crowd in applause for Kitty, then introduce the next performer while Mallory picked up Kitty's discarded wardrobe.

The stage went to black, and Rodeo walked out. She followed a few paces behind him and looked around for Kitty's clothes. Her heart was pounding, and the lights were so bright she couldn't focus. She saw one glove…and a stocking. Oh God, this was going to take forever.

"Another round of applause, ladies and gentlemen, for Kitty Klitty's debut performance." The crowd erupted, encouraged by the whistling and stomping of the other Blue Angel girls. "And how about a hand for our new stage kitten, Moxie."

The swell of applause calmed her, made her hands stop shaking as she reached for Kitty's dress near the edge of the stage. She felt their eyes on her, and she couldn't bring herself to glance at them. She reminded herself that they weren't looking at *her*, they were looking at Moxie. It helped to think of it that way, and it let her feel like Moxie, a woman who wore corsets and six-inch heels and lived in a world that took place behind a blue velvet curtain. Thinking of it this way, she felt emboldened to take a look at the audience.

And there, in the front row, was Patricia Loomis.

Mallory dropped the clothing. She backed slowly away, and when she was far enough from the audience that she could no longer see the fury in Patricia's face, she ran backstage.

"What the hell are you doing?" Bette said, grabbing her arm.

"Oh, my God, Bette! My boss is in the audience—my *boss*. How is this even possible? What is she doing here? Why, why, why did I do something so stupid?"

"Okay, chill the fuck out. First, you have to go back out there and get the clothes, or Agnes is going to kick you out of here."

"I can't."

"Moxie—do it," Bette said. She looked Mallory in the eyes, holding her shoulders. "Show me what you've got."

Mallory took a deep breath. She could hear Rodeo still talking, stalling until someone cleared the stage for the next performer. The damage was already done—Patricia had seen her. She probably thought Mallory had been moonlighting all along. And she'd never liked her anyway. But Bette was offering her something new and wonderful—and Bette believed in her and didn't judge her.

Mallory walked back onstage.

"Stage Kitten Moxie, did you forget to take some things backstage?" Rodeo said, winking at her. "Ladies and gentlemen, even the most seasoned professionals can lose their wits when confronted with all of this hotness in one place."

Mallory gathered the pile of clothes back in her arms. She kept her eyes lowered, but couldn't help glancing at Patricia. This time, her seat was empty.

Her mind went into overdrive as she dropped the clothes backstage. This made no sense whatsoever—why would Patricia be there? Mallory doubted she was a secret burlesque fan. And even if she was, she knew her boss's work ethic would never allow being out on a weeknight when she could be at the firm working. And then to show up at this particular club, on the exact night Mallory happened to debut as a stage kitten?

"Did you forget how to pick up clothes and bring them back here, lawyer?" Agnes said.

"Sorry ... I ... something happened."

"I don't have time for this. If you do that again, I won't even let you sit in the audience, never mind set one foot on that stage."

"It won't happen again."

She noticed Poppy watching them from her perch at a vanity, a strange smile on her face. It was as if she were watching something she expected to see. And then Mallory knew, without a doubt, that Patricia Loomis had not appeared at the Blue Angel that night by some fluke of fate.

After the show. Bette invited her to join the rest of the crew at Elixir.

"The girls want to buy you drinks," she said. But Mallory wasn't in the mood to celebrate. The temporary high of stepping on stage, of slipping into the shoes of a glamorous creature named Moxie, was tempered by the reality that she was messing with her career. And on top of that, she suddenly missed Alec with a ferocious ache in her gut.

She walked to a quiet corner of the club, not far from the table where she had sat with Alec and Billy on her birthday. That night seemed like a year ago. Dialing Alec's cell, she was almost as nervous as she had been stepping onto the stage.

"Hi. It's me. I miss you, Alec. I think we should talk…or something. This feels all wrong to me. Give me a call, okay? I love you. Bye."

Bette waved to her from across the room.

"You coming?"

"I can't. I have to get up really early," she said. "But thank you for everything. It was amazing."

"Aside from your little freak-out, you did good. I think Agnes likes you. I'll talk to her—see if she wants you back this weekend."

"Oh, Bette, I don't know. This was just a onetime thing. You know, to have the experience."

Bette gave her a look she couldn't begin to decipher.

"Hey, are you coming out with us? I want to buy you a drink," Kitty Klitty said. She was such a pretty girl—and would be beautiful if there had been even a hint of intelligence in her wide green eyes.

"Oh, no. Thanks, Kitty. Not tonight."

"Having you step in tonight made me feel like a real performer," Kitty said to her. "If one of the other girls had to take my job tonight instead of performing, I wouldn't have felt as good about it."

"Maybe we can convince her to do it again," Bette said with a wink.

"Of course she'll do it again! It's the Blue Angel."

The elevator door slid open, and Mallory stepped onto the fifteenth floor of Reed, Warner with relief. It had been an excruciating ride up from the lobby. She thought of the book *The Devil Wears Prada,* in which the editor-in-chief of the magazine made people vacate the elevators for her to ride alone. She wished Harrison had that policy. Because she had been stuck on the elevator with him after everyone else vacated for their floors, and either she was paranoid, or he had been looking at her with disgust.

"Good morning, Ms. Dale," Blanca greeted her.

"Good morning, Blanca."

Maybe everything would be fine. Maybe Patricia Loomis was just as embarrassed to be busted at a burlesque club as Mallory was upset about being busted performing at one. If Patricia told the partners about it, she would have to admit to being there herself.

Unless... Again, Mallory thought of the smirk on Poppy's face. But it was unfathomable that Poppy would somehow get Patricia to the club just to make trouble for Mallory. She would have to be truly paranoid to believe that.

She logged onto her computer, fighting the urge to check her BlackBerry for the twentieth time since waking up at 5:30 in the morning—nothing from Alec. And now she had twelve hours of research ahead of her. At least she could just throw herself into work and try not to think about him until she crawled into Julie's sofabed, exhausted. Maybe that was what her life would be for a while—working until she was too exhausted to think about Alec.

"Good morning," Patricia Loomis said, barely two steps into her office. She peered in like someone visiting a patient in quarantine.

"Oh, hi, Patricia... I'm just working on the..."

"Harrison would like to see you in his office." She turned on her heel before Mallory could say a word.

This is not good, Mallory said to herself, over and over like a mantra as she looked around her office.

It was possible he was calling her in to talk about the Koomson memo. She'd done a pretty good job on that—even in her ultracritical mind-set about her legal work lately, she was proud of the Koomson research.

Harrison's office was on the twenty-first floor. The reception area had more flowers than most weddings, and his secretary, septuagenarian Erma Gold, was a stern gatekeeper.

"Do you have an appointment?" she asked, glancing at a wide DayMinder calendar on her desk. Erma refused to use a computer, so she had an assistant to handle all of Harrison's e-mails.

"Patricia said he wanted to see me."

"I haven't even had my coffee yet," Erma grumbled as she picked up the phone, as if this was Mallory's fault. "Do you want to see Mallory Dale?" she barked. Harrison clearly gave her an earful, or at least more than a simple yes, because she nodded and made thoughtful little noises and, Mallory was certain, even a clucking sound.

"Yes, Mallory," she said, focusing her milky brown eyes on her as if seeing her for the first time. "Please go right in."

Patricia was already seated in one of the chairs facing Harrison's desk. How she got there so quickly was beyond Mallory—she must have used her broomstick.

"Have a seat," Harrison said, from behind his desk.

Harrison Reed was as round as he was tall, with a surprising amount of silver hair. He wore small, clear glasses perched on the bridge of his sharp nose like a prop, and she had never seen him wear anything but a gray or black suit.

"I assume you know why we are here," he said.

"To talk about the Koomson memo?" she said hopefully, feeling more naked than she'd ever felt at the Blue Angel.

Harrison and Patricia exchanged a look.

"No, Mallory. We are not here to discuss the Koomson memo. Obviously, Patricia told me that she saw you performing at a strip club last night."

Mallory's first impulse was to tell him that the Blue Angel was not a strip club. But she didn't think that would do much for her case.

"This is disturbing information, Mallory. As I'm sure you can imagine."

Yeah, she bet he liked imagining it.

"Well, Patricia, I hope you also told him that I did not strip or take my clothes off in any way. I was just there helping a friend—filling in for someone who couldn't help out between acts."

Harrison leaned forward, placing his hands on the desk with his palms flat.

"Mallory, perhaps I need to explain this to you, although one would think this would not require explanation: Reed, Warner is one of the oldest law firms in this country. We service some of the largest and most prestigious corporations. This firm has employed Vanderbilts, Astors, and Rockefellers. We are awarded the business of companies like Koomson—which provides us with millions in billings each year because of our reputation and our pedigree. Are you following me?"

"Yes," Mallory said.

"How do you think Paul McGowan, CEO of Koomson, would feel knowing that one of the attorneys we placed on his team was a sex worker?"

Oh, my God, he had to be kidding. And a company that manufactured paint that made people sick—or dead—was going to judge her for wearing a skimpy outfit on stage?

"I am not a sex worker! Look, with all due respect, I understand that you're not happy about my being at that club, but I object to the way you are categorizing..."

"How do you think Anderson Blount, opposing counsel for *The People versus Koomson*, would categorize it in court?"

Mallory slumped back in her seat. On the plus side, she wouldn't have to worry about the bar exam anymore. "I understand your concern. I'm just wondering why Patricia was at the club if it's such a bad reflection on the firm."

Take that, bee-atch.

Harrison sighed deeply, as if the labor of continuing the conversation was almost too much to bear.

"Ms. Loomis was at the club because she was told you would be there. She did not believe it, of course, but knowing what a sensitive matter this would be if it did turn out to be true, she used her extremely valuable time to see for herself before leveling such serious allegations against a member of this firm."

"Someone *told* you? That's ridiculous," Mallory said, turning to face Patricia directly for the first time since stepping into Harrison's office.

"It *was* quite ridiculous, actually. I had to take the call for someone looking for you, who said your voice mail was full, but she had to get you the urgent message to..." She unfolded a piece of paper in her lap. "Quote 'not forget my pasties again. The club can't risk getting busted if she shows her tits again' unquote. And when I inquired where I might catch your performance, your colleague was kind enough to inform me."

Mallory resisted the urge to put her head in her hands.

"Security will escort you out," Harrison said. "Your office is being boxed up as we speak, and your belongings will be sent via messenger. Do you have any questions?"

"Just one," she said, turning again to Patricia. "Did you enjoy the show?"

"I'm glad you find this amusing," Patricia said.

"Amusing isn't the word I'd use."

"Oh? And what word would you use?"

"*Svoboda.*"

13

The bravado Mallory had showed in Harrison's office lasted approximately fifteen minutes after she walked out the front doors of Reed, Warner, Hardy, Lutz, and Capel for the final time.

By the time she reached the subway she was fighting back tears. Her only consolation was that she didn't have to go home and admit this debacle to Alec.

"Julie, it's me," she sniffed into her cell phone.

"What's wrong?"

"I got fired."

"What? Why on earth would they fire you?"

"It's a long story."

"Come to my office—I can't sneak away for coffee or anything but we can talk in my cube."

Mallory reversed direction and walked the few blocks to the HarperCollins building at 53rd between Fifth and Madison, where Julie was the assistant to a top editor who published literary fiction. Julie's boss was often out of town, joining famous authors at their readings or taking them up on invitations to visit the sets of the films that were being adapted from their books or traveling to foreign rights book conferences in London and Frankfurt. It seemed incredibly glamorous to Mallory, though Julie assured her it wasn't.

"Andrea works like a dog, believe me," she'd said more than once.

Mallory signed in with security. *I wonder what he'd think if he knew security had just escorted me* out *of a building.*

"So what happened?" Julie said, pulling her into Andrea Tolen's office and closing the door. Mallory immediately began examining the wall of books.

"Can I take one of these?"

"Yeah, but first things first—what *happened*? This wasn't because of the bar exam, was it?"

"I wish," Mallory said. "Are you sure we can sit in here?"

"Yes—stop talking about Andrea's office and spill it."

"Okay, here goes." She gave the unabridged version of the events—including her theory that Poppy had gotten her busted. Julie looked slightly shell-shocked.

"Mal, this might seem like an obvious question—but what possessed you to *do* that?"

"I don't know. I was curious, I guess. And it was fun—if this hadn't happened today, I'd be really excited about it."

"Okay, this is what we need to do. We're going to call Allison and get her new hotshot boyfriend who is majorly connected in this city to find you a job with a new firm. I'm sure he has some favor he can call in."

"I don't know."

"What don't you know? Don't worry about it—that's the way things happen. It's no big deal."

"I mean I don't know if getting another legal job is what I should do. Maybe this is a sign."

"Yeah, a sign you should stop hanging out with those crazy dancers before you ruin your life!"

"That has nothing to do with it."

"How can you say that? In the few weeks you've been hanging out at the Blue Angel, you and Alec have broken up, and you've lost your job. Even I can do that math."

"There were problems with Alec and with my job before I ever set foot in the Blue Angel. I just didn't realize how bad the problems were."

"Well, now you know, and now it's time to fix them. So go to my apartment; get your resume in order. We'll ask Allison how to deal with this Reed, Warner fiasco, because she is good with damage control. And get some sleep. You look like shit."

"Gee, thanks." Her BlackBerry rang. "Oh, my God, it's Alec."

She put her fingers to her lips for Julie to be silent, and answered with her heart pounding.

"Hey," she said.

"Hey. How are you?"

"I'm okay. How are you?"

"Okay. I got your messages. Sorry it took me a while to get back to you."

"That's okay."

"I've just been thinking a lot."

"Me too."

"Maybe you're right. We should talk."

"Really?"

"Yeah. Come to the apartment tonight after work?"

After work. Oh, what had she done!

"Um, sure. See you later."

She put her phone back in her bag and looked at Julie.

"Alec?" Julie said. Mallory nodded.

"Why do you look so upset? I thought you were dying to talk to him."

"I was. . . . I am. But now on top of everything else, I have to tell him about getting fired."

"It's just a job, Mal. You'll find another one."

"You're not listening to me. I seriously don't think I want another job in law. It sounds crazy, but I think all this stuff happened for a reason."

"Just talk to Alec tonight. Fix that. The rest will follow."

Mallory wasn't so sure. But then, she wasn't sure of anything anymore.

The minute she set foot in the apartment, she ached for Alec in a way she had managed to stave off for the past few days. Every part of her wanted him. She couldn't sit still waiting for him to walk through the door. She retouched her eyeliner, rinsed the dishes in the sink, paced the living room, flipped through ninety cable channels. And when she finally heard the key in the lock, her heart started racing.

He dropped his gym bag on the floor and moved toward her, pulling her into his arms without a word. A sob caught in her throat. She hadn't forgotten the way he smelled, but it was as overwhelming and surprising as if she were experiencing it for the first time. She had told him not too long ago—and this was true—that if someone could bottle and sell his scent, it would be the best aphrodisiac for her. He had replied, "That's love, baby."

They kissed hard, and he pulled her into the bedroom. He kissed her face, her neck, all the while unbuttoning her blouse while she wiggled out of her pencil skirt. He pressed his face between her legs, and she felt his warm breath through her thin lace panties. She started tugging them down, and he helped her, kissing her inner thighs on the way back up. She pulled his face into her pussy in that shameless way she had never done with anyone before him, and he obliged her, licking her, his few days of stubble rough against her slippery wetness. She couldn't help thinking that while she had enjoyed being with Bette—there was something new and soft and taboo about their bodies pressed against one another—it could never be this: strong arms encircling her waist, rough skin against her softness, a hard cock pressed against her, signaling how much she was wanted.

"Come here," she said, pulling at him to move up. She wanted to say, *I want you inside of me,* but she had a hard time expressing things like that—talking dirty. Of course, she didn't have to say a word—he knew what she wanted. He pulled up next to her and she stroked his cock.

"I don't want to rush," he said. "I've missed you so much.... I just want to take you in."

She felt the same way, and what she wanted even more than to feel that first push of him inside her was to take him in her mouth.

"Lie down," she said, and he lowered himself next to her. She kissed his chest, running her tongue over his nipples, then down to his belly button, further until she reached the base of his cock. She ran her tongue along his shaft, and he groaned, roping his fingers through her hair. After she moved up and down the length of him a few times, she closed her lips around the tip, circling it with her tongue, then taking him into her mouth. She used her hand to stroke him in rhythm with her mouth, and she tasted the first bead of semen. She worked her hand and mouth faster, taking him deep into her throat, but trying to control him so that he didn't push too far. She remembered once she had been giving Alec a blow job, and she had gagged a little and felt embarrassed. But Alec told her it turned him on—the fact that it was something uncomfortable for her made it hotter somehow. "I don't want you to be upset or hurt or anything, but sometimes little things change the dynamic or make it more intense."

She'd shared this little tidbit with Julie and Allison, who were appalled.

"First of all, there is a difference between giving a guy a

blow job and a guy fucking your mouth so hard you almost puke," Allison said.

"There's a name for that, you know," Julie had put in.

"Yeah—fellatio."

"No. When you give fellatio, that's the woman being active and the guy being passive—receiving. Some guys can never be passive in bed, so even when you are trying to give them a blow job, they are essentially fucking your mouth, and that's called irrumation."

Mallory didn't tell them that Alec was into irrumation sometimes. She could tell by the way they were talking that they viewed it as overly aggressive. But that was one of the things that got her so hot about Alec. He was such an alpha dog. She loved that he pushed her around in the bedroom a little. But at the same time, he was incredibly generous and was so tuned in to her body, he sometimes knew what she wanted better than she did. Like right now.

"Get on my cock," he said, his voice hoarse. She slid up and hooked her legs around his hips, lowering herself slowly on top of his penis. She felt like it was throbbing inside of her, like he could come at any second.

"You feel so good," she breathed, bracing her arms on either side of him, moving her pelvis so he could go deeper inside of her.

He moved his hand to her ass, his finger circling her anus while she rode his cock. She felt the first wave of spasms in her pussy, and he must have felt it too, because he pressed his finger into her ass at the exact same moment, making her come in shudders that shook her entire body.

She pressed her head against his chest, his cock still hard inside her. His heart was pounding almost as fast as her own.

"Oh, my God," she said. "That felt so amazing."

"Come here, baby—turn around."

She slid off of him, and he pressed her gently onto her stomach. From behind her, he pulled her hips up so that her ass was readily available to him. She braced herself on her forearms, not sure what he wanted. Did he want to fuck her in the ass? They didn't have anal sex often—she couldn't take anything more than his finger without it hurting. A few times she had almost relaxed enough to feel good, but those moments were few and far between. For the most part, she did it for him—because she couldn't say no to him. She didn't *want* to say no. In her mind, a good sexual partner was someone who was willing to go places even if there wasn't a physical payoff—even if it hurt. Maybe even especially if it hurt.

She felt his face against her ass, his tongue licking the outer lips of her pussy from behind. He pressed one finger deep inside her while his tongue worked outside, and she felt herself start to come again. Sometimes it was like that with him—he got her to this plateau where she was so turned on, she could just orgasm repeatedly. Once she was in that state, he could do anything to her; those were the times when she could let him fuck her in the ass, and it almost didn't hurt.

But he wasn't going for that tonight. Instead, he eased his cock into her pussy with extraordinary slowness. She reached behind her and grabbed for him, trying to signal him to go all the way inside her. He knew what she wanted, and he was ignoring her—it made her crazy.

She pulled away and flopped over on her back.

"What are you doing?" he said.

"You're teasing me."

He lay next to her, stroking her hair.

"God, I missed you so much. We have to work this stuff out, Mal."

"I know. I'm miserable."

He kissed her face, then her breasts, cupping them and running his tongue over her nipple.

"I want you to come," she breathed.

"Wow. You're almost talking dirty," he said. "If a few days apart gets you talking dirty, maybe a little arguing is okay now and then."

"Shut up!" she laughed. And then his hand moved between her legs, and she couldn't talk anymore. Her breath quickened.

"You're so wet," he said.

"You keep making me come."

He moved on top of her, and she grabbed his ass as he entered her. As he moved inside of her, he looked into her eyes, and the intensity of feeling she had for him in that moment almost brought tears to her eyes. She loved him, there was no doubt. Whatever issues there were, they had to figure them out. She couldn't lose him.

She felt his cock pulsating inside her, the way it did just before he came. She felt herself cresting one more time, and it was the most intense sensation she'd ever experienced. She felt flooded with love for him, an absolute certainty that she was his and he was hers.

He cried out as he came, and her physical pleasure was intensified by hearing how good she made him feel, too. When he collapsed on top of her, she wrapped her arms around him, and he kissed her forehead, her nose, her brow.

Her body was covered in his sweat when he rolled off of her. They lay side by side, and she looked over at him. This was always when he looked the most beautiful to her—his cheeks were flushed, his blue-gray eyes bright.

She hooked her arm over his chest. He leaned over and kissed the top of her head.

"I don't even know why we were fighting," she said.

He sighed.

"What?" she said.

"This all goes back to that original conversation—I think you've been feeling insecure about this relationship ever since you moved to New York, and now you're insecure about your job because you failed the bar, and you're questioning both, even though both are just as right for you now as they were last year."

"First of all, I love you, Alec. There's no question about that. And I'm not second-guessing our relationship. I tried to tell you I was rethinking my career in law, and you jumped all over me and turned it into a referendum on my character."

"I wasn't judging your character. I think you were being reactive to some recent bumps in the road, and I wanted you to put things in perspective. And instead of thinking calmly about all of this, you ran off and did something crazy and impulsive and hurtful with that dancer."

"You're right—I wasn't thinking calmly. But I wasn't trying to hurt you, either. You constantly talk about other women, about wanting to see me with another woman; you take me to a burlesque show on my birthday. I didn't think that what I did was outside the scope of our relationship."

"Okay, well, let's try to put that behind us. No more burlesque craziness. I'm ready to focus on you and us, and I hope you can do the same. And I think it's important that you give this job a chance, Mal. You're so smart, and you're good at this—I know you are. We both need to be strong in our careers in order to be strong in this relationship. You always said you wanted an equal partnership, and I think work is a big element in that. So promise me—no more Blue Angel. Focus on work and us."

This is not good, Mallory thought.

"Yeah. About that. I . . . got fired today."

Alec pulled away and sat up.

"What are you talking about?"

"Harrison fired me."

"Yeah, I got that part. Why?"

"It's kind of a long story."

"Mallory, just tell me what happened."

"Okay, just hear me out before you freak." She took a deep breath. "I was hanging out with Bette, and she gave me the chance to participate in the show last night—just picking up between acts, nothing major. Not dancing or anything. It was fun—I got to wear a costume, and they even gave me my own burlesque name...."

He looked at her stone-faced.

"Um, so it was all fine, except when I looked out at the audience—you won't believe this part—Patricia Loomis was there."

She thought it best to leave out the part about being set up by Poppy. Let him think it was just an unfortunate twist of fate.

"You've got to be kidding me."

"No. So she told Harrison, and they fired me."

"Mallory, what were you thinking? You have the bar exam soon, and this is how you're spending your time?"

"I really don't need you judging me—again."

"Anyone would judge this! It's so stupid!"

She jumped off the bed and started pulling on her clothes.

"What? Did you think I was going to tell you they were crazy to fire you? Mallory, you're at one of the best law firms in the country. Excuse me, you were at one of the best law firms in the country."

"No, I didn't expect you to take my side in this. In fact, this is exactly what I expected—and that's the problem. It's supposed to be you and me against the world, Alec. Remember that? But I guess that was only as long as I was doing what you approved of."

Alec reached out for her.

"Sit down. Don't run out again. That isn't solving anything." She sat on the edge of the bed, her clothes balled up in her lap. She felt like crying. Alec ran his fingertips across her back, and it made her shudder. "I'll help you find another job—maybe a smaller firm. We'll figure it out. The important thing is to move on from this."

"I don't know if I want another law job," she said.

He stopped touching her.

"Did you sabotage your job on purpose?" he asked slowly.

"No! You think I somehow got Patricia at the show to get busted? I'm mortified! I would never..."

"No. Not what happened last night. Did you tank the bar exam?"

She shook her head. "No. I'm upset that I didn't pass the bar."

"Maybe on some subconscious level you didn't want to pass."

"I don't think so."

"Well, what's done is done. I think you should still take it again in February."

"No, I'm not going to."

"When did you decide that?"

"I don't know. Today. Just now."

"You're making a mistake."

"I don't think so."

He sighed.

"What do you want to do? Maybe Allison can hook you up with a job?"

"Maybe. The thing is...I know it sounds crazy, but I can't stop thinking about performing. It felt exhilarating to be on that stage. I'm not sure I want to settle into corporate life just yet."

"You're thinking about going back to the Blue Angel? I thought you said it was a onetime thing."

"It doesn't have to be."

"Mallory, this is irrational. You're acting out over something, and I don't know what it is. But I don't want to be a part of it."

"You're breaking up with me because I want to try something new?"

"How can I rely on you, plan my life around you, if you are someone who can just throw away a three-year investment in a legal career? What happens when you decide this relationship is too tough, or someone bright and shiny comes along and you don't want to do the work in this relationship anymore? Oh—wait. Someone already did. And you fucked her."

"You are the one who is being irrational. God, Alec! This isn't about you. I'm still figuring out my life. Just because you were lucky enough to know from tenth grade that you wanted to be a journalist doesn't mean the rest of us can't stumble a little along the way."

But she could tell she was wasting her breath. Alec turned completely away from her and started pulling on his clothes. "So that's it?" she said.

He shrugged. "I love you, Mallory. But I'm not happy."

"I'm not happy either. But I don't want to break up over this."

"There's no 'this.' It seems to be everything lately. We're in different places. Or, I should say, you seem to be looking for something, and it doesn't feel like something that's going to make this relationship work. I'm going for a walk. I think maybe you should be gone when I get back."

She lay back on the bed and covered her eyes with her arms. She didn't let herself start crying until she heard Alec leave the apartment, the door closing with a sharp click behind him.

She woke up at Julie's in the morning with the depressing realization that she had nowhere to go—and would not have anywhere to go for a while.

Julie was great, as always. Talking to her late into the night, assuring her she would help her find a new job—or not, whatever she wanted was okay with her (but just for the record she really thought Mallory ought to get a job, not just for money, but for her sanity's sake). But now Julie was at work for the next eight hours, as was Allison and every other normal person she knew. Of course, there was one person she knew who wasn't normal, and looking for her BlackBerry to text her was the only thing that got Mallory out of bed.

I've got "svoboda," *all right: no job, no boyfriend. Now I'm wondering, what comes after* svoboda?

Of course, it was only nine in the morning and too early for Bette to be among the conscious and functioning. She had called being awake before 11 a.m. "obscene." Funny how her definition of obscene differed from Patricia Loomis's.

Mallory sank back into the sofa bed. She jumped when her phone rang.

"Hello?"

The first thing she heard was a languid yawn.

"I'm going to sleep for a few hours," Bette said. "Come to my place at two. And then we'll talk about your freedom. Time to figure out yourself."

And she hung up.

Herself. When had she ever taken the time to think about "self"? It seemed to her that "self" was a set notion, a fait accompli, determined and shaped by her parents and school and the ironclad sense of what a girl like herself did with her life. But those notions weren't so hard and fast after all, because, with one step onto the Blue Angel stage, that feeling of who she was started slipping so fast she felt like the ground beneath her was shifting. It was exhilarating, and even though she knew she should be worried about the future and about money, there was something so right about this feeling, she just had to go with it for now. She just wondered why she had to lose Alec over it.

Why couldn't they make it through this? It felt like she was being forced to choose between the man she loved and, well, herself. If she stepped back from where her life was taking her just to assure Alec that she was someone he could count on, or the same girl he fell in love with, or whatever it was that was freaking him out so much, how could she trust him? How could she be in a relationship that didn't allow for mistakes and trying new things in life, changing course every now and then?

Intellectually, she knew she had to let him go. But it hurt so much. She was tempted to call Allison and ask her to help her get a new job as soon as possible, to not see Bette this afternoon but instead beg Alec to meet her for lunch so they could work this out. And yet as she worked out that scenario in her mind, something in her gut told her it was the wrong way to go. It sounded safe, but it was in fact the most dangerous thing she could do.

She pulled herself out of bed and looked at herself in the wide, bronze-framed mirror next to Julie's bookshelves. She looked tired and washed out.

What would Moxie do?

And then she had an idea of how she would spend her first afternoon as a liberated woman. She texted Bette to meet her on East 56th Street.

When a woman moves to New York, she needs her friends to hook her up with two key things: a good gynecologist and a place to get a haircut. Mallory found both thanks to Allison, who introduced her to Christine Catora, M.D., and Bumble and bumble salon on East 56th Street .

She stood at the check-in counter of Bumble. It was a spare, industrial space, and the stylists were young, clad in all black, and attractive with an edge. A very different scene from the fancy, feminine salons her mother took her to when she was growing up on Philadelphia's Main Line.

"Are you here to check in?" a thin guy with a white-blond buzz cut asked her.

"Yeah. I have a two-thirty color appointment with Galit? Annie referred me to her."

"You're Mallory? Okay, you are checked in. Go in the back to get changed and then up to the third floor color studio."

She was about to explain that she needed to wait for her friend, but Bette managed to breeze in at that precise moment. Even in this jaded, hipster beauty mecca, heads turned.

"So what are we doing here?" Bette asked.

"I'm going to dye my hair red, and I need you to help me make sure I'm doing the right shade."

"Phenomenal! Why didn't you say so in your text? This is momentous. I would have brought champagne."

They took the elevator to the third floor, checked in at another reception desk, and were met by a Kristen Stewart look-alike wearing denim overalls and black patent leather heels. Her left bicep was covered with a Vargas girl tattoo.

Mallory could have sworn she heard Bette gasp.

"Hey, I'm Galit. Which one of you is Mallory?"

Mallory introduced herself and then said, "And this is my friend Bette."

"Cool. You here for moral support?"

"Technical support, actually," Bette said. Mallory noticed the eye lock between them.

Galit showed them back to seats in front of thin, white-framed mirrors. It looked like a salon designed by Apple.

"Did you bring any photos of the shade you had in mind?"

"Um, no. Is that a problem?'

"Not at all. I'll show you some swatches."

Galit brought out a binder with pages filled with synthetic hair colored every shade from platinum blond to black. She opened to a section of red, and pointed to a soft auburn.

"This would look pretty on you," she said.

Mallory looked at Bette, who, without hesitation pointed to a swatch the color of maraschino cherries.

Galit looked at Mallory, then at the color, then back at Mallory.

"That's bold, but she can pull it off. You were born to be a redhead, babe," she said.

"Wow. That's really ... red. Maybe I should ease into it a little?"

"If you're going to do it, just go for it. If she hates it, you can tone it down, right?" Bette said to Galit.

"I can always tone it down. But I think you should only do the color if your heart is in it. It's a gorgeous color, but you have to own it."

"I'm going to do it," Mallory said.

"Great. Let my assistant know if you want coffee or a menu from the café while I go mix it."

Mallory looked at the glossy swatch of faux red hair, numbered 242. It was attached with Velcro, so she pulled it out and held it up to her face.

"Jesus, she is smokin' hot," Bette said.

"Yeah, she's really pretty. She looks like that actress Kristen Stewart. Or Joan Jett. They look the same to me ever since I saw that movie, *The Runaways*. You should get her number."

"I don't have time to date."

"What does that mean?"

"It means I intend to be famous as soon as possible. Having a girlfriend is a distraction I don't need."

"I think love is important." Mallory's eyes teared up, and she dug around in her bag for one of the tissues she'd been relying on nonstop for the past twelve hours.

"Oh, no. What happened?

"First, I got fired."

"Because your boss saw you at the show?"

"Not at the show, in the show. And yeah, that's why."

She was tempted to tell Bette that she knew Poppy had set her up, but she didn't want to start even more trouble. Besides, she couldn't prove it.

"Well, fuck it. You hated that gig anyway. Now you can do something you want to do. And you should start by working at tomorrow night's show. Agnes digs you even though you had a minor freak-out. When I explained why, she understood—sort of. Besides, she doesn't have anyone else. All the girls who come to her want to get billing as performers."

"I don't know. I'm not in the right headspace. Alec broke up with me, and I'm really...I can't believe it."

"Maybe you need a break."

"That's what my friend Julie says."

"I have an idea—something that will take your mind off of Alec. I'm going to LA for a long weekend. Come with me. I'm being put up at a sick hotel in West Hollywood. All you have to pay for is your plane ticket. Everything else will be picked up. I went last year, and it was one of the best times I've ever had."

"Who's paying for it?"

"A guy named Justin Baxter. He used to come to the Blue Angel all the time, then started hiring me to perform at his birthday parties and Christmas parties, that sort of thing. He's loaded and has places in LA and Miami and London...and a ridiculous apartment here on Bond Street. Seriously, just say yes. It will take your mind off of things, and maybe being in a different place will help you figure things out."

"Maybe."

"You need a debut as a redhead. Come on—I won't take no for an answer. Let yourself have some fun. You'll have plenty of time to worry when we get back."

"I'll make a deal with you: I'll go if you get Galit's phone number. I'm not taking a leap if you don't."

"You drive a hard bargain, Moxie. Get ready to pack your bags."

* * *

Poppy knocked on the door of the Blue Angel. She had a fitting with Agnes for the first costume the owner had offered to make for her. She was thrilled about this, of course—finally, she was starting to feel that she was becoming accepted as a real Blue Angel.

Agnes opened the door, looking annoyed.

"This isn't a brothel, you know," she said.

"What do you mean?"

She followed Agnes to the dressing room, where an outrageously large bouquet of dark red poppies was arranged in a square vase.

"What is that?" Poppy asked.

"They came for you this morning." She stormed out of the room. God, she was so rigid. This couldn't be the first time a performer had been sent flowers at the club, could it? And it's not like she could control what customers did.

She opened the card.

Thanks for a fun night. We hope to see you again soon.
Justin and Martha

Ugh! The nerve of him. She wished she had his phone number so she could give him a piece of her mind.

She pulled out her BlackBerry and dialed the number for the florist, Ovando.

"Hi, this is Poppy LaRue. I just received a gorgeous delivery from you guys from a customer named Justin Baxter. I don't have his number, and I'm dying to thank him. Could you give me that information please? I want to tell him what an amazing job you guys did with the flowers."

She jotted down the number and didn't wait more than a beat to dial.

"This is Justin," he said.

"This is Poppy LaRue."

"What a pleasant surprise! Delighted to hear from you, dar-lin'. I hope you're a fan of your namesake."

"You know what I'm not a fan of? Your little bait and switch the other night. And, for the record, I'm not a prostitute."

He laughed. Bastard!

"You didn't seem to have a problem taking the money."

"Yeah, well, I'm broke, and you seem to have plenty to throw around, so I'm not going to lose sleep over it."

"You absolutely shouldn't."

"Okay ... well. As long as we understand each other."

"Wait—don't hang up. I don't want there to be any hard feelings. Although, hearing your voice, I do feel hard. ..."

She couldn't help laughing.

"Let me make it up to you," he said. "We're hosting an in-credible private show tonight. Strictly A-list." He rattled off the names of the actors, musicians, and socialites who would be attending. "Please join us. It's at the apartment, ten sharp. Cocktail attire."

Poppy knew she shouldn't go—that she should have some pride, or at the very least stay out of trouble. But she couldn't help thinking that if she went to the party, she might be invited on the LA trip. She knew Bette and two girls from the Slit were going, and she felt completely left out.

Agnes reappeared in the doorway. "I'll try to make it," Poppy said quickly, and hung up.

Agnes stood in the dressing room doorway, white satin fab-ric in her hands and pins pursed between her lips. She placed the pins side by side on one of the vanities and pulled a tape measure from her pocket.

"Are you ready to do costume or am I interrupting social hour?" she said.

"Sorry," Poppy said. She stripped down to her underwear and Agnes knelt beside her, taking measurements.

"The problem with you girls is no focus! When I was your age I was practicing ballet ten hours a day. No talking on the phone, no drinking at night. And no men! You know who my relationship was with?"

Poppy shook her head.

"My feet! An artist lives for her art. What do you girls live for? Money? Romance?"

Poppy didn't say anything. Fine, so Agnes was a great dancer in her day. But what did she have to show for it? She was old and alone. Poppy wanted to be the best performer at the Blue Angel, but what was the point if she was going to be alone for the rest of her life? Without love, she would feel like a failure. But if she was a famous burlesquer, of course she would find love. Or love would find her.

"I think romance is important," Poppy said.

"Fine. You want love, good luck. But if you're going to be with a man, make sure he's a rich man. Love don't pay the rent," she said.

14

Poppy stood outside the spectacular gates of 40 Bond. She shifted in her heels, and wondered if she'd made the right decision. And then she saw an Academy Award–winning actress breeze past her, and she followed discreetly behind.

In the entrance foyer, she added her shoes to the carefully arranged footwear left by each of the guests. She could estimate at a glance that she was looking at twenty grand worth of shoes.

Up ahead, the girl in the fishbowl had evolved from coed chic to polished vamp. And just below her, Justin Baxter looked even better than she remembered—and Martha, even worse. Poppy shuddered.

A glass table was covered with folded seating cards. The only time she had seen that before was at her cousin's wedding. She hoped she wasn't seated at the Baxters' table, but was sure that was filled by the remarkable number of boldfaced names circulating in the foyer, sipping champagne served by handsome young men in tailcoats.

She took a glass, knowing it would be phenomenal. As she brought the flute to her lips, Justin caught her eye and smiled.

"Have you seen anyone serving something other than champagne?" a short, pretty blonde asked her. She had a pixie haircut and a smattering of freckles across her nose, and Poppy immediately recognized her from the latest Anne Hathaway movie.

"Um, no—but I haven't really been looking."

But the blonde had already spotted someone more important to talk to. Luckily, the crowd seemed to be moving to the assigned tables. Poppy downed her champagne, and followed the herd until she could bench herself at table six.

"Hey, I know you," said the guy next to her. He was good-looking in an affected sort of way. He had thick, shiny brown hair that was slightly feathered around the sides, and he wore mint green suspenders with a matching cashmere sweater tied around his shoulders. "Poppy LaRue, right?"

"Um, yeah."

"Billy Barton—nice to meet you. I caught your show a few weeks ago. Brava."

"Thanks." Why did his name sound so familiar?

"I've never seen you at Justin and Martha's before. I can't believe I would have forgotten a face like yours."

"I just met them recently, so I haven't really been here before."

"Well, you're in for a treat."

"Oh, yeah? What's the show?"

"One never knows. It will be interesting, have no doubt about that. And the food will be sublime. Somehow Justin always manages to lure some top chef away from his hot, recently opened, and impossible to get into restaurant for the night. God only knows what they pay these people."

"I can't imagine," Poppy said, shifting uncomfortably.

The cadre of Calvin Klein model / waiters began circulating with platters. One spooned something unrecognizable onto

Poppy's plate, while another poured her glasses of red and white wine.

"Don't they usually ask if you want red *or* white?"

"I'm seeing the combination serving more and more lately. Some people swear by it—breaks up the flavors, so the palate stays excited."

The tables were arranged in a loose circle, so that there was a large space left in the center of the room with a slightly elevated platform. An extremely thin blonde with defined, ropy muscles stepped onto the platform. She wore only a black sports bra and black boy shorts underwear. In contrast to her sporty body and attire, her nails were long and painted deep, glittery maroon, and her eye makeup was sweeping and dramatic, borderline garish.

The light classical music that had been innocuously filling the background of the evening changed to an ominous, carnivalesque song. The woman began twisting her body into positions that did not seem possible unless she were made of rubber.

"I just love contortionists, don't you?" Billy said.

"Um, yeah. I guess."

"So, were you interviewed for the piece *Gruff* magazine is doing on the burlesque scene in New York?"

So that's how she knew his name! He was the guy Bette had been so focused on the night she pulled Mallory on stage.

"No, actually. And I probably should be, since I'm the hottest new girl at the Blue Angel. And everyone knows the Blue Angel is the best club in the city."

Billy looked at her.

"I agree! Plus, you are staggeringly pretty. I want to get some photos of you for the piece. And I'll have the writer get in touch with you—Alec Martin. If it's too late for him to work you into the article, I'll make sure we have shots of you for the editorial spread."

Alec Martin. Mallory's journalist boyfriend. Finally, a break—something to give her some leverage. Although what that leverage was...she didn't know yet. The first thing she needed was to get Alec Martin alone. Then she was sure she would figure it out.

"I hope your writer has some time to work me in. I have lots of insider stuff and a different perspective on the scene than the older girls."

"I'll talk to him. Shouldn't be a problem."

A handsome Latino waiter replaced her plate with another, and again she wasn't sure what she had been served.

"What is this?"

"Braised short ribs," said the hottie.

"I'd like to braise his short rib," said Billy.

She laughed.

"You're not drinking your wine," he said.

"I only like champagne."

Billy immediately summoned a waiter and asked for a bottle of champagne.

"A bottle? Isn't that too much?"

"This is a Baxter party. There's no such thing as too much."

Across the table, a bald black guy in a sharp black suit and white tie called over to Billy. They began an animated conversation about some politician Poppy had never heard of, so she fixed her eyes on the platform and waited for her champagne.

The contortionist untwisted herself, and somehow managed to walk off the platform. Poppy wondered if her legs felt like Jell-O after that performance. She considered sharing this thought with her new bff, but he was laughing with the dude across the table.

A waiter appeared with a bottle of Krug and poured her a glass.

"Thanks. Billy, do you want some?"

"Why not? Poppy, this is Dominick Monde, head of Tout Le Monde Films. Dominick, Poppy LaRue, burlesquer extraordinaire. Oooh—this show just got good."

One of the waiters was now on the platform. Wait—was that one of the waiters? All these beautiful guys were starting to look alike, with their phenomenal bone structure and taut, muscled bodies and thick heads of hair. This one was on the slim side, with a short blond buzz cut and Siberian husky blue eyes she could see even from the distance of the table.

The music changed yet again, this time to something that sounded like Moby meets dance / trance. The guy removed his clothes, unbuttoning his shirt and tossing it aside, then easing down his trousers to reveal that he was not wearing underwear—and sported a big erection.

"I love the Baxters! You can always count on them for sausage with dinner," Billy said, and the few people who heard him at the table laughed.

A second guy joined the first on the platform, fully nude, holding what looked like a fly swatter. He was Mediterranean-looking and broader shouldered, with longish dark hair, high cheekbones, and an Angelina Jolie mouth. His right bicep was fully tattooed, and he was, overall, one of the hottest guys Poppy had ever seen.

The dark guy stood in front of the blond buzz cut, who immediately knelt and took his erection into his mouth.

"Jesus," Poppy breathed.

"Jesus Luz?" Billy said. "He looks like him, but trust me, honey—even the Baxters don't have that much money. That's Derek Dart. I've seen him in films. But I have to say his theatrical performance promises to be much stronger."

The buzz cut guy worked Derek Dart in and out of his mouth, gripping his muscled ass with one hand, the other working his thick shaft. Poppy wondered how long it could possibly be before Derek came, and wondered if she was mentally prepared to see a guy come in another guy's mouth. She could tell by the movement of Derek's pelvis that he was probably getting close, but then he suddenly pulled himself out and turned the buzz guy around. Buzz cut bent over, and Derek started spanking his ass with the fly swatter. She couldn't help staring at Derek's cock, which was nearly purple in its heightened state of erection and glistened with saliva.

The blond guy was moaning from the ass-swatting in a way that Derek hadn't done even when having his dick sucked. Poppy couldn't believe she was watching this in a room full of people having dinner, and the strangest part was that the vibe in the room hadn't changed from when it was simply a contortionist on the stage. She was afraid to really look around, because she didn't want to catch anyone's eye, but she wouldn't have been surprised if some of the guests were still eating and talking.

And then Derek spit on his own cock, spread his saliva around on it, and pressed it into the other guy's asshole. Poppy wanted to look away, but she was riveted. She'd only had anal sex twice and found it painful—and neither guy had been as big as Derek. She couldn't imagine how this could feel good to the blond guy, but his face was absolutely rapt with ecstasy—unless he was the world's best actor, in which case he deserved an Academy Award.

Derek pumped his dick into the guy with fast, hard thrusts, and the exertion made the muscles on his chest and arms stand out. Poppy was surprised at how turned on she was—couldn't believe that her pussy was starting to throb.

Derek pulled his cock out and started pumping it with his hand until spurts of jizz fell like rain on the other guy's buttocks.

Everyone at the tables started to clap politely, as if a piano concerto had just concluded.

"If they're serving that with the main course, I can't wait to see what's for dessert," Billy said with a wink. Poppy was tempted to say something about not forgetting to put the writer in touch with her, but she didn't want to sound desperate. "Give me your cell number," he said. "So I can pass it on to my writer. I want him to get on this. I think the issue is closing soon."

Trying not to smile, Poppy recited her number, and he programmed it into his iPhone.

Justin appeared beside her seat and touched her shoulder.

"Glad you could make it. Are you enjoying the show?"

Somehow, the way he asked the question made her feel dirty, and this annoyed her. But her pussy was wet, and she couldn't help thinking of how good he was at eating her out.

"Yes. Thanks."

"A stellar evening so far," Billy chimed in.

"Glad you're enjoying. I hope you don't mind if I borrow your tablemate for a moment?"

"By all means. "

Justin winked at Poppy and gestured for her to follow him.

He led her to the bar, a room she remembered the last time she was at the house.

"What did you think of the show?"

"It was interesting."

"Just interesting? I bet you're wet."

She did not think honesty was the best policy at this particular moment. "I enjoyed it, okay? Now I'm going to go back to the table."

"Did I offend you in some way?"

"You offended me the last time I was here. I told you."

"Let me make it up to you. I'd love to lick your pussy."

"No, Justin! Seriously, I'm not some fuck toy for you and your wife."

"I'm not talking about my wife. Just you and me this time."

"I've got to get back to the table," she said. She knew she was probably blowing her chance at an invitation to the LA trip, but so be it. She already had something more important on deck: the interview with Alec Martin.

Then, as if reading her mind, Justin said, "Maybe your table-mate would like to watch us. You know how curious those journalism types can be."

And then she realized she could seal the deal for LA and the magazine with one shot.

Justin took her silence as a yes. She watched him walk to her table and whisper something in Billy's ear. Sure enough, he returned with Justin, and the three of them rode the elevator upstairs without a word exchanged.

Justin led them to a sitting room on the third floor. It was all black and white—three low-to-the-floor black couches, a white shag carpet, and a few retro silver floor lamps. A baby grand piano was in the far corner, and Poppy wondered if anyone actually played it or if it just suited the color scheme.

Billy sat on one of the black couches that directly faced another identical couch. The light was on a dimmer, and Justin set it lower before steering her to the couch across from Billy. He knelt in front of her, hiking her dress up and easing her panties off. She rested her head against the back of the couch, trying not to think of the full view of her pussy currently on display for Billy Barton. But then she thought of how intent Bette was on getting his attention; she was sure she had it in a way Bette never had.

Justin pushed her legs apart and brushed his thumb against her clit. She remembered his technique from last time, the way he pressed his fingers inside her first and then followed deeply with his tongue. Just the thought of it made her squirm, and she touched his hand that gripped her thigh, pulling it toward her pussy. He let her guide his hand, and slowly inserted his middle finger deep inside her. She moaned and arched back, forgetting all about her audience. Just as she was starting to peak, he stopped.

"What are you doing?" she said.

"Why don't you finger fuck yourself for us," he said. Before she could respond, he sat next to Billy on the couch. The two of them looked at her like they were in front row seats at an off-Broadway play.

She was so close to coming she had to finish herself off anyway, so she decided she would simply pretend they were not there. She put her head back, closed her eyes, and stroked her clit, but she was so aroused she didn't need any warm-up and moved straight to pressing two fingers inside herself. As she worked herself up toward an orgasm, trying not to think about Billy and Justin watching her, she realized the fact that they were there actually heightened her excitement. She moved her fingers faster and harder, thinking of the publisher of *Gruff* magazine and the millionaire playboy who could be anywhere doing anything choosing to watch her masturbate. With this thought, her orgasm broke, and it was so strong she cried out very loudly. She shuddered against her own hand, and only then did she allow herself to look at her audience.

Justin moved to stand in front of her. He immediately knelt down, took her wet fingers into his mouth. Then he pressed her thighs apart further, and lapped at her pussy like a cat at fresh cream. She glanced over his head at Billy Barton, and saw that his pants were around his ankles, his cock in his hand.

And that's when she realized she didn't have to worry about getting the interview. In fact, she was going to push for the cover.

15

Mallory stepped off of the plane and into the sunshine. It was incredible—you spend a couple hundred dollars and five hours on a plane, and suddenly winter was gone. It was just heat, palm trees, and dry air. She felt instantly relaxed, couldn't stop smiling. Alec, the law firm, sleeping fitfully on Julie's couch... it all seemed a million miles away.

"The air smells different out here," she said to Bette.

"I know. Better, right?"

A driver met them at the luggage carousel, and carried their bags to the black town car for the twenty minute drive to their hotel in West Hollywood.

The Palihouse was a boutique hotel with an entrance so discreet it looked like a private club. The driver carried their bags down a short flight of wide, wooden stairs that led them into a wonderfully atmospheric lounge.

"We're *staying* here?" Mallory said, taking in the vintage chandeliers, Moroccan tiled floor, distressed leather couches, and idiosyncratic design touches like antique birdcages.

"I know—I love it here. It's Paris meets LA," Bette said.

The check-in desk was just a simple wooden table manned by an adorable young guy who greeted them cheerfully. He handed them each a room key—an actual key, not the plastic card she was used to—and told them that all the information they needed for the weekend festivities was in their suite.

They rode the mirrored elevator up to the fourth—and top—floor. Bette opened the door to the room, and a song Mallory vaguely recognized was playing at low volume.

"What song is this?"

" 'I Feel Cream' by Peaches. Which is a crazy coincidence, or maybe a good omen, because I'm performing Saturday night to her song 'Lose You.' "

"This place is incredible," Mallory said. "I'm not going to want to leave."

"You can take the bedroom," Bette said. "I don't plan on spending much time asleep."

Their room was like a hip urban apartment, with a huge living room with black carpet, exposed brick, moody photography, two white couches, and enough side tables and chairs for a small party. They had a full kitchen complete with a marble island in the center, a bedroom with a king-size bed, and enough closet space for a family. There was an ultra-sleek bathroom with black tiles, lots of mirrors, and a glass enclosed shower. "I feel like the coolness of this place is seeping into my pores."

"Ooh—a gift basket." Bette unwrapped a bottle of Dom Pérignon, some products from Bliss Spa, and a medium-sized black box.

"What's inside?" Mallory asked. Bette handed it to her.

"Take a look."

Mallory removed the lid, and inside was a pink satin pouch. She untied the pouch drawstring to find a hard, rubbery ball that was translucent; inside was another ball, like a little weight. The bizarre object had a looped, firm string attached. "What the hell is this?"

"It's the famous Pike Kegel Ball!" Bette laughed.

"You're joking."

"No—I'm not. Martha made millions on that thing. Many satisfied customers will tell you that you are now holding in your hand the secret to having a super pussy."

"I don't get it—you stick this thing up your vag and then what?"

"You have to flex your pelvic muscles to hold it in place. It's resistance training for your vagina."

Mallory laughed and threw it at her. Bette ducked, and the ball landed on the couch.

"You have to try it before the trip is over. Stop being so closed minded!"

"I'm not being closed minded...but I am being closed vagina-ed."

"With that kind of attitude I'm going to send you right back to New York."

Mallory laughed and walked into the bathroom to wash her face and apply sunscreen, and was surprised once again to see her deep, cherry red hair. But she loved it—her skin tone looked entirely different, and she barely needed any makeup; her hazel eyes looked green; her under-eye circles seemed somehow diminished; and the natural flush to her cheeks was enhanced.

Bette waved an envelope at Mallory.

"He booked me a massage at Equinox on Sunset. I'm going to call and see if they can fit you in, too."

"Oh, don't worry about it. I'll go later."

"No! It's more fun if we go together."

"I don't know. I just lost my job—I shouldn't be spending money like this."

"I'll put it on Justin's tab. I told him I'm bringing a friend. It's not a big deal. I'm calling now, and I won't take no for an answer."

* * *

Two hours later Mallory was wearing a white robe, sipping cucumber water, and relaxing on a lounge chair next to Bette on a deck overlooking Hollywood.

"My gym in New York overlooks a Gap and a hotdog vendor," Mallory said.

"It's pretty sick out here. Every time I'm here I think about moving."

"Why don't you?"

"The burlesque scene isn't as strong. At least, not as supportive as what I've found in New York. Maybe that's just my experience. Besides, you don't want to be broke and struggling in LA. You want to be established and have money. New York on the fringe is cool and artistic. LA on the fringe is desperate."

"Moxie and Bette?" A woman in an Equinox staff T-shirt called to them.

"You gave them my burlesque name?" Mallory said.

"Yeah. Out here you're Moxie. All weekend. I'm serious—try it."

"I'll try it if you tell me your real name."

"I'm offended you'd even ask," she said, smiling.

Two women led them to the massage room, introducing themselves as Jessica and Amy. They left Mallory and Bette to get comfortable on side-by-side tables. Mallory shed her robe but left her underwear on and quickly climbed under the tightly folded white sheet.

"You have a hot body," Bette said. Her robe was off, and she sat up on the massage table, stretching. Mallory couldn't help looking at her perfect breasts—they still amazed her. She could barely believe she had touched them, held them in her hands, and had her mouth on them. It was as if she'd had a painting from the Met in her apartment for a few hours.

"You're one to talk," Mallory said.

"I still don't get why you never wanted to hook up after that night. You seemed into it at the time."

"Shh—they might hear us,"

"Who? The massage girls? They don't care. Why are you so edgy all the time? You're like a nervous little Chihuahua."

"Oh, my God, I am not. I just don't want to talk about this here."

The masseuses returned and quietly took their places beside Mallory and Bette. Soothing music filled the room. Mallory closed her eyes, melting into the massage table as the woman pressed her warm, well-oiled hands into her sore muscles. Her mind clicked into floaty, stream-of-consciousness mode, and that meant that the thoughts she had been working so hard to keep at a distance found their way in: she missed Alec. She should be with him, getting ready for dinner together on a Thursday night, maybe stopping by Barnes & Noble on the way to dinner to buy two books that they would read and swap. On the way home they would stop by the bagel store to get bagels and lox, so they didn't have to wait on the long, Saturday morning line. And they would debate whether they should make omelets or sandwiches and continue the ongoing debate about how long you can keep cream cheese in the refrigerator. Instead, she was stretched out on a massage table in a strange city next to a woman she barely knew, and who knew nothing about her. Her life with Alec felt like something she'd imagined, a dream she'd woken up from and wanted to go back to sleep to return to.

She felt tears, and willed them back. This was ridiculous— she was on a fabulous vacation in LA. She was traveling with a new friend, an interesting friend who was opening life up to her in a way she had never experienced. Bette didn't care if Mallory failed at work, didn't ask her how and when she would get a new job. And she was a friend who made her feel beautiful, showed her how to be beautiful.

The masseuse's hands kneaded her neck, and she thought about how Alec used to make her feel beautiful. He was the first person to give her an orgasm. He was the first guy who told her that he loved her. And even though he sometimes checked out other women—blatantly checked them out—he used to tell her she was the hottest girl in the room—even when it wasn't true. And yet he meant it.

But somehow they had stopped working.

She couldn't pinpoint when it had happened. Julie had said something about it not being right since she got to New York at the end of last summer, but that wasn't exactly accurate. It had been so exciting when she first moved into the apartment he had been sharing with his office buddy, Jared. Then Jared got a job working on Wall Street and didn't need a roommate anymore, and she got the formal job offer from Reed, Warner... and it was perfect. They went shopping at Bed, Bath, and Beyond. They cooked dinner a few nights a week, and met for cheap dinners out at places like Two Boots pizza or a neighborhood diner. And at first, the only problem was that they didn't sleep enough because they would wake up in the middle of the night and reach out, excited by the novelty of sleeping in their own bed, and make sleepy love like in a dream. Or in the morning he would step into the shower with her when she was getting ready for work and soap up her back... and her front.

But then things got busy at the magazine. And once her initial excitement at having a job wore off, she was exhausted by the monotony of her research work at the firm. And then Billy Barton invited them to more and more parties, where the women were "model hot" and dressed like they got all their clothes from Barney's or Jeffrey or Scoop—which they probably did. She noticed how Alec looked at them—like they were untouchable but infinitely desirable. When they went home on the nights of these parties and he didn't try to make love to her, she took it personally. She wondered if she just didn't "do it" for him anymore. Was it because he was comparing her to all that New York had to offer, or because they had been together for four years and that's what happened to couples who had been together that long and then started living together?

And then he'd brought her to that show on her birthday. Even though she was annoyed at first, the truth was, she liked that he would choose to do something unconventional. Any guy could take her to a place like One If By Land or a Mario Batali restaurant. Alec was always surprising, and she liked that, even if he pushed her in ways that made her uncomfortable. When he'd asked her to dance for him that night, it made her embarrassed but excited at the same time. She had read once that in the brain, the feelings of fear and the feelings of love are closely related. Somehow Alec had a way of setting her on edge that heightened her love for him. She'd never experienced that with someone before, and she wondered if it was possible to have it ever again.

"Turn over slowly onto your stomach," the masseuse said softly. Mallory complied, flipping over while the woman held the sheet discreetly above her. When she was settled, the masseuse placed hot rocks at certain pressure points along her back. Mallory sighed, wishing she could stay on the table forever. She felt that if she could just have Jessica work on her knotted muscles long enough, she could figure out the whole mess her life had become.

When the hour was up, the masseuses left Mallory and Bette to relax and get their robes back on. Jessica told them to take as long as they liked, that they should let themselves "slowly reawaken their minds and bodies."

Mallory felt incredible. Her mind was quiet, her body felt limp, but every inch of her buzzed.

"You know what's great at a time like this?" Bette said.

"No—what?"

"A good fuck."

"Bette!"

"I'm serious. Have you ever had sex right after an intense massage? Your muscles and nerves are already primed—you will come in two seconds."

"I'll keep that in mind for next time."

"Why wait?" she said, sliding off her table. Her beautiful body glistened with massage oil.

"We talked about this. It's not a good idea," Mallory protested feebly. The truth was, she had been thinking about being sexual with Bette again, even if it was just one more time. She had been so nervous and upset about Alec the first time, she couldn't fully enjoy it. But it had felt good, and she found herself thinking of the way Bette touched her and of the way it felt to touch her back—especially feeling her breasts, and feeling Bette's soft lips and small tongue between her legs. She loved Alec too much to be with another guy—she couldn't even think about it. But she needed the release of sex, and somehow letting Bette make her come didn't feel like she was violating her relationship—even though she technically didn't have to worry about that anymore.

"*You* said it's not a good idea. I don't remember agreeing."

Bette moved to retrieve her handbag from the small table where she'd left it, and stood next to Mallory, where Jessica had stood during her massage. Mallory sat up but Bette pressed her gently down. "Don't get up yet. You need to get your money's worth."

"I didn't pay for this—the Baxters did, remember?"

"Well, then, let them get their money's worth. Believe me— they would consider it a rip-off if one of us didn't *get* off."

"Bette!"

"And look what I brought." She pulled the Pike Kegel Ball out of her handbag.

"What on earth did you bring that for?"

"I knew you'd never try it on your own—and you really should."

"Put that thing away."

"I thought you were going to be open to new experiences out here?"

"I'm not that open."

Ignoring her, Bette tugged Mallory's underwear off. Mallory smiled as if humoring an unruly child.

Bette rolled the ball over Mallory's nipple, which was already erect just from Bette's proximity. She controlled it with her palm, moving it between Mallory's breasts, then down her stomach and between her legs, where she rubbed it against Mallory's outer lips. She pressed it up against Mallory's clit, moving it in small circles. Mallory's breathing quickened, and she closed her eyes.

Bette continued the gentle pressure of the ball while she pressed her tongue inside of Mallory. Mallory's pelvis rocked in barely perceptible motions, and she willed Bette to just finger her, to trigger the release she knew was so close to the surface.

"I can't believe you won't try this little ball. You're being such a bad girl," Bette cooed, pressing the ball closer to the entrance to Mallory's pussy. Mallory reached for Bette's hand, pulling it toward her hungry opening, and she moaned when Bette pushed the Kegel ball inside of her. Then, just as quickly, Bette pulled it out and replaced it with her fingers, pressing deeply and rhythmically. Bette had been right about the massage prelude making her primed for an orgasm: within seconds, Mallory came with such intensity chills washed over her body.

Bette moved onto the table, lying next to her. Mallory propped herself on her elbow, then bent down to suck on Bette's breasts. She felt so much more relaxed than she had the last time she got to touch her—maybe it was from the orgasm, or maybe it was because she was far away from her real life. Whatever the reason, this time, touching Bette felt like she was a kid running loose in a candy store. She didn't feel pressure to make Bette come—she knew Bette was happy just to see her relaxed enough to explore her body.

Mallory trailed her hands down Bette's belly, touching her gently between her legs. It felt weird to put her fingers inside of her—like she was invading her space or something. She knew it was illogical—she tried to remind herself how good it felt when someone did it to her. And it was amazing how smooth and soft Bette's pussy was. Aside from the one time she tried it, Mallory didn't wax, she shaved, so her skin was only that soft for a day at the most. And she didn't take all of her hair off the way Bette did.

She felt Bette's pussy contract against her fingers, and this excited her in a way that was unlike anything she experienced with guys. It was as if Bette's body was communicating with hers in the most intimate way, and it was so natural for her to respond by touching her with more confidence. She could sense that Bette was going to come, and this made her so turned on, she pressed her own pussy against Bette's leg, grinding against it in tandem with Bette's pelvis thrusting against her hand. And then Bette reached for her, finding her open wetness with two fingers. Mallory burrowed her face in Bette's neck, trying not to make too much noise as they came together.

"Oh, my God," Mallory said.

"Hate to say I told you so." Bette smiled.

Mallory started to get off the massage table.

"Not so fast," Bette said. "I carried this in, now you carry it out. Hold it for me until we get to the locker room." And she pressed the Kegel ball back into Mallory's wet pussy.

"I take that as a challenge," Mallory said, touching the looped thread that peaked out from her lips.

"Impress me," said Bette.

Mallory curled up on the couch with a Palihouse blanket and a paperback she'd started reading before all hell broke loose in her life. Seeing the cover, remembering the day she'd bought the book for two dollars off a street stand in the Village while walking around with Alec, she got upset again. Who would have thought on the day she bought the book that by the time she was halfway through, she would be broken up with Alec and reading it halfway across the country?

"You sure you don't want to go? It will be so fun. I promise."

Bette and two other girls who were in town for the Baxter party were going to a club called Voyeur. Bette was dressed in a black corset and tight white jeans with white platform mules. Her fingernails and toenails were painted a gunmetal gray/black color that Mallory was crazy about; Bette told her it was a discontinued Chanel polish that she could only find on eBay.

"Yeah, thanks. I'm exhausted. I'll go to bed early and be rarin' to go tomorrow."

"You don't even want to have dinner with us?"

"No—I'm fine. I'll order from downstairs."

Bette sat next to her.

"Are you okay?"

"Yeah. I just miss Alec."

"Oh, honey. Aren't you having a good time?"

"I am—but somehow that just makes it worse. I wish I could call him and tell him all about it. I know it sounds crazy, but I wish I could tell him about the Kegel ball thing.... He's my best friend. I just don't know what happened."

"If it's meant to be, it will be. I'm sorry to be trite, but I think that's the truth."

"Can I ask you something? When's the last time you were in love?"

"I don't know if I've ever been in love."

"Really?"

"Yeah. I've had lots of lovers and some girlfriends I really liked, but I never felt that connection like, this is my soul mate."

"When's the last time you had a girlfriend?"

"Two years ago, maybe."

"That's a long time."

"What do I need the hassle for? I get laid when I want; I have fun. I have friends. Look at you—it's a gorgeous night in LA, and we're going to the hottest club in the city, and you can't even get your ass off the couch you're so depressed. I need to live my life and a relationship will only hold me back. There aren't many gals who can roll with me, Moxie."

"Yeah. I can see that."

Bette kissed her on the cheek.

"Get some rest. I'll see you in the morning."

As soon as the door clicked shut behind Bette, Mallory dialed Alec's cell phone. It was eight o'clock at night in New York, but the call went straight to voice mail. Where was he? She didn't leave a message.

16

Poppy wasn't sure what to wear for her "interview" with Alec Martin. On the one hand, it was business. On the other hand, it was a Thursday night, and that was a big night out in New York—maybe even bigger than Friday night. She wanted to look hot, but not in a way that overtly said "I would be happy to fuck you"—although she would be happy to fuck him. If she remembered correctly from the first night she had seen him with Mallory at the show, he was hot. And there would be a certain fairness to it: Mallory was living it up in LA with Bette, no doubt fucking her brains out all across Hollywood. If something happened between Poppy and Alec... Well, that's life. And if it upset Mallory, then maybe Poppy would be willing to strike a little bargain: stay away from the Blue Angel, and she'd stay away from Alec.

She was in a retro mood and decided to channel Jackie O meets Coco Chanel. She pulled on a black trench dress with oversized buttons to the waist and a belt to cinch it. She pinned one side of her bob away from her face with a rhinestone barrette that made her feel girlish. She finished off her ensemble with red lipstick—MAC's Russian Red—and a light spritz of Chanel Allure.

He'd told her to meet him at the bar at Gemma, the restaurant attached to the Bowery Hotel. When she arrived, he was already there, drinking vodka and sitting at a small table for two next to the long bar. It was early and not terribly crowded, and she spotted him immediately.

"Billy speaks very highly of you," Alec said when she sat across from him. There was nothing ironic or playful in the statement, so she assumed Billy had exercised discretion when he'd arranged the interview. She wasn't sure if this surprised her or not.

"He's an interesting character," Poppy said.

"I don't know if Billy told you but I'm actually almost finished with the piece. I spoke to one of the other dancers at the club last month—Bette Noir. But Billy seemed to feel my portrait of the Blue Angel would be incomplete without a few words from you." He smiled, and it was a boyish, utterly disarming smile. He had the faintest dimples and a slight gap between his two front teeth. She had the urge to stick her tongue in it.

"Bette and I work closely together—I guess you could say she's my mentor," Poppy said.

Alec ordered a beer, and Poppy asked for a glass of champagne. The waiter brought them a glass filled with extremely long, thin, crunchy bread sticks. Poppy was starving and quickly devoured one, then reached for another.

"I love those things. I think they are the only reason I keep coming back here," Alec said.

"I can see how they could be addictive."

She could tell from their eye contact that he found her attractive. Game on! He asked her questions about how she got started as a performer, and about the culture at the Blue Angel, and she felt pressure to say things that were different and more interesting than what Bette might have said. It was a lot of pressure, actually, and she got tired of it quickly.

"Do you have enough to get a good quote?" she said. She was on her second (or maybe third) glass of champagne.

"I think so. Why—do you have to leave?"

"No, not at all. I just thought it was getting boring."

He laughed. "I hope my readers don't think so."

"Oh, they won't. I'm sure you know how to keep things exciting." They locked eyes on that comment, and he broke contact first. Poppy knew it was time to step it up. "So have you been to the Angel since Mallory started with the show?"

His expression clouded over, and she wondered if she had made a mistake by going there. But then he seemed to relax back into his chair, took a sip of his beer (his third, but who was counting?) and shook his head.

"No. I haven't."

"You don't want to?"

"Mallory and I broke up. Didn't she mention that?"

"Not to me. We're not exactly friends. But, sorry to hear that. I mean, breakups suck."

"Are you and Bette friends?"

"I don't know," she said, smiling. "Frenemies, maybe."

"I thought you said she was your mentor."

Busted! He was good. Did they teach that at journalism school?

"Okay, I guess I exaggerated. I want her to be my mentor. She should be—honestly, I'm the best one there after her, and I just started. She's been there two years and you'd think she'd want to help someone else get established." *Someone aside from Mallory, who doesn't even deserve it.*

"Is there a lot of rivalry between the girls at the Blue Angel—or on the burlesque scene in general?"

"I can't speak for other girls or the scene in general. Besides, I thought you said you had enough for your article."

"Did I say that? I don't think I said that."

"Yes, you definitely did." She smiled her most alluring smile, and he couldn't help but smiling back.

"Okay. No more questions. You're a tough negotiator, Ms. LaRue."

No more questions? Did that mean he was going to get the check? But no, he seemed to settle back in his seat and even flipped through the menu.

"Have you had dinner yet? I'm starving," he said.

"Um, no." Did that mean he was offering to buy her dinner? Because there was no way she could pay for the food on that menu. Plus she'd just spent thirty dollars on feathers for next month's costume.

"Great. Then let's get some food." When she hesitated to pick up her menu, he winked at her and said, "It's on *Gruff*."

By the time they finished their porcini ravioli, the restaurant was jumping with a loud and eclectic crowd of hipsters and tourists. Poppy finished her third (or maybe fourth) glass of champagne, which was her absolute limit because anything more was too fattening, and she would be puffy in the morning. Alec seemed to want to have another drink, but she was ready to get the show on the road. And she knew where she wanted that road to lead!

"It's getting late," she said.

He signaled for the check.

At the door he helped her with her coat. It reminded her of how long it had been since she'd been on a proper date.

"I'll get you in a cab," he said, looking down the street to see if any were approaching.

"I think I'll just walk," she said.

"Where do you live?"

"Near St. Marks."

"It's freezing out. I'll get you a cab. I'll even keep you com-

pany in the cab if that would make you feel better—" He
smiled that lazy, sexy smile of his.

"Okay." She knew he thought she was hot; over dinner he'd
told her she could be a model, which she already knew, but
she'd tried it once and found the go-sees so demoralizing her
psyche couldn't handle it. She preferred the guaranteed adula-
tion of burlesque. And now he was taking a cab with her.

It was crazy. She wanted to hook up with him to get back at
Mallory for taking Bette's attention away from her, maybe even
to have some leverage to get Mallory away from the Blue
Angel—you stay away from my club; I'll stay away from your
man. But she actually liked him. He was cute and charming,
and he treated her like a lady. Mallory was so lucky. How did
she screw things up with him? Poppy was dying to know so she
wouldn't make the same mistake.

It would be nice to have a boyfriend in New York.

Mallory couldn't imagine why Alec didn't answer his phone
all night. She even texted him, and he ignored her.

Sitting in the hotel room was agonizing. She kept running
through the time calculations—now it's ten o'clock in New
York; now it's midnight. . . . She was losing her mind.

She had no interest in partying, but meeting Bette at the club
had to be better than sitting alone and obsessing over Alec.

Of course, she had no idea how to get a cab in this town.

She took the elevator to the lobby. The place was packed
with people, every table of the restaurant atrium filled. In the
corner, a DJ spun, and clusters of great looking people stood
holding exotic cocktails and talking intently.

The boyishly handsome guy at the desk greeted her with a
smile. She'd never been at a hotel where the front desk was just
feet away from the bar, but maybe that's how it was in LA.

"How can I help you?"

"Can I get a cab?"

"Sure. Where are you going?"

"7969 Santa Monica Boulevard."

"Ooh! Sounds like someone has a good night planned. But honey, I suggest you step up the ensemble a notch."

"What?"

"Yes. Trust me. March yourself back upstairs, and slip on something short and black and hot. You can rock it. The cab will be waiting for you."

Mallory hesitated a minute, then said, "Fine. I'll be right down."

From the outside, the club appeared to be a nondescript white building. If it hadn't been for the name "Voyeur" on the side of the door, she would have thought she was in the wrong place.

"Club's closed tonight for a private party," the guy at the door told her.

"Yeah, I know. I should be on the list. Mallory Dale?"

The guy spoke into his headset and then waited. He shook his head.

"You're not on the list," he said, and she could tell he wanted to shoo her away. Mallory's stomach dropped. She couldn't go back to that hotel room and worry about Alec for the rest of the night. She was all dressed up, and she was here.... She had to get into this stupid club. Bette had promised her name would be at the door.

And then she realized her mistake.

"Try the name Moxie," she said.

"What?"

"Moxie. I'm on the list under the name Moxie."

The guy spoke into his headset again and opened the door for her.

Mallory texted Bette, *I'm here...meet me inside the front door?*

She stood nervously inside the entrance hallway, and even in that space she could tell she was out of her depth. Walking slowly into the club, she knew this place was going to make the Blue Angel look like the Olive Garden. Sure enough, as she made her way inside the club, she felt like she'd wandered into a sex dungeon in Versailles. Above her hung enormous metal chandeliers with spiked lights; the drapes were black leather; the first room she turned into was wallpapered with filmstrip from a vintage-looking erotic photo shoot.

Two women brushed by her holding hands. They were dressed in identical corsets with black garters, thigh-high black patent leather boots, and carrying whips. A guy lounged on a Chesterfield sofa, totally nude except for a mask.

A text came through from Bette, *Meet me at the photo booth.*

What was she talking about? She would have to ask the nude guy.

"Excuse me—is there a photo booth here?"

"Yeah—you passed it already. Go back the way you came in . . . near the women's bathroom."

She backtracked, and sure enough there was an old-fashioned photo booth—the kind she used to go into with her friends at the mall or in the beachside shops at the Jersey Shore. And there was Bette, who had somehow added a black cape to her outfit.

"Hey—so glad you made it out!" Bette said. Mallory could tell even from a few feet away that Bette's usual cool demeanor had been dramatically defrosted: her cheeks were flushed; her eyes shining; and her smile was giddy as a school girl's. Mallory wondered if she had taken drugs.

"Are you okay?" Mallory asked.

"Oh, my God, I'm better than okay. I'm in love."

"Are you high?"

"I don't do drugs. I thought I told you that."

"Maybe someone slipped something into your drink. You

have to be careful at places like this. Here, look at me.... I'll tell you if your pupils are dilated."

"I'm not on drugs! Listen, if anyone can understand this, it's you. I met my soul mate."

"Your soul mate? Here?"

"Yes! I know—it sounds crazy. But it finally happened. We started talking, and I just felt this connection.... It's beyond attraction. It's like I've known her forever."

Mallory hated to be a buzz-kill, but was tempted to point out that Bette had only been at the club for two hours.

"Look," Bette said. "Here are some pictures we took in the photo booth."

She pulled a ribbon of photos out of her bag. Mallory bent close in the darkness of the room to get a good look at Bette's new love interest.

The woman had dark skin and light eyes and cheekbones you could ski jump off of. Mallory would have recognized that bone structure anywhere: it was the pop star Zebra.

"You are kidding me!" Mallory said.

"No. It's crazy, right? She performed on that stage over there. And then afterward a bunch of us went over to talk to her, and she recognized *me*. She was at the Angel almost two years ago—before she was anybody. She said she saw me perform to an Amy Winehouse song, and she thought about it for days."

"Zebra. I can't believe it."

"I know. I told her I just performed to 'Through the Looking Glass' last week! She said I have to come to her hotel and show her my routine."

"Yeah, I'll bet she wants you to come to her room and show her something. But it's not your 'routine'!"

"I'm in love. Seriously. I can't wait to get out of here and just be alone with her." Bette smiled. "You don't mind that I'm telling you this stuff, do you?"

"No—why would I mind?"

"I don't know. Because we're sort of lovers. And I don't want you to feel bad."

"Bette, I'm the one who's been moping about Alec this whole trip. I want you to be happy—I've been telling you all along that you should find someone you can have a relationship with. I just never thought that person would be the biggest pop star in the world."

"Are you going to be okay if I sleep out tonight?"

"Of course. I'm a big girl. Go—have fun."

"I want you to meet her."

"I don't know if I'm going to stay here very long. This is a bit intense for me at the moment. And I'm exhausted."

"You're leaving?"

"Yeah. I wanted to get out for a bit, and seeing you here was enough. I'm ready to go to sleep."

"No! Come to the back and meet Zebra and some of the girls who will be at the party Saturday night."

"I can't." Suddenly, she felt near tears. She didn't know if it was the jet lag, the fact that Alec surely had gotten her messages and was not calling back, or that Bette was about to fall in love and leave her more alone than ever; whatever it was, she couldn't process it all in the middle of this over the top club.

"Just come with me to meet Justin Baxter, and we'll get his driver to take you home."

"I don't think I'm in the right frame of mind," Mallory said.

"Trust me—some day you will be happy you met Justin Baxter. Just humor me," said Bette. "Have I steered you wrong yet?"

The cab pulled up in front of Poppy's dilapidated building. The old lady from 4G was sitting on the step, smoking as usual, with her cat on her lap. Poppy could never understand why the cat didn't scamper away. Maybe it was too old to run.

She wondered if Alec lived in a big fancy building.

"Do you want to come up?" she asked.

"Sure," he said. *That was easy,* she thought.

They walked past the old lady, and neither she nor the cat seemed to notice them going by.

"That cat must be sedated," Alec said.

"I never thought of that."

Poppy could imagine them as a couple. They already had this in common—their shared interest in why the cat from 4G didn't run. She wondered how long he and Mallory had been together. A year? Longer? Poppy's longest relationship had lasted a year. His name was Trent, and they were together her entire freshman year at Arkansas State. He had shaggy blond hair and blue eyes and looked like an Abercrombie model. She had lost her virginity to him in his dorm room closet. It wasn't the big life-changing event her friends had said it would be. She didn't even come, and then two months later she was tired of him.

"This building is old-school," Alec said, as they climbed the stairs to the third floor. The staircase was wide with a thick wooden railing. The tiling along the wall and ceiling was elaborate and decades older than she was.

"I like it, but my apartment is tiny. And my roommate is annoying, but she's in London for the month."

"What does she do?"

"She's a student at NYU. I get the sense that her parents are loaded, and she's slumming it here for a year or two before she gets her own place in Tribeca."

She opened the door, and her roommate's cat greeted them excitedly at the door, until it realized they weren't her owner. She slunk back to the master bedroom.

"I see there's a feline vibe in this building."

"Yeah. And I hate cats. My mother told me they carry evil spirits, and it's hard to shake that sort of thing off just because you move to a city where they are everywhere. The first time I went to one of those Korean delis and saw a big fat cat in the corner near the potato chip display, I almost had a heart attack."

She gave him a tour of the place, ending with her small bedroom off of the kitchen.

"So that's it. Do you want a drink? We might have a bottle of wine here."

"No," he said, and the way he was looking at her, she knew he was going to kiss her. She put her arms around his neck, and he pulled her close. He smelled good, and he was at least five inches taller than her, which was a rarity and really turned her on. She wondered how Mallory the Mouse had scored a guy like this.

They sat on the edge of her twin bed, and he pressed her back, his body tight against hers. He unbuttoned her dress, kissing her neck, moving down to take one of her breasts in his mouth.

"You're perfect," he breathed.

She said nothing, because "yes, I know" probably wouldn't sound right.

Poppy reached for his belt, fumbling with the buckle until he just took his jeans off himself. She felt him hard against her legs, and she was surprised by how much she wanted to take him in her mouth.

His hand was moving between her legs, stroking her clit. She moaned, and she pressed his hand deeper, wanting his fingers inside of her. An image of Bette flashed in her mind, and she imagined it was Bette's hand touching her. But it felt nothing like Bette's touch, and this distracted her. Alec moved his finger in and out with sharp, quick strokes, and she was dying for him to eat her pussy—that was the way she always came the fastest. But he didn't seem to be moving in that direction. She thought maybe she should lead the way, and she wriggled free of his touch so she could maneuver herself on top of him to suck his cock. She kissed his chest, working her way down to his cock. She slid her tongue along the shaft, and he made a noise, his hands in her hair. Like Justin Baxter's, Alec's cock was bigger than she was comfortable with for blow jobs, but she wanted the satisfaction of making Mallory's boyfriend come in her mouth. And then she wanted him to put his face between her legs and eat her pussy so she could come in his mouth. And then she would get on top of him and fuck him.

The thought of this made her even more wet as she sucked his cock. She pressed her pussy against his leg, grinding it gently in a way that could sometimes make her come. She worked her mouth around the tip of his cock, her hand stroking his thick shaft in a way he seemed to like. Her pussy throbbed, hungry for an orgasm. Plus, her mouth was getting tired. She wondered if she should make him come with her mouth or get on top of him and fuck him. But before she could decide, he pulled away from her.

"It's okay," she said, slightly dazed. "You can come in my mouth."

"Um, no. It's not that," he said, sitting up.

"Then what? Did I do something wrong?"

"No! No, absolutely not. You are incredible." He sat back against the window and pressed his hands against his forehead as if thinking about a complicated math problem. "The truth is, I'm just so fucked up about my girlfriend."

"Mallory? I thought you broke up."

"We did. But I can't...I thought maybe with someone like you—so gorgeous and cool. But I can't."

She couldn't believe this. That bitch was thwarting her at every turn!

"Do you want to just...talk or something?"

"No," he said, pulling on his jeans. "I'm really sorry, Poppy. This has nothing to do with you. You gotta know that."

And then he left.

17

Mallory woke up in the big Palihouse king-size bed alone.

The first thing she did was slip on her UGGs and pad around the suite to see if Bette had ever made it home. Apparently, she had not. But that was fine—expected, actually. She hoped maybe Bette had found her other half. It happened to everyone at some point. Some people were just better at holding on to happiness than others.

She made a pot of coffee and then brewed up the nerve to turn on her BlackBerry and see if she had any message from Alec. It was eleven in the morning in New York. If he was ignoring her still in the calm light of day, there was little hope.

There it was—the message icon. Heart pounding, she clicked on it to see the phone number.

Alec Martin.

Her hand shook as she dialed into her voice mail.

Hi, Mal. It's crazy you left me that message last night because I was thinking about you so much I could hardly stand it. I had my phone turned off, and when I got home I saw your message and it was like... this gift from the universe. I wanted to call you last night but at the same time I wasn't sure what to say. Then I woke up this morning and realized I was being an idiot—all I had to say was that I miss you. I really do. Call me when you can.

Mallory pushed the buttons on her phone as fast as she could type.

"Hey," he said.

"Hey." She caught sight of herself in the mirror across from the bed and saw she was grinning like a lunatic. Love made people crazy, but maybe sanity was overrated. "Thanks for calling me back."

"I'm glad you called and texted me last night. I was ... thinking about you a lot. Maybe we should get coffee or something later today?"

"I wish I could! I'm actually in LA."

"What are you doing there?" he asked suspiciously.

"Well, I haven't found a new job yet, and Bette had an all expense paid trip and invited me along. Just for a change of scenery."

Silence. "We're just friends, Alec. Really. I have been so upset about losing you ... about our relationship. I couldn't sit on Julie's couch crying for another week."

"I don't want you to be that upset. I think we should find a way through this."

"So do I!"

"So you're really just out there to clear your head? This isn't some crazy burlesque convention or anything?"

"No. I mean, Bette is performing at a private party. But I'm just hanging out. I'm going to try to find a way to the beach later today."

"When do you get back?"

"Sunday night."

"Okay. Let's talk when you get back."

"Great. I love you."

"I love you, too, Mal. I really do."

She put down her BlackBerry and cried with relief. That was how Bette found her when she walked in the door.

"What's wrong? Jeez, I shouldn't have left you alone!" She dropped her sequined clutch and rushed to Mallory's side. Bette was still wearing her corset and jeans, but her face was clear of any makeup, her cheeks were flushed, and she looked as fresh and beautiful as a preschooler at her first ballet recital.

"Nothing—nothing is wrong. Everything is great, actually." Mallory wiped her eyes. "Alec called, and we had a great conversation."

"Oh, honey. I'm happy for you. See? Being apart did you both some good."

"Tell me about your night!"

"Oh, Mallory. I've got it bad. She is literally perfect. I'm in love. Seriously."

"That's amazing! Why do you say it like it's a bad thing?"

"I don't know when I'll see her again. I just had the best night of my life, and I'm afraid it's a one-and-done."

"Why? Did you get the sense she doesn't want to see you again?"

"No. In fact, she invited me to come to Vegas with her tomorrow and stay for the week. And get this—I showed her my routine to 'Through the Looking Glass,' and she said she'd love for me to do it onstage. Can you image? Performing in front of thousands and thousands of people a night?"

"Oh, my God, you have to do it!"

"I can't! I have to do the Baxters' party tomorrow night. I can't bail on them. I don't even know if any other burlesquers are going to perform. I know they have a few different types of performers, but I think I'm the only burlesque dancer. There are two girls from the Slit, but they are doing some crazy knife act. I know Justin really likes at least one big, beautiful dance routine. I can't let them down. Even if I wanted to bail, I can't afford to reimburse them for this trip."

"They wouldn't ask you to pay them back for the airfare and room, would they?"

"I don't know. It's pointless even to think about it, because I can't let them down. I've been doing Justin's birthday for the past four years. The Baxters booked me before I even had a regular gig at the Blue Angel. The money I've made on these parties has helped me avoid getting a day job to support myself."

"What can I do?"

"Nothing. There's nothing to do."

They sat in silence. Mallory looked up and saw herself in the mirror, still surprised at the red hair. She thought about Justin's comment last night when Bette had introduced them: he said it had been a long time since he'd seen such a beautiful redhead. Then his wife launched into a whole conversation about how they thought Nicole Kidman was miscast as Satine in *Moulin Rouge*.

"They could have found someone hotter," Justin had said.

"Like you," Martha had said to her.

Now Mallory looked at Bette, who was close to tears. She had never seen Bette emotional before, and it moved her.

"I can do your routine for you," Mallory said.

"What?"

"Teach me your routine. I can learn it in a day. I was a ballet dancer—I'm a fast learner. I met Justin and Martha last night. They told me they thought I was hot and even said weird stuff like that they would have rather seen me cast in *Moulin Rouge* than Nicole Kidman."

"They said that?"

"Yeah."

Bette seemed to consider it.

"That's really amazing of you, Mal. But I don't know how I

can expect you to learn this in a day and perform for the first time in front of hundreds of people at the Baxters' party. No offense, but you freaked out the first time you walked on stage as a stage kitten."

"That was because my boss was there! No one knows me here. I really will just be Moxie. Seriously, I won't blow this. Let me do this for you. You've done so much for me."

Bette looked into her eyes. "I don't know what to say," she said.

"Say yes. It's time for Bette Noir to go on tour with Zebra. And it's time for Moxie to make her debut."

In the morning, Poppy did something that was, by any measure, colossally stupid: she called Alec and asked him to breakfast.

"I don't think that's a good idea," he said.

"I'm not trying to hit on you," she said. "I mean, come on—I do have my pride."

"I'm not sure of the point then," he said. Men!

"I want to talk."

"Okaaay. Can you come uptown?"

Poppy felt like she had vertigo anywhere above 24th Street. Alec named a diner on 81st and First Avenue.

"That's sort of out of the way," she said.

"Not for me—I live on 83rd."

"Okay," she agreed. After all, she was the one who'd suggested breakfast. She hoped it was a cute place, like the one called Friend of a Farmer with the amazing French toast. Or the French country one called Danal. Come to think of it, that place had a cat roaming around it, too. Maybe she should suggest it—keep the vibe going from last night. But no—this wasn't about hooking up. She wasn't going to fight a losing battle. But she did have to know why Mallory was better than she was—to everyone and in every way.

She couldn't waste money on a cab and the 6 train took forty-five minutes. By the time she arrived at Gracie Mews Diner, she was cold, tired, and cranky. Making things worse, it was just a plain old Greek diner. They could have gone anywhere!

"So what's up?" Alec asked. He was already at a booth near the window. The waiter poured her a coffee without even asking if she wanted any. That scored some points, at least.

She wore leggings, a long-sleeved black T-shirt, knee-high UGGs, and faux-fur coat. With her aviator sunglasses and careless, unwashed blond bob, she was by far the sexiest looking woman on the Upper East Side. Alec barely seemed to notice.

"I feel weird about last night," she said.

"I'm sorry," said Alec. "It's my fault. I shouldn't have gone back to your place. It's not that I'm not attracted to you—because I am. Who wouldn't be? Christ, look at you."

Poppy smiled.

"But like I said last night...I'm really hung up on Mallory. I spoke to her this morning, though. I'm hopeful maybe things will work out."

"So why aren't you having breakfast with *her*?" Bitchy much? Okay—but she had a point, so that made it okay.

"She's in LA."

Poppy felt her stomach tighten. The coffee sloshed around like acid.

"She's not there for the Baxter party, is she?"

He shrugged. "It's some sort of party, I think. I don't know. Bette Noir was invited out, and Mallory tagged along. I guess she needed to clear her head, too. This has been a really tough time for us."

Poppy's head was spinning. How did Mallory get invited instead of Poppy—after she'd let Justin fuck her like crazy?

"Is Mallory performing?" Poppy asked. If so, she was going

to make thousands of dollars. And Bette would probably like her even more.

"God, no," Alec said.

"How do you know?" she pressed.

"She's not a burlesque dancer, Poppy. Okay, so she likes hanging around that club, but I think it's just a phase. She resents moving here and feeling like she's in *my* life. I think she feels like she needs to prove that she's her own person or something. And she's being reckless and stupid about the whole thing. But when I spoke to her this morning, she sounded like her old self."

"I don't understand why everyone loves her so much!" Poppy wailed.

"Who's everyone?"

"You. Bette. Agnes. Justin Baxter. I just want to know why. Can you tell me?"

"Who is Justin Baxter?"

"The guy hosting the party in LA."

"Mallory has nothing to do with that party. I told you that."

"Well, I wouldn't be so sure. The Baxters have a way of sucking people into their craziness." She signaled the waiter and ordered more black coffee.

"What does that mean?"

"They have these wild parties, and let's just say it's easy to get caught up in the moment. Besides, I can't believe Justin would pay for her to fly all the way out there and not ask her to perform. He's not running a charity."

"I told you, she's not a burlesque performer. And she told me she wasn't there for the party, and I believe her."

"Whatevs. Anyway, if you had any doubt, I'm sure you could ask Billy Barton to give you the lowdown on the party."

"What does Billy have to do with it?"

"Nothing, except I know he's going to be there." She could tell Alec was thinking hard about that little bit of information.

"She has no reason to lie to me."

"Except she knows you don't like her hanging out at Blue Angel. Or any other burlesque scene. And why is that, by the way?"

Alec sighed. "It's hard to explain."

"Try."

"For one thing, it's hypocritical: she never liked when I went to strip clubs or watched porn because she said it made her feel like she wasn't enough for me. Then she wants to hang out at a place where it's all about titillating other guys? How am I supposed to feel about that?"

"That's not what burlesque is all about."

"Okay, spare me the post-feminist deconstruction of burlesque. I'm a guy, and to guys it's hot women taking off their clothes. Period. We don't care about the music and the costumes."

"Fair enough," Poppy said. "Now tell me one more thing: what does she have that I'm missing? No offense, but I'm ten times hotter than she is. You said it yourself last night—I could be a model."

"First of all, to me she is the most beautiful woman in the world. Period. *And* we're amazing friends, *and* we have great sex. And whenever I think of my future, she is the one by my side. I can't explain it any better than that. I can't imagine anyone making me as happy as she does."

Poppy blinked at him. Would anyone ever feel that way about her?

"What do you mean by 'great sex'?" she said.

"Oh, come on, Poppy. I can't get into this with you."

"Seriously. I have great sex. And it never amounts to anything. It's like, just a good feeling that evaporates—like eating candy."

"Maybe it's because you don't have the emotional connection. You know, like when you think about someone all the time and can't wait to talk to him or her."

She did feel that way—about Bette. And now Mallory was in LA with her and the Baxters having God only knew what kind of crazy orgies. And Bette was probably falling in love with Mallory just like Alec had. It was so unfair.

"I do feel that way about someone. But I don't think that person feels it for me."

"You are probably underestimating him."

"Her."

"Her?"

"Yeah."

"Oh. I had no idea."

"I've never had a girlfriend before. I've only liked guys. But I just can't stop thinking about her. At first I thought it was because I wanted her to help me with getting ahead in the burlesque scene. But even when I was with you last night, I was thinking about her."

"Ouch!"

"No—I mean, I was into being with you. Until you got up to leave."

"I guess we were both thinking about other women."

He smiled at her. She could imagine what it would be like to be in love with him, and how much it would suck to lose that. For the first time, she felt a little sorry for Mallory.

And then she realized something: If Alec and Mallory got back together, she could get Mallory away from Bette and still have a chance herself.

"I don't think you should mention to Mallory that we hooked up last night," she said quickly.

"Yeah, I was going to say the same thing to you. I was hoping we could maybe just pretend that never happened. No offense—it's just that after talking to her today, I realize how much I want to try to make things work."

"That's a good idea."

He shrugged. "But now that you're telling me how she must be partying like a lunatic at this guy Justin's place, I'm thinking I don't know what is going to happen. Maybe she's already moving on."

"No! No, I'm sure she's not moving on. Forget what I said about the Baxter parties. That was just my experience. You can't go by me."

"I guess only Billy Barton knows for sure. And believe me: if Mallory is at that party, I'm going to hear about it."

"It's just a party," Poppy said weakly, backtracking as fast as she could.

"If she is lying to me about why she is in LA, how can we work on our relationship? And I hooked up with you. God, it's so fucked up."

"No! It's not. Look, we didn't have sex. And Mallory is probably just in LA shopping and trying not to be sad."

Alec looked at her, his head cocked to one side as if he was trying to figure out a puzzle.

"Why are you suddenly on her side?"

"I dunno," she said with a shrug. "Maybe I'm a romantic."

"Ah, the proverbial 'hooker with a heart of gold.'"

"I'm not a hooker!"

"Sorry—stripper with a heart of gold."

"I'm not a stripper."

"Okay: burlesquer with a heart of gold. That doesn't have the same ring to it. At any rate, I'm still going to check in with Billy Barton."

Poppy looked down at her coffee cup.

18

With the help of Mason from the front desk and two of the porters, Mallory and Bette moved most of the furniture from the center of the living room to a far corner, to make an open space. They borrowed a huge mirror from one of the other suites and propped it against one wall. In this makeshift dance studio, they got to the work of preparing Mallory to perform at the Baxter party. But three hours into their "rehearsal," Bette had still not shown Mallory one step from the act planned for the party that would take place in twenty-four hours. Instead, Bette insisted on painstakingly teaching her the foundations of burlesque. Bette spent close to an hour just on the art of removing a glove. Mallory realized that the powerful effect of the burlesque performance was built on the tiniest motions, that it was about slowness and the reveal.

"Now you need to learn the bump 'n' grind. I'm going to teach it to you the way I learned it from Jo Weldon."

"Who is Jo Weldon?"

"A great performer who also runs the New York School of Burlesque. Now pay attention—it's simple. Stand with your feet apart, knees slightly bent. Now, imagine an apple hanging from your right hip, an orange hanging from your left, and a coffee bean hanging between your legs. Okay, now bump the apple with your hip. Bump the orange. Now rotate your hips in a circle around the coffee bean."

Mallory followed her directions, feeling stiff.

"Now do it in the opposite direction."

She repeated it.

"Okay—good enough."

"It doesn't look as good as when you do it."

"You can practice later. We have to keep moving. Now take off your shirt."

"Why?"

"You're going to try on some pasties, and I'm going to show you how to twirl the tassels with your breasts."

"I can't do that."

"Of course you can. Everyone can."

The pasties were gold sequined with fuchsia tassels. Bette whipped out some false eyelash glue from her cosmetics bag and coated the back of the pasties. When the glue was slightly tacky, she pressed them onto Mallory's breasts, covering her nipples. Mallory was mesmerized just looking at herself wearing them, but she knew Bette was impatient.

"Okay, now shimmy."

She shook her torso like she was trying to get a mosquito off her shoulder.

"Don't just shake them—the tassles need to go in circles, not side to side. Open up your rib cage. That's it. Try to isolate your ribcage from your hips."

"I can't—if I move my ribcage, my hips move. They're attached."

"They're not attached. Here, sit on this chair. Now shimmy your shoulders."

Mallory moved her shoulders and, sure enough, the deep pink tassels were airborne, twirling in circles.

"Oh, my God! It worked!" She stood up, maintaining the motion with her shoulders. She looked at herself in the mirror. With her red hair, bare, tasseled breasts, and twirling ability, she felt Moxie coming alive.

"There are a few variations I want to show you, but we need to keep moving. I wish we had a week to do this. Okay, we have to move on to using the fans."

"Fans?"

"Yeah. I have big feather fans that I use for the act I'm doing."

"Does that mean you're finally going to show me the routine?"

"No, not yet. We have to do the basics of fan dancing. Then we'll talk about the routine."

"Can you at least tell me what song you're using?"

"No. I don't even want you thinking about the performance right now. I want you to learn."

"I'm learning! So where are the fans? I didn't even see them here."

"One of my suitcases is all costume stuff, and I have them packed in there. I'll be right back."

While Bette went to retrieve the fans, Mallory practiced twirling her tassels. She imagined facing a crowd of people as she did it, and it felt okay. It didn't feel like it was herself, Mallory Dale, standing there with bare breasts with only sequins between her nipples and a bunch of strangers. It felt like she was in a play or a movie, like she was inhabiting a character who had nothing to do with her actual self. And yet, the character was in some ways the purest form of herself.

"Check these out. Gorgeous, right?"

The fans were not at all the small, Asian variety Mallory had imagined. Instead, they were giant, shell-like wings of black feathers.

"Wow. You got those in your suitcase?"

"Yes. Carefully. They're collapsible. Ostrich feather."

"Where did you get them?"

"Agnes has a friend who makes them. Okay, now watch me. And notice that with the fans, as with the gloves, it's about the reveal. The fans only work if you are effectively concealing something with them. Make the audience want to see. Just waving them around randomly does nothing. You have to be strategic."

She cupped the fans around herself as she moved, letting Mallory have only a glimpse of her leg, her arm, the arch of her back while her ass was concealed. Mallory knew that while it looked easy, she was going to struggle.

"You know what—before we get started I want to show you something. Do you have a laptop with you?"

"No. Why?"

"I have to show you just a gorgeous example of fan usage—sort of the effect I want you to go for when you perform tomorrow night. Let's go downstairs and see if Mason will let us use his computer for a few minutes."

Mallory changed into sweats, and they traipsed down to the lobby and found Mason at his desk on the phone.

"Sorry to bother you again."

"Not at all! Anything in the name of art. What can I do for you ladies?"

"Can we check something out on your computer?"

He stood up and gestured for Bette to go ahead. She logged onto www.msticklearts.com and cued up a video on the home screen.

"Sit, watch, and learn," she said to Mallory.

Mallory bent toward the screen, watching the dancer begin slow, deliberate movements. She suspected, by the arc of her back and arms, that the dancer had serious dance training. The music was slow, melodic, and haunting. The dancer moved with excruciating precision, her body perfectly attuned to the song. From what Mallory could tell from the poor quality video, the woman's white costume was an elaborate bodice with a broad skirt of feathers not unlike the ostrich fans Bette had just shown her.

This performer was nothing like Bette, who led with her sexuality. This woman, with her slow, delicate movements, was like a ballerina. The music moved toward its first crescendo, and the dancer pulled off the sides of her skirt, revealing them to be, in fact, large fans.

The audience in the video howled and clapped, and while that made perfect sense at the Blue Angel, it annoyed Mallory while she tried to take in this performance.

The dancer used her fans to conceal her body, at one point cupping one overhead and one underneath so that she was like a baby bird just beginning to emerge into the world.

"That's the Clam Shell," Bette said. "I'm going to show you how to do that next."

Mallory barely heard her. She was mesmerized.

The music peaked again, and this time the dancer pulled the fans apart to reveal her body. She wore a spangled bikini top and bottom, and she gyrated her body like a belly dancer. The audience screamed and hooted, and again this seemed entirely inappropriate to Mallory. This woman deserved silent reverence.

When it ended, Mason spoke first.

"Is that you?"

"No!" Bette said. "But tomorrow night, that will be her." She nudged Mallory.

"Cool," Mason said.

Mallory looked at them like they were both crazy.

When they rode the elevator back upstairs, Mallory checked

out her reflection in the mirrors. She straightened her back and held her fingers loosely posed in "ballet hands." She remembered, as a child, how her teacher explained to her that the best way to remember ballet hands was to pretend you had to hold a fluffy cotton ball between your thumb and middle finger without crushing it.

She could tell Bette had never danced ballet.

"How did you get started doing this?" Mallory asked.

"It was a random thing. I was at NYU, stripping and nude modeling for tuition money." She said this casually, as if she had said she had been waiting tables. "One of the photographers came to see me strip, and then she invited me to see a show at the Slit. I thought it was cool. The photographer introduced me to Penelope Lowe. She's this rich society brat who owns the club. I auditioned but didn't get it—they always want girls to do crazy things like stick knives up their pussies, and I was just trying to learn how to perform. It was a disaster. "

"But if you needed money, why would you leave stripping for burlesque? Strippers must make so much more money. You told me Agnes barely pays."

"I think the idea started one day when I was reading a magazine I found in the trash compactor room of my building. One of my neighbors had a subscription to every magazine you could imagine—*Vogue, W, Vanity Fair, Us, Cosmo*...I think she worked for a magazine or something. Every few months she left a massive pile in the trash room. I always read *Vogue* and *W* because I ripped out the best photos to hang in my apartment. This was before I could pay for prints. I love photography, you know."

"Yeah. The first thing I noticed in your apartment was the photographs."

"Anyway, there was a gorgeous editorial spread of Marilyn Manson and Dita Von Teese at their wedding. It was gothic, and the spread looked like they were covering a royal wedding of the underworld. Dita Von Teese wore an incredible, dark violet Vivienne Westwood gown. I've never seen anything like it. But the point is, they never would have featured her so prominently if she were a stripper. But she was a burlesque performer and had made a name for herself doing a routine in a giant martini glass—props can be a big part of defining yourself as a performer, but we don't have time to get into all that now. Anyway, I knew that was what I wanted and what I would go for: the *Vogue* spread, the celebrity wedding. A name of my own. You don't get that as a stripper. When a celebrity marries a stripper he marries a punch line. But a burlesque performer... she's a creative equal. So I eventually made a name for myself at the Blue Angel. The only thing missing was the famous boyfriend. And believe me, a few musicians and actors have come through the Angel. I knew I could sleep with them once or twice. But I'm not good enough at faking it to have a whole relationship with a guy."

"I guess that's where Zebra comes in," Mallory said.

"Why do you say it like that?"

"I thought you said she was your soul mate, and you were in love and all that."

"She is. I am."

"I don't know. Maybe she just conveniently serves as the famous lover you need to take you to the next level of your career," Mallory said.

"Oh Mallory—you're such a cynic. Look, I am crazy about her. And there is the potential for something real there—I know it. But yes, it helps that she is an extremely visible celebrity. That's part of the attraction."

"That's not what makes a relationship work."

"I know, hon. Not for you. And it's great that you and Alec have been in love since you were kids. There's a purity to that.

But it's more complex for me. I've never been in love before. And I know that being with a woman like Zebra is my best chance at feeling in love *and* getting what I want out of life."

"Being in love is the best feeling in the world—better than any audience can give you," Mallory said. She felt tears coming. "I miss him so much."

"I know you do. But you had a good conversation this morning. Things will work out. But put him out of your mind for now—we have fan dancing to learn."

It was eleven at night before they finished.

Mallory sat on the couch, every muscle in her body aching. She had spent the past six hours learning variations of the bump 'n' grind, tassel twirling, glove peeling, showgirl posing, and ten different fan dance techniques. She was grateful that Bette had taken the time to show her the Ms. Tickle performance—when she had moments of feeling that she was just going through the motions with no end in sight, she drew upon the mental image of that magnificent dance, a dance that pulled all the pieces together to make magic.

And then there was Bette's choreography for the Baxter party performance. Just watching it had left Mallory breathless. The dance was a perfect combination of Ms. Tickle's grace and subtlety and Bette's signature, fierce sexuality. It was the most ambitious performance she had ever seen, and she felt like a fool for thinking she could just step in to Bette's place.

"You think I can do that? Why didn't you tell me it was the most intense performance I've seen yet? I'd imagined something simple, like your Alice in Wonderland dance. Oh, my God, what have I gotten myself into?"

Bette opened a bottle of red wine.

"Don't stress. See, that's why I didn't want to show you at first. Just take a step back and think of the pieces of the performance. It's just the things I showed you strung together. And the costume helps, doesn't it?"

Luckily, Bette's black satin corset and black Ostrich feather skirt fit Mallory almost as well as if they had been made for her. The only thing she didn't have was shoes, because Bette's were too small, but they would find replacements at the Hustler store on Sunset. Even Bette's black sequined pasties were the right size because they both had small, delicate nipples. "I really appreciate your doing this for me, Mallory. It was a stroke of genius, and it's giving me the chance to have something with Zebra. So here—cheers. To friends and lovers."

They touched their glasses together.

"And to tomorrow, the debut of Moxie."

"Wait—what's the date tomorrow?" Mallory said.

"I don't know, February 3? Why?"

"Unbelievable. That's the retake date for the bar exam. If I'd done what I was supposed to do and gone for it again, I would have been up tonight cramming for that test."

"Did you forget?"

"No! I would never forget something like that if I had any intention of retaking the test. But I knew a while ago—maybe even subconsciously as long ago as the day I registered to take it again—that I wasn't going to. And so tonight, instead, I'm cramming to learn your performance. How crazy is that?"

"I guarantee tomorrow is one test you will pass—big-time."

"Bette, I can never thank you enough for opening my eyes to all of this. I was so stuck before. I couldn't even admit to myself how much I was second-guessing my decision to be a lawyer. I really thought Alec was the one who would have an interesting career. I was just settling."

"Do you think you want to do this for real?"

"What do you mean?"

"Audition for the Blue Angel?"

"I don't know."

"You're not interested?"

"Let's see how things go tomorrow night."

"I wish I could see it! I just hope someone records it with a phone, and it ends up on YouTube."

"Don't even say that!" She could just imagine Alec hearing from one of his friends that she was naked on YouTube.

"It's no big deal. We all end up on there eventually."

"That cannot happen tomorrow night!"

"Why? What difference does it make?"

"I swore to Alec I was just here to relax—that I had nothing to do with the party."

"Why did you say that?"

"Because at the time, it was true!"

"So tell him you've decided to perform. Not a big deal."

"It is a big deal. He broke up with me because of the night you and I hooked up. He blames the Blue Angel for my losing my job at the law firm. The combination ... you, the club. He sees it as a threat. I'm lucky he took the news that I'm out here with you so calmly."

"Guys are such babies. They can dish it out, but they can't take it. I'm so glad I don't have to deal with that bullshit. I mean, don't get me wrong. Women come with their own crap. But it's crap I can at least understand."

Mallory put her head in her hands. "I'm exhausted. I can't believe I'm going to try to do this tomorrow night."

"Get some sleep. All this stuff will sink in overnight. You'll wake up owning it. Trust me."

Bette kissed Mallory on the forehead.

"You're leaving?"

"I'm spending the night with Zebra. I'll be back first thing in the morning to take you shoe shopping and to run through the routine a few more times before my flight to Vegas. Sleep well, Moxie."

19

The Lincoln Town Car pulled up to a mansion perched on the edge of the Pacific Ocean.

When Bette had told her that the Baxters had a beach house, Mallory had somehow envisioned something quaint and rustic like her parents' summer home at the Jersey Shore. She was not prepared—although she should have been—for the sight of the Italian Renaissance mansion, with its triple-arched entrance flanked by palm trees. Her stomach tightened like a fist.

The night had begun a few hours earlier, with the phone call from Bette to Justin. She's told him she was sick, but that the redheaded burlesque dancer he'd met at Voyeur was happy to perform in her place.

"He was fine with it," she told Mallory from her cell phone. She was on Zebra's private plane waiting to leave for Vegas.

"I guess he had to be, considering the party starts in three hours."

"No, he was really okay with it. He said he remembers you from Thursday night, and you're hot. He asked if you wanted to hang out at the party before you perform but I told him no—just to send a car for you to arrive a half hour ahead of time. That's what I always do. If you want to stay after and mingle, that's fine, but I never see the audience before I perform."

"Okay," Mallory said. She knew she would not want to mingle with the audience at all—not before, and especially not after.

"Break a leg," Bette said. And then she was gone.

Pulling up to the entrance, the car circled a Venetian fountain surrounded by Bentleys and Ferraris. Mallory would have given anything to have Bette riding shotgun, even just to walk her inside. The only two thoughts that helped mobilize her out of the backseat of the car were that first, she was not Mallory Dale tonight. She was Moxie, and no one would know anything different. Second, the sooner she got through the performance, the sooner she would be home in bed so she could wake up the next morning to a flight that would take her home to Alec.

"I'll be waiting here when you're ready to leave," the driver said, opening the door for her.

She grabbed the bag with her costume in it, a large Juicy Couture overnight satchel. It was Bette's, and someone had personalized it for her with the word *Noir* in pink rhinestones. Or maybe she had just found a bag that came that way.

"Welcome! Are you a guest or a performer?" a woman greeted her in the entrance foyer.

"Performer," Mallory said.

"What's your name?" She looked at a clipboard.

"Mallory...I mean, Moxie."

She spoke into a headset. "Moxie has arrived." And then, "Mr. Baxter will be right with you."

Justin appeared. He wore a black suit, black shirt, and black tie. He looked the way some of the slick agents looked standing with their A-list clients at the Academy Awards.

"Hey, Moxie. So glad you could fill in for Bette. Is she doing okay?"

"Yes. Fine. She's . . . resting." *On Zebra's jet.*

"Poor thing. Was it something she ate?"

Mallory missed Alec with a sudden pang. If he were there, he would have deadpanned, "Yes, something she ate really got to her," and they would have shared a private laugh.

"I'm not really sure," Mallory said.

"Well, you're an angel for stepping in at the last minute. Everything you need should be in the dressing room upstairs. I have hors d'oeuvres and a few bottles of Perrier and champagne but if you want anything else, just let Maria here know. You're on in a half hour. When you're ready, Maria will call the party producer to escort you to the performance area. The producer has your song cued up, so when you step onto the floor it will be ready to go. It's not an actual stage, so there's no curtain or anything—I hope that's okay. I mention it because it throws some of the girls at first if they don't know. But trust me, it works beautifully. We've done dozens of shows here, and by the end the girls tell me they like my room more than any club."

"Thanks. It will be great, I'm sure."

"Can't wait to see you out there." He kissed her on the cheek, and left her to climb the stairs alone.

Mallory stepped onto the performance space, which was a wide, hardwood floor that had surprisingly professional-looking lighting overhead. It had the effect of obscuring the audience somewhat. She knew the space was surrounded by tables for ten and that still more people were milling around, but she couldn't see specific faces the way she could see the front row at the Blue Angel.

She positioned herself with her back to the audience, so they were looking at the intricate lacing of her corset, her arms outstretched in long black gloves. Her hands were shaking so hard she wondered how she would be able to remove the feathered skirt.

The first beats of the Peaches song "Lose You" overtook the room. She couldn't tell if the crowd fell silent or if the music was covering the sound of voices, but either way, between the lights and the music she was able to get her mind in the game.

When the lyrics began, she spun around twice, walked toward the front of the "stage," and slowly peeled off one glove. Bette had choreographed a lot of spinning in the dance—she said the song begged for movement—and with each turn Mallory had to get her hands in position to remove another section of her costume. The one thing that was excruciating to her was that at the very end she had to remove her pasties. Bette had told her that Justin liked full nudity in his shows, but she could get away with just being topless since she was new and only filling in for her. But to compensate for this, Bette had added a spanking to the ending: Mallory would turn her back to the audience in a final turn, while wearing only a white sequined thong, bend over, and hit her ass with a black paddle.

The audience was quieter than the Blue Angel audience, but they clapped and occasionally whistled as she moved through the first steps of her performance. She pulled off the section of her skirt that doubled as fans, and she moved into her Clam Shell pose. She exaggerated each gesture, careful not to rush through the motions. She was again grateful that Bette had showed her the Ms. Tickle performance, which gave her the confidence to have moments of near-stillness.

She used one fan to obscure her waist and then removed the rest of her skirt, tossing it aside. The audience clapped their approval. Now the hard part: she did another turn, dropped the fans, and unzipped the side of her corset, then turned again, removing it in one motion. She felt a rush of heat through her body in those first moments standing there in just a thong and the pasties. She froze for half a beat, then forced herself through the motion of twirling the tassels. The audience erupted in applause and whistles, and something clicked inside of her; she stopped hearing Bette's instructions in her mind, and she moved because her body launched into the steps as automatically as her lungs pushed out each breath. A sense of absolute control came over her, control of the room, control of herself. It became a game to elicit noise from the audience, and by the time she had to remove her pasties, she was happy to have some way to up the ante.

The music built to its finale, and she took two more turns, getting her ass in position for the audience to have a full view of her spanking. She reached down for the carefully placed paddle, then brought her arm out in an exaggerated motion before smacking her ass hard enough to leave a mark. Bette had told her she was lucky she was fair skinned—it wouldn't be hard to get a red mark. Mallory had to trust her on that. From the shrieks of the audience—no more polite clapping, it was full-on yelling now—she could imagine they were seeing something.

The song moved toward its final beats, and she dropped the paddle and froze in a pose that mirrored her original position, back to the audience, arms outstretched.

The room went wild, and Mallory felt flooded with relief and a joy so pure it almost brought tears to her eyes.

As Justin had told her, there was no curtain to signal the end of the performance, but the party producer escorted her off stage and handed her a robe.

"You are incredible!" she gushed.

"Thanks," Mallory said, slightly breathless.

"Moxie! Oh, my God, there are no words. You are a star." Justin met her at the foot of the stairs.

"Thanks, Justin." Her heart was pounding, and she felt like hugging him for giving her the chance to take the stage.

"Thank *you*. The Marigold twins are on next, but I suspect you stole the show. Bravo. Where do you perform in the city?"

"Um, I'm just starting at the Blue Angel. I've done a few shows just helping out between sets."

"I'll call you when we get back east. We'd love to have you perform again. Do you have a card?"

"Not...on me."

"I can reach you through Agnes or Bette. Okay, then. You're welcome to join the party. Hope to see you soon."

This time, he kissed her on the cheek *and* squeezed her ass.

She shook her head and started up the stairs.

"Mallory!"

She turned to find Billy Barton looking up at her. She froze.

"Oh, hi, Billy." She tried to sound casual, but her heart was racing. She knew the polite thing to do was to go back down the stairs and say hi to him, but her adrenaline had her in fight-or-flight mode, and she just wanted to run away.

"You were fantastic! I had no idea you were a burlesque performer. How could Alec not mention this—he's writing a feature story on it, for God's sake. And I like the red hair, by the way."

She slowly descended the stairs.

"Thanks. Listen, the reason Alec never mentioned it is because he doesn't know yet. And if you don't mind, I'd like to be the one to tell him."

"Sure thing—no problem. I hope you talk to him soon, though."

"Why?"

"He's been moping around the office like a lovesick teenager. What are you two fighting about?"

"We're not fighting," she said.

"He said you broke up."

"We're just...working some things out."

"I'm sure hearing about your new hobby will cheer him up."

"Billy, I don't want you to mention it, okay? Things are

complicated right now, and I don't think he needs this news at the moment."

"My lips are sealed," he said. They looked at each other for just a beat too long. She felt certain she couldn't trust him.

She climbed back up the stairs.

The Blue Angel was empty for a Saturday night. Poppy wondered if maybe it was because Bette wasn't on the bill.

"I don't like her doing these parties," Agnes muttered. "I never should have agreed."

"She'll be back on Tuesday," Kitty Klitty said reassuringly. Agnes muttered something in Polish.

Scarlett Letter was headlining in Bette's place that night. Poppy thought it should be her, but of course Agnes still looked at her as a newbie.

"Don't you start getting involved with those parties," Agnes told her.

"I won't if you let me headline one night."

"You show me something worthy of a headline!" she said. "And for your smart mouth, you can do the tip jar tonight."

She couldn't win with that woman.

Poppy watched Scarlett from the side of the stage. Her eyes wandered to the audience, and she recognized a woman in the first row. She had stringy brown hair and wore a business suit. Looking at her, Poppy thought the same thing she'd thought the first time she'd seen her: that woman needs a makeover. She knew there was significance to the woman, but who was she?

Then she realized who she was. It was Mallory's boss!

But why was she back at the club? She couldn't be trying to bust Mallory—Mallory had already been fired.

When Scarlett finished, Rude Ralph reminded everyone to tip generously on the way out. Poppy hated holding the tip jar. She felt the performers should be elusive after the show, and the stage kitten should hold the tip jar. But Agnes said the audience tipped more when it was one of the performers. They also tipped more when the girl stood there wearing nothing but pasties and a thong, which Poppy opted not to do that night. She was in a pissy mood, so she put her bustier and tulle skirt back on. Still, the bucket filled with tens and twenties. And then the stringy-haired woman put two fifties on the pile.

"You were amazing," the woman said.

"Thanks." Poppy smiled. Finally, someone had something positive to say!

"And . . . you're gorgeous."

"I'm Poppy." She held out her hand. The woman might need a makeover, but at least she had good taste.

"Patricia," the woman said, shaking her hand. To Poppy's surprise, she felt a pulse of excitement when the woman closed her cool fingers around her own.

"Want to get a drink?" Poppy said, surprising herself.

"Sure."

Poppy handed the tip jar off to Kitty Klitty, grabbed her coat and handbag, and left with Patricia Loomis.

Outside, there was an awkward silence.

"We could go to Dogstar on Avenue A?" Poppy said. "Or B Bar. That's right around the corner."

"I live uptown," said Patricia. Poppy knew an invitation when she heard one.

"Okay," she said. Patricia hailed a cab.

Patricia lived on 72nd Street off of Lexington. It was a third floor apartment in a quaint brownstone. Poppy noted how serene the streets were compared to the action in the Village.

"So you're the one who got Mallory fired," Poppy said. She figured she might as well make small talk since Patricia wasn't particularly chatty.

"Are you friends with her?" Patricia asked.

"Not really," said Poppy.

"Are you the one who called me that day?"

"Yes," she said. "You didn't have to fire her, you know."

"I didn't fire her—our boss did. And it wasn't only because of the dancing."

"Then why?"

"We didn't think she had sufficient long-term potential."

Finally! Someone who wasn't enamored with the great Mallory Dale. Her night was looking up.

"You don't have cats, do you?" Poppy asked.

"Yes—a tabby. Is that a problem?"

Okay—so nothing was perfect.

"No," Poppy lied.

The apartment was decorated in French country—super cute. Poppy wondered if she would ever have enough money to have a nice apartment in New York.

Patricia asked if she wanted a glass of wine, and Poppy said sure, even though she only drank champagne.

"I have a great Malbec or Shiraz if you like red," Patricia called from the kitchen.

"Um, sure." As far as Poppy was concerned, Patricia was speaking a different language. But she would roll with it.

Patricia returned with two full glasses. She sat next to Poppy on the couch. An orange cat circled her leg, and she pushed it away with her foot.

"Cheers," Patricia said, touching her glass to Poppy's. "I have to confess—I've been thinking about you since that night I went to the club to see what Mallory Dale was up to."

"Really?"

Patricia nodded. "You wore that trench coat with the red lacy thing underneath."

Poppy saw the reverence in her eyes, and it was the biggest turn-on she'd ever experienced. It was like what she got from the audience when she was on stage, but times a thousand.

She set her glass on the wood coffee table, and took Patricia's glass from her hand. As soon as Patricia relinquished the glass to her, she felt in control and knew what she wanted to do. Leaning forward, she put her mouth on Patricia's, and, to her shock, the rigid lawyer responded like she had been shot out of a cannon.

Patricia moved on top of her, and within half a minute flat she had managed to remove Poppy's sweater and skirt, her hands as practiced as those of Trent at Arkansas State when he took Poppy's virginity. But this time, Poppy was not nervous. She welcomed the firm, practiced touch teasing her nipples, and loved the feeling of Patricia's body pressing against her own.

Patricia removed her pants and blouse, and Poppy was surprised to find that the woman's breasts were large and round, with areolas the size of quarters and the color of pale tea. She was dying to suck them. Patricia lay back next to her, and Poppy propped herself up on one elbow, tracing Patricia's large, dark nipples. She was amazed by how much they turned her on, and bent her head to suck them. Patricia had a surprisingly slammin' body—full breasts, womanly hips, but a flat belly and long legs. Who knew you could hide all that under a business suit? And finding it under the navy pinstripe skirt and tailored jacket was somehow much sexier than finding it under a pair of tight jeans and a sweater. She imagined going out to dinner with Patricia, and no one else at the restaurant guessing what was waiting to be unwrapped at home.

But she was getting ahead of herself: she had to make a lasting impression. Alec said the reason none of her hook-ups amounted to anything was because she didn't have an emotional connection. But that part of relationships was a mystery to her. The only thing she could control was being beautiful enough to attract love, and being good enough in bed to keep people coming back for more. But even sex didn't seem to be working lately.

She couldn't worry about that now.

She brushed her mouth across Patricia's breasts, her hands

sliding down to rub her pussy. It felt strange to touch her pussy at first: Patricia had more of a bush than she'd seen in a long time. Nothing crazy—it wasn't like she was in a 1970s porno or anything. But it was clear that the words "Brazilian" had never crossed her lips. Surprisingly, this didn't bother Poppy. She was really into Patricia's body—the way it looked, the way it felt, the way it smelled. For the first time, she understood the expression "animal attraction." There was no reason for it, but she wanted nothing more than to explore this woman all over in every way she could.

Poppy maneuvered herself so she was positioned on her side with one leg over Patricia. She bent her head to take one breast in her mouth, circling her tongue over the nipple. Patricia made a soft noise, and Poppy felt heat between her legs. She pulled her panties down so she could feel Patricia's leg against her bare pussy. The urge to grind against the woman was so strong that she let herself, even as she wondered if it was okay. Then, Patricia grabbed her ass, pulling her even harder onto herself.

"Move up a little," Patricia said. Poppy complied, and she felt Patricia's finger slip inside of her from behind. Poppy moaned. Patricia's hand moved in and out while she kissed Poppy's neck.

"Don't stop," Poppy said.

"I won't. Come, baby." The combination of Patricia's touch—her fingers gently caressing her outer lips, but firm and deep inside her—and the term of endearment sent Poppy into her first orgasm. When she stopped quivering, Patricia pulled her up so they were face-to-face.

"You are so beautiful," she said.

Poppy smiled, and asked, "What do you want me to do?"

"Come to my bed."

She led her into a bedroom right out of a Ralph Lauren ad, in the center of which was a king-sized, high wooden sleigh bed covered with a richly colored floral comforter and half a dozen throw pillows. Poppy hesitated, but Patricia told her to get on and lie down.

"Let me look at you," she said, and Poppy happily complied. It felt good to be objectified, to be someone's ideal. For the first time since moving to New York, she felt like the prettiest girl in town.

Patricia soon moved from looking at to touching her: she dipped her head between Poppy's legs, licking her outer lips slowly. Poppy reached down and played with Patricia's hair while the woman's tongue moved in circles around the rim of her pussy. Poppy knew how wet she was, but Patricia didn't seem to mind. She used her fingers again, then, just as Poppy felt close to coming for the second time, Poppy pulled herself up so she was lying directly on top of her, their pussies kissing. Somehow, this felt almost more intimate than intercourse with a man. They rubbed against each other, a slow but intense grind that brought Poppy to the edge of climax. Then Patricia switched positions so that she was above her, bending down to eat Poppy's pussy while pressing her own cunt into Poppy's face. Poppy held Patricia's ass while gingerly running her tongue inside her pussy, and she felt Patricia do the same to her. Even though the outside of Patricia's pussy had hair, the inside was smooth and easy for Poppy to lick. When Patricia pressed her tongue inside of her, Poppy did the same thing, so they were simultaneously fucking each other with their mouths. Poppy worked to keep up with Patricia, but she felt herself sliding into an orgasm, and she could only put her head back and let the waves rock through her body. She cried out, and Patricia slid her fingers inside her, bringing Poppy to a feeling she had never experienced before.

"That was amazing," Poppy said when she was finished.

Patricia moved off the bed, and Poppy thought maybe she was tired of fooling around. Failure—again! But then Patricia pulled something out of her nightstand drawer. Something purple. And big. A big, thick, veiny, purple penis.

She returned to the bed and placed the dildo next to Poppy. Immediately, she resumed attending to her, licking her breasts and stroking her arms, her belly. She pressed the dildo into Poppy's hand.

"I want you to use this on me," she said.

"Um, are you sure?" It seemed a bit unnatural to her, but then she remembered how when she was hooking up with Bette she had craved penetration.

"Yes—don't be nervous. I'll show you what I like," Patricia said.

She guided Poppy's hand with the dildo, pressing the thick head along her outer lips, then circling her clit. When Patricia relaxed and moved her hand away, Poppy continued the motion on her own.

"Now press it against my clit. Yes, just like that. Now rub it up and down on that spot." Poppy followed her directions. Patricia's head tilted back, her breathing heavier. "Now inside," Patricia said, moving the dildo toward her wet center. Poppy gingerly pressed the tip inside.

"Fuck me, Poppy. Fuck me the way you like to be fucked," Patricia said, thrusting her pussy up toward her. Good lord! Poppy felt way out of her depth. It seemed just entirely wrong to stick this object inside someone.

"I . . . can't," Poppy said, her hand clutching the purple penis in a frozen position.

"Of course you can."

"I'm afraid I'm going to hurt you. This thing is huge."

Patricia sat up.

"I'm sorry," Poppy said.

"Don't worry about it." Patricia stood and walked to the door of the bedroom.

"Are you leaving?" Poppy said, aghast.

"No! I'll be right back."

Poppy hugged her knees to her chest and hoped she hadn't just blown it. But Patricia quickly returned, holding out a black box the size of a small shoebox.

"Open it," she said.

Poppy removed the lid and found a plastic cover, and underneath that a black satin pouch and in it a sleek, black oblong object that was smooth and tapered at the front.

"What is this?"

"Gorgeous, right? It's the LELO 'Ella' dildo. I haven't even used it yet. I thought maybe you'd be more comfortable with this one."

Poppy held the object in her hand, turning it around a few times. It did seem more inviting, with its flawless finish and delicate shape.

Patricia resumed her position on the bed. Poppy sat next to her, and Patricia pulled her down, kissing her, her hand moving between Poppy's legs. She stroked Poppy's clit and told Poppy to finger her at the same time. Poppy complied, and as she worked her finger in and out of Patricia's slick cunt, she found herself wondering what that LELO would feel like. Patricia kept the pressure on Poppy's clit, refusing to move inside of her. It was as if she wanted Poppy to feel the absence of penetration, to be deprived the way she had deprived her of the purple dildo.

Poppy pulled Patricia's hand lower, trying to get her to finger fuck her, but Patricia refused. For a second, Poppy stopped the motion of her own hand, distracted by her frustration.

"Don't stop!" Patricia said, and Poppy immediately resumed her in and out fingering, feeling Patricia begin to contract against her hand. Her pussy muscles were strong, and Poppy experienced the orgasm against her hand in a way that was remarkable and exciting. Her own pussy was throbbing now, and she was dying for the type of release that she had managed to give Patricia.

When Patricia finished climaxing, she kissed Poppy hard on the mouth, and pressed the LELO into her hand.

"I want you to be comfortable with this stuff," she said hoarsely. "We will have fun with it. Try it. Make yourself feel good, and let me watch."

Poppy was so excited, Patricia didn't need to ask twice. She spread her legs and stroked herself with the LELO a few times before pushing it deep into her cunt, then drawing it out slowly and pressing it in again. She moaned and didn't even care that Patricia was watching this incredibly intimate act. Then, wordlessly, Patricia took it from her. She licked Poppy with a long, practiced stroke of her tongue, then worked the LELO firmly inside of her.

"Does it feel good?" she said.

"Yes," Poppy breathed.

"Do you want it fast or slow?"

"Fast."

Patricia worked it in and out, and Poppy felt her pelvis moving with the LELO as she would move with a guy on top of her. When her orgasm came, it was so sudden and strong it forced a scream out of her, and she was startled at her violent response to being fucked in that way.

Patricia lay next to her and pulled her close. They held each other for a minute, and Patricia laughed.

"I don't think you were scared of fucking me with that," she said. "You just wanted it all to yourself." She kissed the top of Poppy's head.

"I had no idea it could be that good."

"Baby, that was nothing. Tomorrow, I'm taking you shopping."

Poppy liked the sound of that. Tomorrow. But she knew that for now, she should go. But when she stood to get her clothes on, Patricia grabbed her hand.

"Where are you going?"

"It's so late. I should get home."

"I wish you would stay," Patricia said.

It was the first time anyone had asked her to stay the night since she'd moved to New York three years ago. Poppy sank back into bed, pressing herself against Patricia, who put her arm around her.

"Does your cat sleep in the bed?"

"I'm a one-pussy woman, Poppy. The bed is just yours and mine tonight."

Mallory closed the door to her suite at the Palihouse. She sat on the couch, where just twenty-four hours ago she had sat worried that she would not be able to pull off Bette's routine. But she had not only done it: she had done it, and loved it.

She pulled her phone out of her bag and dialed Bette's cell.

"It's me," she said.

"Let me go somewhere quiet—hold on!" Bette said over the sound of club music. Mallory waited, sifting through her bag. She found the envelope Justin had left for her in her dressing room, which she had yet to open. "Okay—tell me!" Bette said.

"Where are you?"

"The Bellagio. Zebra's hotel room. She's having a little get-together. Now tell me."

"It went great. Amazing, actually. I remembered everything you taught me—it all came together. By the middle of the performance I was barely thinking except for the logistics of getting the costume off—my body just knew what to do. And I love that song, and your choreography is perfect for it. I was thinking of adding one last turn at the end, but there was nothing else to take off, and I remembered you saying each movement has to mean something for the overall reveal so I didn't mess with it...."

"Did you remember what I said about not mingling with the guests before your performance—about staying elusive?"

"Yes."

"I'm proud of you! I just wish I could have been there to see it. Oh, Zebra says she is proud of you, too."

Mallory shook her head. How had her life come to this—the biggest pop star in the world was being supportive of her burlesque debut!

"How are you?"

"Mallory, this is it. I feel my life in motion. The paparazzi photographed me leaving the hotel with Zebra. I guarantee I will be in *Us* magazine next week."

"How are things with you two?"

"She's unbelievable in bed."

Mallory smiled. "I'm so happy for you."

"I'm happy for you! So when do you want to audition for the Blue Angel? That is what you want now, right?"

"Yes, " Mallory said, admitting it for the first time, even to herself. "Can you help me?"

"Of course I'll help you. We'll talk when I get back."

"When are you flying home?"

"I don't know, Moxie. But you'll be the first to hear."

Mallory could imagine the devilish look in her beautiful blue eyes.

"Be good," she said.

"I'm always good," said Bette.

Mallory ended the call, then sank back in the sofa. She looked at the time, then calculated New York hours. In less than twenty-four hours, she would be with Alec.

20

In the earliest hours of the morning, she fumbled for her phone in the dark and dialed Alec.

"Hey," he said. "What are you doing up so early?"

"I'm too wound up to sleep," she said, which was true. "I'm excited to see you tonight."

"I'm excited to see you, too," he said. "I miss you."

"You do?"

"Of course I do! Call me when you land," he said.

"Okay. I love you, Alec."

"I love you, too, Mallory. You know that's not the issue."

"So what is the issue?"

"I don't know. Trust? I never went outside our relationship for anything the entire time we were together. I know I pushed you to do things that sometimes you were hesitant to do, but we always explored those things together. And it made us closer. Then the minute we had a fight, you went to someone else—physically and emotionally you went to that person. You made decisions about your job that affect both of us as a couple without talking to me. I felt very excluded, Mallory."

"Okay," she said. "I can see how you would feel excluded. And I'm sorry, Alec. I really am." She knew she had to tell him about the Baxter party, and about her plans to audition at the Blue Angel. But she wanted to do it in person. "Let's continue this conversation tomorrow night. I want to be able to put my arms around you and show you how much you mean to me."

"I like the sound of that. I can't wait to see you."

She hung up, feeling like the luckiest girl in the world. And then she remembered the envelope from Justin Baxter. She quickly opened it, and pulled out a check for five thousand dollars. She wouldn't have to worry about getting a temp job next week or even next month. This bought her time to focus on the Blue Angel.

There was no turning back. Moxie was part of her now. She would just have to find a way to help Alec see that Moxie loved him, too.

The plane landed, and the captain told them they could turn on their wireless devices. Mallory dialed Alec before she even pulled her bag out of the overhead bin.

"It's me—I just landed," she said, nearly breathless. "I'll meet you at the apartment?"

"Please don't," he said.

Mallory was sure she'd heard him wrong. Her ears must be clogged from the descent.

"What did you say?"

"I don't think you should come over, Mallory."

"Okay. Do you want to meet for dinner? I'm starving."

"I don't want to meet at all."

"What are you talking about? We just had a whole conversation this morning about what was bothering you and moving ahead with our relationship..."

People were pulling down their luggage, a line was forming in the aisle to deplane.

"Yes. A whole conversation in which you failed to mention that you stripped at a party in Malibu last night. Apparently, Billy Barton was quite impressed with your performance."

Oh, no.

"I wanted to tell you about that in person," she said.

"You lied to me—again! You said explicitly that you were not involved in that party—that you were just in LA to clear your head."

"I can explain. Bette needed to go to Vegas and . . ."

"Yeah. Somehow Bette is always involved. I don't see how there is room for us to have a relationship when clearly Bette has more to do with your life these days than I do."

"You're not being fair," she said. "I think we need to talk about this face-to-face."

"I don't want to see you."

"If you are ending this, you at least owe it to me to see me," she said, starting to cry.

"I don't want to end it, Mallory, but I can't be in a relationship where you lie to me, and I can't trust you. I will never know who you are with or what you are doing as long as you're hanging around that club. The only way this is going to work is if you stop going there and promise me you will stay away from Bette."

"You're making me choose between you and the Blue Angel?"

"Is it really a hard choice? I can't believe you say it like that."

She watched the line of people start to leave the plane. All she could do was sit hunched in her seat, clutching the phone.

"We've been together since we were twenty-two. We've both changed and taken on new interests along the way. I didn't get upset when you got so involved with *Gruff*, when you started hanging out with Billy Barton and going clubbing."

"The difference is, I found a way to include you in that world. I could have gone to burlesque shows for that article and never mentioned it to you, but instead I brought you to a show so we could share the experience. And fine, maybe I pushed too hard for the three-way, but at the end of the day it was still something we would do together. You, on the other hand, go off and sleep with a woman alone the night we have a fight; you get involved with this club without even mentioning it to me. You never thought to tell me so I could watch you or somehow feel it was a part of our life and not totally outside of it. That is why the relationship is ending, Mallory. Not because I can't deal with your changing."

"I want to include you!"

"It's too late," he said. And hung up on her.

Poppy sat curled against Patricia on her pillow-laden sleigh bed. They were watching a DVR marathon of *The Good Wife* (Patricia loved legal dramas) when Poppy's phone rang.

"I'll pause it," Patricia said.

"Hello?" Poppy didn't recognize the incoming number.

"Hey, it's Alec Martin. Can you talk?" When it rained, it poured! Too bad for him he was a day late and a dollar short, as her mother would say.

"Sort of. What's up?"

"You were right—Mallory did perform at that party."

"Oh, Alec, it's not a big deal. I mean, it's just a party," she said. Patricia stroked her inner thigh.

"Can you meet me somewhere for a drink? I just need to talk," he said.

"I don't know—" She looked at Patricia. "When?"

"Now?"

"Hold on a sec." She covered the phone and told Patricia that Mallory's boyfriend wanted to talk to her. "He sounds traumatized," she said.

"Go—but don't be too long. I'm already feeling possessive." Patricia bit her shoulder lightly.

"Okay," she said to Alec. "I'm in your neighborhood. Pick a

place, and I'll be there in ten. But only for a little while. I have plans tonight."

"Good for you! Is it *her*?"

"Who?"

"The woman you were telling me about at breakfast."

"Oh—no. Someone better." She smiled at Patricia. "Much better."

She met him at Wicker Park, a loud sports bar on Third Avenue. He was sitting in a booth near the door and looked like someone had run over his dog.

"Thanks for meeting me," he said.

"Sure. What can I do?" He was so obviously forlorn she felt bad and forgot all about Patricia waiting for her back at the apartment.

"I wish you could somehow help me understand this world that has pulled Mallory in so strongly. She tells me her interest in burlesque has nothing to do with me, but it feels like there is a third person in our relationship suddenly. She never lied to me before, and now I can't trust her at all."

"I don't know that much about relationships. I never have good ones."

"Do you think I have something to worry about? Is she having an affair with Bette?"

Poppy felt a tug of jealousy just at the thought of it. Then she remembered how good it felt to be with Patricia, and she let it go.

"I don't know. I doubt it."

Her phone rang. Strangely, the incoming number was Bette's.

"Speak of the devil," she said. "I'm going to take this outside. Be right back. Hello?" she said, pulling on her coat and walking outside.

"Hey, Poppy. It's Bette. I need a favor. Can you cover my shifts this week?"

"What's wrong?"

"Everything is great—never better. But I'm away, and I'm not going to be back for a few days."

"Agnes is going to freak,"

"I know. But this is a good development for you, Poppy. You can fill my place—it's a chance for you to be in the spotlight."

Poppy's mind raced, imagining herself headlining the show every night.

"Agnes might fire you for this. Missing one show for a private party is one thing—but bailing on a whole week? And the Valentine's Day show is coming up. Will you be back by then?"

"I don't know, so I need one more thing from you: get Mallory an audition with Agnes. I would set it up myself, but she is going to be too angry with me to listen and give Mallory a chance. Without me around, she will be looking to you to lead things. I'm counting on you to make this happen, Poppy. Can you do it?"

"Yes," she said, excited and confused at the same time. "I don't get it, are you quitting?"

"Just get Mallory the audition. And be ready to rock your performances this week so Agnes doesn't miss me too much, okay? The show must go on, and all that."

"Where are you?"

"Vegas. Go to Popbaby.com, and you'll understand."

The line went dead.

Poppy went back inside.

"Do you have an iPhone?" she asked Alec.

"Yeah. Why?"

"Go to the Web site Popbaby.com."

He pulled up the site. "What am I looking for?"

She took it out of his hands and skimmed the posts. "Holy shit! Look at this: *Zebra Changes her Stripes: the perennially*

private pop star is seen out and about with new gal pal, bur-
lesque performer Bette Noir. She's hooking up with Zebra!"

"That's just a gossip site. That stuff isn't always true."

"Look at this photo." She showed him a picture of Bette and
Zebra kissing at a Vegas Starbucks.

"I guess she's not with Mallory," he said.

"See? It's all cool. Just call Mallory up and work it out."

"It's not that simple. She still cheated on me. She slept with
Bette when she was never willing to do that with me as a couple."

"Maybe she needed to do it for herself before she could do it
with you."

"I don't know. I still think the club is a bad influence on her.
She's blown her whole legal career."

Poppy took a deep breath.

"I have a confession to make: I set that up. I got her busted."

"Why the hell would you do that?"

"I was jealous. All I wanted was for Bette to teach me everything, to help me become someone at the club. And she showed
more interest in this random woman who didn't even want to
be a performer! It was so unfair. Even Agnes seemed to like her.
So I wanted to throw Mallory off her game. And maybe get her
in trouble so she stopped hanging around the club. I never
thought she would get fired. And it just made things worse because without the job she started hanging out at the club more.
And now she wants to be a performer."

"No, she doesn't."

"Yeah, she does. I have to get used to it, and so do you."

Alec actually looked frightened. "I can't believe this is my
Mallory."

Poppy shrugged. "It's not a big deal. But I guess you have to
see that for yourself."

"How?"

"I'll think of something," she said. "But now I have to get back to my new girlfriend."

She loved the feeling of the word *girlfriend* on her lips, and it made her even more eager to hurry back...and feel Patricia on her lips.

For the first time in as long as she could remember, she was happy. The least she could do was help Alec and Mallory feel the same.

21

The Blue Angel was unusually empty and quiet. No one was practicing, and the dressing room was dark.

Mallory sat at a table with Agnes, uncomfortably fidgeting with her handbag. She had been summoned there with a curt phone call, and now Agnes was barely speaking. The owner of the Blue Angel appraised her like she was a side of beef.

"I like the red hair."

"Thanks," Mallory said.

"You know why I called you?" she asked, lighting a cigarette. Mallory suddenly felt as if she was in a Polish espionage film.

"Um, no."

"You can work as stage kitten tomorrow night?"

"Sure," she said.

"You know I fired Bette."

Mallory felt her stomach drop.

"Why?"

"To me, loyalty, a person's word, is everything. She stopped showing up; she is done here."

"I'm sure she can explain," Mallory said.

"Enough of that. What do you want?" she said. Mallory was confused. Agnes had called *her*.

"You mean...in life?"

"Don't be coy," Agnes snapped. "Do you want to be a dancer or do you want to watch other people?"

"I want to be a dancer," she said, without hesitation.

"Poppy is going to headline my Valentine's Day show instead of Bette. We need another girl, and Poppy says that girl should be you."

Mallory looked at Agnes as if she must be kidding or mistaken.

"Are you sure?"

"No! Of course I'm not sure! You screwed up your first night as a stage kitten."

"I mean, are you sure that's what Poppy said?"

"Yes. Of course. She was very clear. I was surprised, too. Still, I will take a chance. But...if you screw up, this is the last time you will be on that stage. In fact, if you screw up, I don't even want to see you in the audience. I'm about over it with all of you girls."

"I won't screw up."

"I shouldn't have to explain this to you, but the theme of that night is love. Dance something about love, getting love, losing love, sexy love. Whatever. And show up tomorrow night to help out."

She stood up from the table, and walked off. Mallory waited a few minutes to see if she was coming back. When she was sure Agnes had disappeared, she walked away from the table and immediately called Bette.

"What the hell? You're just dropping out of the Blue Angel?" she said.

"I guess you spoke to Agnes."

"Why didn't you tell me she fired you?"

"It's not that important. Did she ask you to do a show?"

"Yes, actually. Did you set that up?"

"In a way."

"You're not coming back?"

"I am back—I flew in last night. But I'm done at the club. I have to move on, Mallory. I told you from the beginning I want to be famous."

"I need to see you," Mallory said.

"You know where I live."

Bette opened the door wearing a silver lamé jumpsuit.

"I see your love life is influencing your fashion choices," Mallory said.

"You don't approve? I think it's hot."

"You can pull off anything," she said.

They sat on the couch. Mallory thought of the first night she'd come to Bette's apartment. It felt like a million years ago. And she still hadn't managed to make things right with Alec.

"Why aren't you more excited about your gig at the Blue Angel?" Bette said. "A dozen girls would try to fill that slot in a heartbeat."

"I am excited. But I'm so upset about Alec. I got back on Sunday, and he refused to see me. He found out about the Baxter party from Billy Barton, and he thinks I just lie to him constantly and that I go outside the relationship instead of including him in my life. And when I look at it the way he describes it, I can't even defend myself."

"There's nothing to defend. You can't change what you've done, or the fact that you want to be a performer. The only thing you can do is find a way to bring him into this world so he doesn't feel like he's losing you to it. He's just feeling threatened."

"I think the worst part for him is that I hooked up with you. He can't forgive me for that."

Bette took Mallory's hand.

"I think the only way to fix that is to bring him into that part of your life, too."

"What do you mean?"

"He wanted a threesome, and not only did it not happen for the two of you, you went off and hooked up with a woman on your own. Totally emasculating. You need to give him the threesome. That's the only way to set things right."

"And how do I manage that? Dial 1-800-Three-way?"

"I'll do it with you."

Mallory looked at her, searching for some hint that she was teasing her.

"Very funny."

"I never joke about sex. Look, you know I'm not into guys, but I would hook up with you, and he could watch, or if he was dying to jump in I could roll with it to a point. I think it would change everything for you two. Get you back on track."

"I don't know what to say."

"Say you'll think about it."

"How would I even go about bringing it up to him? We're barely speaking."

"You'll figure it out. Either the situation will present itself, or it won't."

"I'd do anything to get him back. Maybe I'd even give up the Blue Angel. But I don't want to have to make that choice."

"I hope you don't have to. But for now, you have to stop thinking about all of this. You're not going to be able to perform if you're worried about Alec. Put it out of your mind. Take the chance—let Moxie have her moment. Then deal with your personal life."

"Okay. I'll try." Mallory looked at the Us magazine on the coffee table. "Are you in this?"

Bette nodded. Mallory flipped through until she found a

photo of Bette kissing Zebra at a Starbucks. "This is surreal," she said.

"The paparazzi will be following me in New York soon. Zebra is coming in two weeks to kick off the East Coast part of her tour."

"So you're just going to follow Zebra around the world? What about your own career?"

"I'll figure it out. Let's worry about you now. You have eight days until the Valentine's Day show."

"I know. I'm not ready to choreograph something that quickly. I'm not sure what to do."

"Why start from scratch? Do the 'Lose You' routine."

"That's yours."

"Not anymore. I've never performed it in front of an audience, and you've mastered it."

Mallory knew what a tremendous gift it was for a performer to share her choreography.

"You're amazing," she said simply.

"I know!"

"Do you think I should change it in any way to match the 'love' theme of the show?"

"The song is about not wanting to lose someone, so that works. But maybe the costume should be campier. Less dark and vampy, more in line with the romance theme."

They thought in silence for a minute.

"Maybe I could dress as a cupid?"

"Yes! A sexy cupid."

"And I have an idea of something I want to add to the choreography."

"Go for it."

"Where will I get the costume? I couldn't sew my own clothes if my life depended on it."

"I'll take you to someone. But you're going to have to pay for it."

"Not only will I pay for the costume, I will pay for the cab. Show me the way!"

Bette picked up her BlackBerry. "Max, it's Bette. Clear the decks—I have an emergency costume situation."

"And one more thing," Mallory said, as they headed out the door. "I need to stop at a Capezio dance store."

"We'll get the supplies at M&J Trimming."

"They don't have what I need anywhere but Capezio. Trust me."

22

_____

Valentine's Day fell on a Friday night. Poppy had never been more excited to have a date. Unfortunately, because she had to get to the Blue Angel to perform, her date was a quickie in Patricia's living room.

"I wish I could take you out for dinner," Patricia said from between her legs.

"Aren't you happy to eat in?" Poppy joked. She had never thought of herself as a humorous person, but Patricia brought out the best in her. She felt that she was finally in on the secret the rest of the world knew: love. It was the world's best mood enhancer.

"I could eat you all night," Patricia said, licking her clit. Poppy reached out and cupped her breast, then leaned down to kiss her.

"I have to get going," she said.

"So unfair!"

"Think of it this way: I'll be dancing just for you. And think of how hot it will be to come back here and fuck after."

"I'd rather skip straight to the fucking part of the evening."

Poppy pulled up her panties and grabbed her costume and handbag.

"Don't forget to swing by Alec's place on your way to the show. I don't want him bailing on this. It's important that he show up. Okay?"

"I won't forget," Patricia said unenthusiastically, still sitting on the floor. "By the way—I meant what I said when you first stayed the night."

"What's that?"

"That I'm a one-pussy type of gal. Do you think you can handle that?"

Poppy bent down and kissed Patricia on the mouth, tasting herself on her lips.

"I can handle it, all right," she whispered. "And I can't wait until you handle me later."

Mallory's hands shook as she brushed one more layer of pink glitter over her eyelids. Her cheeks were fully rouged, and her mouth was painted red with a thick layer of red glitter on her lips. She was still getting used to the dramatic effect color had against her skin now that her hair was red. If she hadn't been sick to her stomach with nerves, she would have felt beautiful.

She stepped back from the mirror to make sure her costume was on right. Agnes had made her preview it for her before the show began, and she had reluctantly clucked her approval. How could she not? It was stunning—a white satin corset top with a short, full skirt created from layers of red feathers. She accented it with thigh-high white stockings, long, white gloves, four inch red patent leather heels, and large, red feather wings that strapped onto her shoulders and could be easily removed for her to use as fans. Underneath it all, she wore a red thong and red sequined, heart-shaped pasties. Most important, she had a pair of red satin *pointe* shoes. She'd only had a few days to break them in, but they would be fine for the five minute performance. And, for the finale, Bette had made her a red, sequined bow and arrow. They'd rechoreographed the ending so she finished the number by pointing the arrow at the audience.

"You look hot," Poppy said. She was dressed in a nurse costume for her performance to Kesha's "Your Love Is My Drug."

"Thanks," she said. She still couldn't get used to this turnaround in Poppy's attitude toward her. It was as if now that Bette was out of the picture, Poppy was her biggest supporter. She would never understand why Poppy had been so nasty to her in the first place, but she couldn't think about it anymore. She had bigger things to worry about.

Kitty Klitty's number was winding down. Mallory's pulse raced. Rude Ralph went into his introduction.

"Our next performer is making her Blue Angel debut. She's the brassiest, ballsiest, hottest redhead since Jessica Rabbit. Please give it up for Moxie!"

Mallory waited for the stage to go dark, then stepped through the curtain. She felt like she was going to have a heart attack. She tried to summon the calm focus she'd felt at the Baxter party, but couldn't.

The music started, and she went into her first turn. She peeled off one glove, and the audience howled. She remembered that the energy at the Baxter party had been so different from the club's energy, and she had missed the noise level. She let the crowd fuel her through the next series of turns, during which she removed one wing and used it as a fan to cover her breasts. She waved it open and closed teasingly as she removed her corset. She held the corset out to the audience, then tossed it aside to howls and hoots. She moved the fan to reveal her tasseled breasts, shimmied them, and the whistles almost made her smile. She shimmied into her tassel twirling, and the room erupted. Finally, she felt a groove. She sat in the chair that had been placed for her in center stage, and slowly removed her high heels with exaggerated movements. Then she carefully placed her feet in the toe shoes, taking a moment to caress her legs with the ribbons. The audience clapped their approval.

She stood up and did a series of *chaîné* turns to the front of the stage. It had been so long since she'd danced in front of an audience—the feeling of movement in the *pointe* shoes, combined with the music and her bare skin, almost brought tears to her eyes.

The audience went wild. With a graceful arc forward, she picked up one of the fans and covered her waist as she removed her skirt, then—with only a moment of hesitation—pulled the fan away, flashing her ass at the audience. Adrenaline raced through her, and she found that mindless space where she was just moving to the music without thinking. Her next step was one of her favorite parts in the routine: the Clam Shell with the fans. As she got into position, she felt confident enough to glance out at the audience.

It was a huge mistake. Like an animal in the wild whose eyes are drawn to the first sign of danger, she immediately spotted Alec in the crowd.

For a few seconds, she stood frozen like a deer in headlights. She couldn't remember what to do with her arms. The audience clapped louder, as if her lack of movement was a choreographed pose. What if she just ended the performance like this? Just let the music play out to her standing frozen like a semi-nude statue? Of course, if she tanked the performance, she would be banned from the Blue Angel. But after this, she'd never want to get on stage again, anyway. What was he *doing* here? How could this be happening to her? The first time she'd stepped out as a stage kitten, she'd seen her boss. Now, it was her first performance and her boyfriend—no, *ex*-boyfriend, who despised the entire scene—was watching. It couldn't be a coincidence, and she planned to find out who was behind it. Who would show up next to see her take off her clothes—her grandmother?

She glanced back at Alec. He looked so handsome, his hair dark and longer than she remembered. He wore a navy blue sweater, and she could imagine what that color did to his eyes.

And then he winked at her.

She moved the fans into position, and closed them around her in the Clam Shell formation. Taking a deep breath, she reminded herself not to rush through it, and again recalled the languid grace of the Ms. Tickle performance.

The music built toward a finish. She got into position and then turned in a pirouette. When she stopped, facing the audience, she twirled the tassels and arched her back with her arms overhead. Then, with her arms still outstretched, she shimmied forward, and with an elegant sweep to the floor she scooped up the bow and arrow. She turned her back to the audience, shook her ass, then turned halfway and drew back the bow, pointing the arrow straight at Alec.

The stage went to black, the crowd went wild, and it was all she could do to catch her breath and find her way back to the dressing room.

"That was unbelievable!" Kitty Klitty told her. "I've never seen anything like it."

"Thanks," Mallory said. She realized, sitting in a chair, that her legs were shaking. She heard Poppy's music begin. Originally, she had planned on sneaking into the audience to watch Poppy's performance, but now she didn't want to move from the dressing room. Ever.

Agnes strode into the room and summoned Kitty to help her with something in the music booth. Mallory waited for a glance from her, some indication of whether or not she was pleased with her performance.

"And would it kill you girls to use classic burlesque music for a change? I can't imagine Gypsy Rose Lee performing to this garbage. What is it with you kids?"

Mallory hadn't realized, until she saw Agnes's tiny frame and dark flashing eyes, how much she wanted not only her approval, but an invitation to return to the stage. She wondered how long her frozen moment had actually been. Maybe no one had noticed. But Agnes did not look in her direction.

Trying not to get upset, Mallory pulled her jeans out of her bag, and noticed the light on her BlackBerry was flashing.

I snuck in to watch. Congratulations! You killed. Nice pause you improvised—very dramatic ☺ *Meet me out front asap...*
Xo B

Mallory smiled. Maybe Agnes liked the performance; maybe she didn't. But the fact that Bette had showed up for her and said she did a good job...That was enough. Even if she never set foot on a stage again, she'd done it. She should be satisfied with that—enough for her to let it go and focus on what really mattered.

She wiped off as much body glitter as she could manage, and pulled on a black sweater. She stuffed her costume into her bag. With a glance in the mirror, she decided to keep her stage makeup on for a little while longer. If this was to be her last night as Moxie, she wanted it to last another hour or two.

"Where are you going? Aren't you going to come out with us?" Scarlett Letter asked,

"Maybe—I'll be right back." Mallory threw on her coat and grabbed her handbag, making her way down the dark stage-side stairs. She wondered if Alec would try to find her.

Outside, Bette paced along the curb talking on her phone.

When she saw Mallory, she ended the call and rushed over to her.

"I'm so fucking proud of you," she said, hugging her. "Did you love it?"

"Yeah, I did, I really did. Thanks so much for coming."

"Are you kidding? I wouldn't have missed it. The ballet shoe thing was brilliant. Your intro from now on should be 'Moxie: the Burlesque Ballerina.'"

"I'm glad you liked it. The choreography felt good but... I freaked out for a moment—that's why I froze. It wasn't planned."

"What happened?"

"I looked out at the audience and saw Alec."

"He's here?"

Mallory nodded.

"Is he still inside?"

"I think so. And Bette, I want him back more than I want anything else."

"I'm telling you what to do: give him crazy sex with you and another girl. It's better than a Hallmark card."

Mallory shook her head.

The door to the club opened, almost banging into her. She moved aside, then realized it was Alec.

"Hey," he said. He held a bouquet of yellow roses.

"Alec," she said.

"I saw you walk out here. Can we talk?"

"Yes! Of course."

"I'll give you two some privacy," Bette said, sauntering off down the street.

Alec and Mallory watched her go, neither saying anything.

"I hope I wasn't interrupting anything," he said.

"Alec."

"What?" he said.

"There's nothing between us to interrupt. I wish you would believe me."

"I don't want to talk about that now. I just wanted to tell you...you were amazing out there. I couldn't believe it." He handed her the flowers, and she felt tears in her eyes. He reached out and touched her hair. "Jesus. Is that your real hair?"

"Yeah."

"You dyed it red?"

"Um, yeah."

"It's hot," he said, smiling that devilish smile she missed so much.

"Alec." She threw herself against him, and he put his arms around her tightly.

"I see why you are into this place, Mal. You look like you belong up there. You look like...someone else."

"I'm not someone else! I'm the same person you love. And I want to have this *with* you—not alone."

"I want that too, but it's not just the dancing. You slept with someone else."

"Um, well..." she looked down the street and saw Bette. "I want to have that with you, too."

"What do you mean?"

"You're right—I was wrong to get upset with you about wanting to have a threesome and then going off and hooking up with Bette myself. I'm sorry. I wish I could take it back, but I can't. But I was thinking maybe the next best thing would be if you and I hooked up with Bette together. Then you'd know at the end of the day, it's still us."

He looked at her. "Are you serious?"

"Yes."

Silence.

"Say something," she urged.

"I have to admit, it's an interesting proposition."

"Then let's go."

"Now?"

"It's probably now or never. Bette's about two seconds away

from becoming the girlfriend of the biggest pop star in the world. I don't know when I'll see her again after tonight."

She waved to Bette to come back. Bette held up one finger—she was on the phone again. Mallory turned and hailed a cab.

"Get in," she said to Alec. Then, to the driver: "We're going to Rivington Street. But first we're picking up that brunette on the corner."

23

Stepping into Bette's white living room while holding Alec's hand was like worlds colliding.

"Nice place," he said.

"Thanks. Can I get you two a drink? I only have vodka." Bette wandered into the kitchen. Mallory sat nervously on the couch, and Alec sat beside her.

"That girl looks like you," Alec said, pointing to the photograph of the redhead. Mallory remembered noticing the photo the first night she was at Bette's and confiding that she had toyed with the idea of dying her hair red. That night, a drastic change in hair color seemed like an outrageous thing to do.

How far she had come.

Bette appeared with a tray of chilled shots. They each took one, and clinked them together.

"To Moxie," Bette said, winking at her. "The hottest body to grace the Blue Angel stage. At least since I left." She laughed a throaty laugh.

"To you—jet-setting tabloid star," Mallory said.

"I'll drink to that," Bette said.

Alec raised his glass, but was silent. Mallory wondered if he was as nervous as she was.

She looked at Bette, who was especially luminous that night, wearing a black sheath dress clinging in just the right places, her nipples pressed against the fabric. Her pale skin was flawless, and Mallory could tell she was barely wearing any makeup, just her smudgy black Sephora eyeliner and matte red lipstick. Her hair was tucked girlishly behind her ears. Even though this night was all about Alec, Mallory had to admit she was still attracted to Bette. After tonight, she knew she would never be with her again. But she was excited to have one last time.

There was an awkward silence after the toast.

"How about one more round?" Bette suggested.

While she disappeared into the kitchen, Alec reached for Mallory's hand. After so much time apart, the casual contact was almost dizzying. She looked up at him, and he leaned in to kiss her. She threw her arms around his neck, and their mouths met so roughly their teeth bumped together. His tongue traced her lower lip, and she sucked greedily at it, wanting to devour him. His hand moved under her sweater, tracing her nipple. She breathed in the smell of him, forgetting where she was, wanting him inside of her so badly she almost lost her breath.

Bette returned, sitting beside Mallory on the couch, but Mallory didn't stop kissing Alec until he pulled away. He nodded toward Bette, and in a daze, Mallory turned to her, and then it was a different mouth against hers, softer and less familiar. She leaned back and let Bette kiss her while Alec continued stroking her breasts. She was incredibly turned on, losing herself in sensation, when Bette pulled back and started kissing Alec.

Mallory was almost startled by this turn of events, but knew on some level that that was how these things went. Alec was still touching her, so she lay back against the couch and tried to enjoy watching her boyfriend and new best friend kiss slowly and deeply. She didn't have to try very hard: it got her incredibly hot. She reached for Bette's breasts, tracing her hard nipples over the thin fabric of her dress.

"Let's move into the bedroom," Bette said.

Mallory felt wobbly when she stood. Alec took her by the hand, and they followed Bette, who pulled off her dress as she walked. She wore only black, lacy boy shorts underneath, no bra. She sprawled out on her bed as if asking, with her body, which one of you is going to fuck me?

Mallory and Alec looked at each other, and he gave her a wink. He reached over and pulled off Mallory's sweater, and unzipped her jeans, which she pulled down over her hips. His hands traced her breasts over her bra, then he leaned forward and unclasped it, kissing her collarbone. She felt an intense rush of closeness to him, and for the first time in a very long time, it felt like it was him and her against the world. In that moment, she wished Bette wasn't there. She adored her beautiful new friend, and she was grateful for the way Bette had so generously opened up the world to her. In a way, she had finished what Alec had started all those years ago at Penn—she'd freed Mallory from the girl her parents had raised her to be, and helped her find her true self. But for now, all she wanted was to put her arms around her man, to reconnect with him and let him know that the most important thing in this new world, to this true self, was their love. But ironically, the way to do that involved making love to another woman—and possibly watching him do the same.

Alec nudged her toward the bed. She lay next to Mallory, and he pulled down her pink panties. Bette bent her head to Mallory's breast, taking her nipple in her mouth, her tongue flicking against it teasingly while her hand moved between her legs. Bette circled her clit with her thumb, and Mallory was already so wet that Bette immediately slipped a finger inside her. Mallory moaned and thrust her pelvis against Bette's hand, all the while acutely aware that Alec was watching. Knowing that his eyes were on her pussy while Bette finger-fucked her made her tremble. All she could think about was getting his cock inside of her, having him fuck her while Bette took a turn being the one to watch.

She felt him move onto the bed, and when he pressed himself against her she knew he was naked now, too. She reached out her hand until she found his hard cock, brushing over the tip and then firmly massaging his thick shaft.

Bette's fingers moved more quickly in and out of her, while Mallory moved her hand to the same rhythm up and down Alec's cock. He kissed her, then Bette leaned down and kissed her, then Bette and Alec's mouths met, both poised above her. Mallory leaned forward so she could tongue Bette's breasts, then Alec pushed her down so he could do the same to her. She felt Bette's hands on her pussy replaced by Alec's. He knew exactly how to touch her, and within seconds of his fingers working in and out of her cunt she started to come.

When her body finally stopped spasming, he pulled back, and startled her by saying to Bette, "Do you mind if we have some time alone?"

"Not at all. Be my guest." She kissed Mallory on the cheek "Be happy," she whispered.

She slipped out of the room, closing the door behind her.

Mallory sat up, her head spinning slightly.

"Why did you do that?"

"Do you mind?"

"No. Of course not. But I thought this was what you wanted...."

"I just want you, Mallory. That's all I ever really wanted. This was fun, but after a month apart, I just want you to myself."

They kissed, and her stomach did a little flip, the way it had since the first time he'd kissed her on Penn's campus four years ago.

"Do you want to go home?" she whispered.

He put her hand on his throbbing cock. "I do, but I don't think I can wait. Don't worry—I'm sure Bette's bedroom has seen its fair share of action. She won't be sweating this."

Mallory smiled, and gently pressed him down on his back. She bent down to lick his balls, sliding her tongue along the length of his cock, licking the tip, and then sliding down again. He moaned and pressed on her head, and she knew he wanted her to take him entirely in her mouth. She cupped his balls while slipping his cock between her lips, sucking slightly to create tension while flicking her tongue against him inside her mouth. She used one hand to stroke the length of him, moving up and down.

"Get on me," he said.

She moved quickly to climb on top of him, pausing for a minute with her wet pussy poised at the tip of his cock. She rubbed him against her clit, then pressed herself down on him so he was completely inside of her. She hadn't realized how much she missed his thick cock filling her up.

"Oh, my God," she said, bending forward so they were chest to chest. She could feel his heart beating, and he grabbed her ass and thrust deeper inside of her. It felt so good she came quickly, her pussy clenching against him in waves. Her orgasm kept going and going, and she felt his cock vibrate inside her in a way that let her know he was going to come soon, too. She watched his face, and his blue-gray eyes locked on hers in a way that made her sure this was it—they were together again. Nothing would change that.

He cried out as he came, his orgasm so strong that she had to brace herself against his movements so she could hold him inside her pussy long enough for him to finish. Then she gently slid off of him, and they lay side by side, slick with sweat; she could feel his cum between her legs. Her pulled her against him so her head was braced in the crook of his arm.

"I love you so much," she said.

"I love you, Mallory." He kissed the top of her head. They breathed against one another, content. "We'll go home soon?"

"Yeah," she said.

"I don't think I can move just yet." He pulled a box of tissues off of Bette's bedside and passed them to her.

I'll have Bette send us the dry-cleaning bill," she said, and he laughed. He kissed her again.

"You know what? You look hot as a redhead, but I kind of miss the beautiful brunette I fell in love with."

"Really? You think I should go back to dark hair?"

"It's up to you. But if you felt that you had to go red because Bette's the hottest dark-haired chick in the room, I can tell you you're very much mistaken."

She smiled at him. "It was fun to try something different. But I will always be the girl you fell in love with."

"You know I love you—more now than ever."

"Yes," she breathed, happier than she could remember. She reached out and stroked his face.

"Can I tell you something weird?" he said.

"Sure. What?"

"I saw Patricia Loomis in the audience tonight."

"Very funny."

"I'm serious. And let me tell you—she looked extremely into it."

Bette knocked on the door.

"I hate to disturb you two lovebirds, but there's a call for you, Mal."

Mallory and Alec exchanged a look.

"Who could be calling you at this hour?" he asked.

"I have no idea. But I'd better find out." She pulled on her clothes, glancing at herself in the mirror on her way to open the door. She looked well-fucked. It made her smile.

Bette handed her a cell phone.

"You didn't answer yours, so she called on mine."

"Hello?" Mallory said, bewildered.

"Moxie, it's Agnes." The Polish accent sounded even thicker over the phone. "Why don't you answer your phone?"

"Sorry. I was ... busy."

"Celebrating, I hope."

"Celebrating?"

"Yes. Your new job. Welcome to the Blue Angel."

The Boom Boom Room was filled with the usual glitterati: the starlets, the star-makers, and the star-fuckers. Everyone had turned out that night to celebrate *Gruff* magazine's "Hot" issue, and its new cover girl, Bette Noir.

Mallory and Alec sat in a banquet in the farthest corner of the room. She watched the scene playing out around her, and was amazed at how in her element she felt. She wore a vintage, crimson Azzedine Alaia dress that she'd bought with part of the Baxter party check; her hair was long and loose; and her only jewelry was her Elsa Peretti heart necklace. When she and Alec had walked into the room, the photographers had actually pushed people aside to get shots of her.

The glossy magazine was piled and fanned out on tables all over the room. She picked up a copy, and ran her finger along the bold white letters written underneath the photo of Bette vamping it up in a black bustier: "Girls! Glitter! Glam! Behind the Velvet Curtain of New York Burlesque" by Alec Martin.

She was so proud of him. The article was already getting a lot of buzz.

"How's my star writer?" Billy Barton asked, looming above them in a white tuxedo.

"Hey, Billy. Great party, as always," said Alec.

"It's not bad, if I do say so myself. And how are you, lovely Moxie? Do you think our cover girl will be a no-show?"

"You never know with Bette," she said.

"Maybe I picked the wrong face for the burlesque feature," he said. "Everyone in the room is asking who *you* are. And now I have to explain why you're not even mentioned in the article. You single-handedly made this piece out-of-date, you lovely bitch."

"That's sweet, Billy," Mallory said, rolling her eyes. "But we both know you got exactly the right girl at exactly the right moment. Photos of Bette and Zebra are in every tabloid on the rack this week."

"Isn't it glorious? I couldn't have planned it better myself. Oh—there's Ms. Poppy LaRue. And who is that unattractive creature with her? She's bringing down the aesthetic of the entire room."

Mallory looked at the door, and, sure enough, there was Poppy making an entrance with Patricia Loomis. She had heard they were dating. Of all the things that had transpired over the past few months, this had to be the most outrageous and shocking turn of events. Their connection explained why Alec had seen Patricia in the audience the night Mallory had made her Moxie debut. It probably also explained how she'd been busted and lost her job.

She watched them make their way into the room, together but obviously trying to appear *not* together. As if anyone in that crowd cared. Although, after what had happened to Mallory in the corporate culture of Reed, Warner, she couldn't blame Patricia for being paranoid. Looking at Patricia now, Mallory couldn't help smiling. In the end, Patricia and the firm had done her a favor.

The two women began heading toward them.

"I'd better steer clear of Poppy," Billy said. "She's still furious with me for not putting her on the cover."

"Why would she expect to be on the cover?"

"Um, it's a long story. Now you must excuse me, love."

Billy beelined it over to a hard-bodied young guy she'd seen in a recent movie trailer.

"Hey," Poppy said. She was positively glowing with happiness, and even Patricia looked remarkably attractive. Her skin was shine-free; her hair was finally loose and cut in an attractive long bob just skimming her shoulders; and Mallory was almost sure she detected lipstick. Now if someone could just get her into a dress…

"Hi, ladies. Glad you could make it," Alec said.

"So you went back to brunette?" Poppy said to Mallory. "I like it. It's darker than it used to be."

"Isn't it gorgeous? I can barely take my eyes off of her. Or my hands…"

Mallory elbowed him.

"Um, Mallory, first of all, I want to apologize for the way things happened at the firm," Patricia said stiffly.

"Oh, don't worry about it," Mallory said. "I wasn't cut out for a career at a place like that."

"No, you weren't," Patricia said. Poppy and Alec looked at her sharply. "What? I'm just being honest."

"It's fine! You did me a favor. Really."

"But what are you going to do for work?" Patricia said.

"I'll figure it out."

"Come on—I need a cocktail," Poppy said.

"Okay, I'll walk right behind you."

"Trust me—no one is watching us here," Poppy said. They walked away, debating their own visibility.

Mallory laughed.

"Ah, young love," Alec said.

Before she could respond, her BlackBerry buzzed.

I'm not going to make it. On my way to Paris with Z. Don't be a stranger. Xoxo Bette

"I just got a text from Bette—she won't be here tonight."

"I'm not surprised. Billy will be disappointed, though."

"I think he'll survive," she said, nodding in the direction of Billy, who had with his arm around the hot actor.

"Do you want a drink?" Alec said.

"I do. But first I have to make a quick trip to the ladies room." They exchanged a long look. She had visions of him pressing her up against the wall of glass. "Why don't you join me?" she said.

"I'd love to," he said with a wink. "Let's give the whole city a show they won't forget."